GAMES
in a
BALLROOM

PROPER ROMANCE

JENTRY FLINT

SHADOW
MOUNTAIN
PUBLISHING

To my husband.

*I will never forget your hilariously shocked
expression and loving words of "Wow. Just—wow.
I had no idea you could write like that, honey!"*

Library of Congress Cataloging-in-Publication Data
Names: Flint, Jentry, author.
Title: Games in a ballroom / Jentry Flint.
Other titles: Proper romance.
Description: [Salt Lake City] : Shadow Mountain, [2022] | Series: Proper romance | Summary: "Olivia Wilde has one last Season to enjoy before her father arranges her marriage to a titled gentleman. Emerson Latham doesn't have a title, but he does have a plan to court Olivia without her father's interference. He proposes they play a game of tag during the various parties they attend, and if all goes well, the girl of his dreams will fall in love with him before he loses her forever."—Provided by publisher.
Identifiers: LCCN 2021038239 | ISBN 9781629729930 (trade paperback)
Subjects: LCSH: Courtship—Fiction. | Tag games—Fiction. | Nineteenth century, setting. | London (England), setting. | BISAC: FICTION / Romance / Historical / Regency | FICTION / Romance / Clean & Wholesome | GSAFD: Regency fiction | LCGFT: Romance fiction. | Historical fiction.
Classification: LCC PS3606.L569 G36 2022 | DDC 813/.6—dc23
LC record available at https://lccn.loc.gov/2021038239

Printed in the United States of America
LSC Communications, Crawfordsville, IN

10   9   8   7   6   5   4   3   2   1

ONE

There had once been a time in Emerson Latham's life when, like most firstborn sons of the gentry awaiting their ascent into responsibility, he lived for the thrill of a game. The next wager, the next risk. But those days were behind him. He was the head of his family now, which put his widowed mother, his troublesome sister, and a country estate that was sustainable but not overly profitable, far above betting books and gentlemen's club rivalries.

Most of his time was now spent in ballrooms, where his ability to spot a bluff allowed him to identify an unsuitable match for his sister in her first Season.

Responsibility. Family. That was his focus, though he felt ill-prepared for the task. He knew it. His father on his deathbed must have known it, yet somehow Emerson stood in yet another ballroom, surrounded by an excessive amount of beeswax candles—he had been amazed to learn about the government's exorbitant tax for every wick—and drinking overly sweetened ratafia when he would have preferred port.

"It would appear Lady Bixbee requires our attention," his mother said with a weary sigh.

He slowed his pace and tucked her arm closer to his side to offer her support. Though his father had been gone for well over a year, his mother still showed signs of frailty, and he worried she would never find her way out of her heartache. He did his best to shoulder the burdens that came with running their London household and a small country estate, but when it came to her grief, he felt useless.

Following his mother's gaze, Emerson found the elderly and cumbersome Lady Bixbee bedecked in jewels and lace, swishing her fan like a general signaling soldiers into battle, but in this case, her forces consisted of a circle of gossipy matrons. He was not certain he would not rather face down an infantry of soldiers.

"Is there no avoiding it?" he asked, attempting to evade making eye contact with the matron. "I do not like her influence over Arabella."

"*Arabella*, can hear you," his sister cut in, knocking her elbow into his side. "And I, for one, like Lady Bixbee. She is not afraid to speak her mind."

"You would not like her using those opinions to find you a husband."

"No, but how fortunate I am that you have chosen to *help* me with such a task." Her eyes snapped to him with annoyance.

"I would not have to step in if I believed you would take

the time to think through the consequences of what you do or say."

"And I would have valued your thoughts if I did not believe you to be overbearing and an utter bore. How both of our opinions of one another appear to have changed."

"That is quite enough," his mother cut in. "From the both of you. Let us see what Lady Bixbee wants, and then we shall find you both dance partners . . . preferably on opposite sides of the ballroom." She said the last half underneath her breath.

Arabella snorted, and Emerson clenched his fists against the urge to continue quarreling with his sister, if only for his mother's sake. Arabella was consistently finding ways to rile him. Their relationship had not always been so strained, but since their father's death, nothing seemed to be the same.

Following his mother's directive, he led them to the ever-watchful Lady Bixbee, who smiled like a queen over her court.

"Ah, Mrs. Latham, I was just telling Lady Masdon how refreshing it was to have you and Miss Latham help in our committee at our last charity event," Lady Bixbee said.

"We were honored to be asked," his mother replied.

"Good." Lady Bixbee's smile was much too wide for Emerson's comfort. "I look forward to asking you both again."

Emerson held in a groan.

"Now," Lady Bixbee continued, snapping her fan, "I have just unearthed the most—"

Emerson ceased listening, his attention catching on the most peculiar shade of salmon standing on the opposite side of the ballroom. His heart picked up its pace, and he found it impossible to look away. Only one woman would wear such a gown: Olivia Wilde. He knew her father's taste in all things ran toward the expensive and the garish, and seeing his childhood friend subjected to such gaudy fashions had been eye-opening to say the least. Though it did make her easy to spot in a crowd.

Not that he needed it. He could find her anywhere.

She was petite in stature, the top of her head not quite reaching his chin. Her hair, twisted and curled into a beautiful chignon, reminded him of the golden wheat field he had, for the first time ever, helped one of his tenant farmers harvest. And her large eyes were the softest shade of blue. To anyone who did not truly know her, she appeared gentle and soft-spoken. But Emerson knew otherwise.

That adorable chin and rosebud mouth had the strength and the power to quickly put him in his place. She was a quick wit and an even quicker learner. She had never been afraid to challenge him—the most recent challenge being that she had blossomed into the most stunningly beautiful woman, inside and out. He could not take his eyes off her.

And this Season, he was determined to ask her to be his.

"I will return before Lady Bixbee finishes," he whispered to his mother, confident that the well-informed matron's tale would last through to the next set.

His mother looked up at him, and something harrowing passed through her eyes before she nodded her consent. Some days for his mother were better than others, but his greatest fear was that she felt all alone.

He quickly reached across his chest and squeezed her hand in his before she could slip it from his elbow. Her gentle smile somewhat eased his worry, and he took a step back so Arabella could take his place at their mother's side.

"Afraid of being married off if you remain in a group full of ladies, Mr. Latham?" Lady Bixbee paused her story to call out to him, her tone laced with far too much amusement.

"Not afraid," he replied with a confident smile. "Merely cautious when it comes to your talent for machinations, Lady Bixbee."

The old matron openly laughed, and the other matrons obediently followed.

Offering a small bow, he left, not slowing to hear whatever else she might say. His interest was more agreeably engaged in joining a much smaller group of ladies, one of whom he would not mind surrendering his freedom to.

"Oh, good. You managed to escape," his friend Bradbury said, stepping into place to walk alongside him. Their other friend, Lord Northcott, also joined them, his broad stature—or, perhaps, his family's oft-whispered-about past—easily parting the ever-moving crowd.

Bradbury slapped his hand on Emerson's shoulder. "Another batch of those prigs from White's believe they can out-sharp Brooks's greatest pairing at whist. What do you say? Shall we meet them in the cardroom?"

"Have Northcott step in," Emerson replied, not breaking his stride. "I have something I must see to."

Bradbury scoffed and cocked his thumb at Northcott. "Beasty, here, refuses to gamble, remember?"

Emerson stopped short, a wave of guilt washing over him. He should have remembered. Would he ever find balance in his life? His new responsibilities were taking much from him, but he had no excuse to neglect his friends—whom he considered more like brothers—who had been by his side through everything, unwavering.

"Forgive me," he said, looking to Northcott and then Bradbury. "I have not been a good friend as of late."

Northcott offered him a sympathetic nod, which was all Emerson expected from his stoic friend. Bradbury, on the other hand, was a whole other matter.

"Good," Bradbury said. "Now that you have got that off your chest, you can make it up to me by coming to the cardroom and helping me take those pompous upstarts from White's for all they are worth." His brows bobbed with mischief.

Emerson chuckled, but shook his head. "I am sorry, but I cannot." He glanced over the crowd, relieved to see Olivia still standing to the side of the room with her mother. "There is something I must do first."

Not for the first time he considered telling his friends about his desire to marry Olivia, but Bradbury always seemed to have an adverse reaction whenever the subject of matrimony was even broached. Then there was the added pressure he would feel should he fail to win her affections. As it stood, he only wanted to be given the chance.

"What could be more important than beating those fools who blackballed us from their club?" Bradbury asked, his mouth turning down into a scowl.

"It is important; trust me," he replied, which brought something else to his mind. "Northcott, would you stand up with Arabella, again? It would alleviate some of my mother's worry in finding Arabella a dance partner."

"Of course," his friend replied. Though Northcott had earned the name "the Brooding Baron" from the *ton* gossips, the moniker had done nothing to deter anyone from noting whom he stood up with. And if Emerson was going to see his sister's future secured by a good marriage, he was going to need all the help he could get.

"You two and your dancing," Bradbury said, shaking his head, exasperated. "Very well, I shall return to the card-room—*alone*—and give them our regrets. But just so we are clear"—he pointed a firm finger at Emerson—"I expect you to make this up to me."

Emerson nodded, not certain when that could even be managed. It seemed his time was no longer his own.

They all parted ways with a plan to find one another later in the evening.

Approaching Olivia and her mother, Emerson cleared his throat and prepared himself for subterfuge. While he did not anticipate any ill will from Olivia's mother, neither did he expect her to willingly defy her husband's edict that their only daughter marry a gentleman with a title—a title which Emerson did not have. No, it was better to keep everyone in the dark until he and Olivia had come to an understanding.

"Mrs. Wilde. Miss Wilde." He greeted each of them with a smile and a bow.

"Mr. Latham," Olivia's mother said with a curtsy. Olivia did the same, her eyes watching him under her long, golden lashes. "How kind of you to seek out your country neighbors."

"Indeed," Emerson replied. It could not be construed as lying if he simply left Mrs. Wilde to her opinion. In saying nothing, he would be able to get closer to Olivia without drawing any unwanted suspicion. "Which brings me to why I have come." He turned slightly to face Olivia. "If you are not otherwise engaged, Miss Wilde, may I claim this next dance?"

"I am not engaged," she replied, and he resisted the urge to ask her if she would like to be. Her tone was encouraging, though her eyes appeared hesitant.

Did she also worry about how her parents would react should they discover their courtship too soon?

"Then shall we?" he asked, holding out his arm to her.

She slipped her hand into the crook of his arm. The feeling of her fingers pressed against the sleeve of his jacket made him feel more at ease than he had in days.

"I shall return her to your side the moment the dance has ended," he added for her mother's benefit. Everything must appear good and proper for this to work.

Olivia's hand twitched on his arm, and he quickly glanced to see if someone might have bumped her or stepped on her foot.

"Are you all right?" he asked, not seeing anyone who could have been close enough to do so.

"Perfectly," she said with a smile that did not quite reach her eyes.

Emerson studied her for a moment, but found no answers to account for her current distress. He would have to add this to the change he had noticed in her demeanor since they had both arrived in London.

At first, he had found her more demure behavior unsettling but decided it was because of the sudden change he was making to their friendship. He was more than willing to give her time to discover and understand her feelings, but she could not blame him for wanting to continue to press his suit.

Only, he was finding it somewhat difficult to do when the usual means for complimenting a woman were not entirely available to him. He could not compliment her on her dress; she would know he was lying. Throughout the Season, she had been open with him and Arabella about her dislike of some of her gowns—this one certainly fit that bill—which forced him to be more creative when giving an acceptable compliment.

"You always hold yourself quite well, considering—" He glanced down at her gown as they made their way toward the dance floor. To actually say the words and call out the dress while also trying to find a way to compliment her seemed counterproductive.

Slowly, one of her delicate, golden brows raised, and she looked at him with amusement.

Very well, he was proving rather abysmal at giving compliments, but he wanted to court her properly for her sake. If it were up to him, he would go about it in a much less formal way that felt natural to their friendship. But she deserved to have a proper London Season. He hoped she felt he was at least trying.

"If this is your attempt at practicing complimenting a lady, Emerson Latham," Olivia said, "might I suggest further study?" Her lips twitched, and he watched as she struggled to hold in a laugh. It felt good to see a glimpse of her old self returning.

"Then please, instruct me so I do not cause such a

reaction ever again," he said, unable to keep his own laughter from his voice. "What is it that a lady wishes to hear from a gentleman?" They reached the edge of the dance floor and waited for their set to begin.

A slight pink tinged her cheeks. "I am certain I am not the best person to ask."

"And yet, I have." He held his gaze steadfast to hers, desperate for her help. He wanted to make her happy.

Her eyes darted away before settling back on him. "If—if it were I receiving such compliments," she paused, slipping her hand from his arm and adjusting her heavily embroidered white silk gloves, "I would not care for trivial words. Society is too focused on appearances. What would matter more to me would be his actions."

"Like, perhaps, asking her to dance?" he asked, wanting to know what she thought of his attempt at courtship.

"Yes, perhaps," she replied with a small smile.

Encouraged, he straightened his shoulders and returned her smile.

The musicians began to play the opening chords of their set. He held out his hand to her. "Well then, Miss Wilde, would you allow me this opportunity to practice?"

She took his hand, and together they stepped out onto the dance floor.

TWO

The Grishams' ball was swiftly coming to an end, and Olivia Wilde had only been able to secure two dance partners. One of those gentlemen was her closest friend's older brother, Emerson, which made her doubt if it should even count—though the dance with him had been far more enjoyable than the other. Emerson Latham had made a habit of rescuing her from the forgotten edges of the ballroom throughout the Season. A neighborly duty she both appreciated and hated. No one wanted to be asked to dance out of pity, but he always tried to make it seem as if she were not another burden thrust upon his shoulders after his father's death.

Sequestered in a small group of chairs along the edge of the lavishly decorated ballroom, Olivia watched as couples bounced, turned, and clapped to the lively tune of a reel. She had found herself in many similar situations during her first Season—and it seemed she was destined to do so for her second.

"Is my mother still watching?" Olivia leaned to ask her friend, Arabella, tearing her envious gaze from the dance floor. Her feet continued to tap along with the music beneath the gaudy layers of lace and shimmering salmon-colored silk that—in her opinion—made her look the actual part of a scaly fish.

Arabella stretched her willowy frame to look over Olivia's much shorter one, her fawn-colored eyes giving nothing away. Until she cringed. Quickly, she covered up her reaction with an awkward smile that was stretched far too thin.

That did not bode well.

"She is talking with Mrs. Fowlhurst," Arabella replied, before biting her bottom lip. "And Mrs. Fowlhurst's two sons."

Olivia groaned softly. "How can I get her to stop?" The fact that her mother was asking—no, more like begging—her friends to pair their sons with her daughter for a dance was humiliating. "I know she fears my father's patience is wearing thin, but this is ridiculous."

"Your father's expectations are ridiculous—and I do not mean that in any way as a slight toward you or your mother. It is because . . ." Arabella paused, again biting her bottom lip.

"Because my father comes from trade," Olivia finished for her. She had been friends with Arabella long enough to know there was no judgment in that fact, but that did not mean the rest of the *ton* felt the same way.

"I was thinking more along the lines of your father's crass manners," Arabella corrected, which only made Olivia cringe.

Her father's tenacity in business and in life was well-known among the gentry and most of the aristocracy. It was why his investments were so highly sought after and his appearance merely tolerated.

Joshua Wilde had grown up on the docks of London, the only son of a merchant ship's chief mate. Through hard work and many risky business ventures, he had raised himself up enough to marry the daughter of a prominent family in trade. With his new connections and the money he received from Olivia's mother's dowry, he had purchased a shipping company of his own. Which, thanks to the war with Napoleon and his cutthroat business sense, had earned him more money than one man could ever spend in a single lifetime.

With all that, his self-importance had likewise grown, which was why he was now pining for the one thing his money could not buy: the direct connection and privilege of a title.

For that, he needed Olivia.

"There has to be something I can do to secure more dance partners," she said. *And my own future,* she thought.

"I could ask Emerson to see if Lord Northcott would dance with you. He is a baron, surely that would help assuage your father."

"Ask your brother?" Olivia shook her head. "He has already done enough in asking me to dance as often as he has this Season. I could not ask more of him." Not when he appeared so weighed down by the responsibility that fell to him following his father's death.

Emerson was much more serious now, at least compared to the tormenting tease she knew him to be from their past. Now, when he spoke it was with purpose, intent. And when she would find him staring at her—or anything, really—she felt like he was looking for something but never finding whatever it was.

"I will find another way," Olivia said, mostly to herself.

"Or," Arabella said, excitement in her tone, "*I* could ask Lord Northcott for you." One corner of her lips quirked up.

"You cannot be serious." Olivia's eyes bulged at the notion. "I may not be a part of the gentry by birthright, but even I know that is too forward."

Arabella giggled as she shrugged. It was so like her to speak her mind. "I will only point out that ever since Lord Northcott partnered with me, I have had more dance partners than I did at the beginning of the Season."

Her friend had a point. Arabella had missed her first Season due to observing the proper mourning period for her father, and coming in now at what should have been her second Season with Olivia, Arabella was at a disadvantage with the other girls their age. But that fact did not seem to matter the moment she stood up with Lord Northcott. A title could solve anyone's problems it seemed.

Unfortunately, Olivia did not feel as confident as her friend to bend the rules of propriety. A lifetime of trying to please one's parents, who had excelled in their own lives, could do that to a person. And she so desperately wanted to make her parents proud.

"You must promise me you will do no such thing," Olivia pressed, knowing Arabella's fearlessness.

Arabella arched a brow. "Have you a better solution?"

"You know I do not. But I am in earnest when I tell you that anything would be better than what you suggest."

Arabella shrugged and smiled.

A noticeable silence settled between them as the music came to an end and the dance floor emptied of partners. There would be no bustle or commotion in their corner as Olivia knew all too well that neither she nor her friend had a partner for the next set.

"What *a sorry sight* we make," Arabella said with a huff, the deliberate inflection in her tone and obvious side-glance informing Olivia she intended to play her little game as a distraction.

Desperate for any kind of fun, Olivia played along. "*Macbeth*," she answered, grateful that the Shakespeare line had come from one of the few plays she had been able to finish. There were far too many of them, and some quite difficult to follow with their layered meanings and twists.

Olivia doubted she would ever read them all, but Arabella had. It was her scholarly glory that by the age of one-and-twenty she had read all thirty-seven of Shakespeare's plays—some of them several times over.

"That was an easy one," Arabella said.

"For which I am relieved," Olivia replied. "But *methinks, thou* likes Shakespeare far too much."

Arabella smiled as if she had been given a compliment. "*Hamlet*. And you would too if you simply gave him a chance. Really, you are always telling me how bored you are at home."

"I am, but I can assure you Shakespeare is not the answer."

"Shakespeare is *always* the answer." Arabella's eyes brightened with mischief.

"Prove it," Olivia challenged, her mind already working on a plan.

"Very well." Arabella squared her shoulders confidently. "Name your game."

"Solve my predicament." Arabella quickly opened her mouth to answer, but Olivia held up a finger and added, "No sleeping potions or mistaken identities allowed."

Arabella huffed. "A mistaken identity is exactly what you need, but I shall continue to play." This time she paused, her eyes drawing down in concentration. Then she looked up and snapped her fingers. "We *fight fire with fire*."

"We what?" Olivia choked out, her eyes darting toward the hundreds of lit candles in the room. She prayed this was one of those Shakespeare lines with layered meaning and not what it actually sounded like.

"It's *King John*," Arabella offered.

Olivia stared at her blankly. She had never read that play.

"It means, if the gentlemen feel they can ignore us, then we shall do the same to them." She beamed as if she had come up with the perfect solution when really all she had done was leave Olivia more confounded.

"I thought the point was to get a gentleman to notice me, not give him a reason to continue to ignore me."

"No, you misunderstand me." Arabella released an exasperated breath. "Have you ever been fox hunting?"

"No," Olivia replied in droll tones. "Have you?"

"Well, no. But that is beside the point." She waved her hand, dismissing the matter. "I know the strategy of it."

"Really? Do enlighten me," Olivia said, arching a skeptical brow.

"The *reason*," Arabella said, drawing out the word, "for why fox hunting is such a popular sport is because of the thrill of the chase. Do you not see?"

Olivia shook her head.

Arabella released another sigh. "By making an obvious effort to ignore them, we will be encouraging them to chase you. Nothing makes anyone want something more than knowing one cannot have it. I, of all people, should know."

"Should I pin a foxtail to the back of my gown to give them the full effect?" Olivia drawled. Certainly this plan would never work.

"Do you think we could convince your father to get you one at your next dress fitting?" Arabella bobbed her slender dark brows as she looked to Olivia's current monstrosity of a dress. Olivia's father had insisted upon it, just to show the *ton* how much wealth he had.

Olivia groaned, fussing with her skirts as if that would somehow fix the problem of how ugly it was. "Please do not give him any notions."

Arabella's eyes twinkled with amusement as she bit her lower lip in an obvious attempt to hide the grin spreading across her face.

"Can we get back to being serious?" Olivia scowled playfully, secretly wishing they could continue to ignore her problem.

Her father's last tirade still echoed inside her head. He had been so angry, his skin turning the deepest shade of red, it could have been mistaken for purple. His yelling had shaken the house, and the many items he had picked up and thrown peppered the room with shattered shards. The broken pieces served as a reminder of the many ways she continued to disappointment him.

"Olivia?" Arabella's concerned tone broke through her thoughts.

She looked up, not realizing her head had dropped down as she stared into her lap. Arabella was watching her, a deep crease of concern running down the center of her brow.

"I am all right." Olivia forced a smile.

Arabella's continued stare told Olivia she was not fooling anyone, but for some reason, her friend chose not to press the issue. "We shall figure something out." She jokingly motioned to the dark corner they occupied. "It is not as if we can do any worse."

"We could be compromised and left to bear the shame of it." In for a penny, in for a pound.

"That is where the sleeping potion comes in." Arabella winked, always the positive one. "We fake our own deaths and start again somewhere new. Just as Romeo and Juliet intended."

"And that is supposed to make me feel better? Arabella, they both died," Olivia exclaimed as she attempted to hold back a laugh at the ridiculousness of it all.

"Yes. But"—a giggle escaped her lips—"that was only because Romeo did not know the poison was a fake. You and I shall know, and so there would be no issue."

Olivia shook her head and released a laugh. Apparently they could not stay on topic to save their lives.

"Come," Arabella said, after collecting herself. "We should at least take a turn about the room. Perhaps an opportunity will present itself."

They stood, looping their arms together, and abandoning the corner society had relegated them to occupy. Even though she did not know where the decision would lead, at least she was doing something.

"And where are you two running off to?" The deep and serious tones of Emerson Latham rose behind them.

They turned around, coming face-to-face with Arabella's older brother. His two closest friends, Lord Northcott and Mr. Bradbury, stood to his left.

"We are only stretching our legs, Emerson," Arabella replied, a scowl crossing her face. "Or do I have to ask for your permission to do that as well?"

Emerson quickly returned her scowl. "I would not have to ask if you did not tend to get into so much trouble."

"You are not my fath—" Her voice broke. "My father." A sheen of tears glossed over her eyes, and Olivia's heart broke all over again for the siblings.

Emerson cleared his throat, averting his eyes before turning back to her with a strained expression. "Nor do I intend to ever replace him. But I will look out for you as an elder brother should."

A stern silence settled over the group, and desperate to ease it, Olivia came to her friend's defense. "Arabella was merely trying to help me."

"Help you?" Emerson echoed, his dark eyes searching her own as if he feared something terrible had happened.

Guilt weighed upon her chest, constricting her lungs and making it impossible for her to lie to him. He obviously felt his role as brotherly protector stretched to her. She did not want to be that sort of weight on him.

"For the same reason you have often felt the need to ask me to dance. I have very few prospects, and we thought if we took a turn about the room, perhaps more gentlemen would feel inclined to ask me to dance."

"Ask *us* to dance," Arabella amended, raising her chin and tightening her arm around Olivia's in support.

Leave it to Arabella to jump back into the fire Olivia had been trying to rescue her from.

But Emerson did not look to Arabella as Olivia thought he would. Instead his eyes remained solely upon her. Was that disappointment she saw in those dark depths?

"That is not why I choose to dance with you," Emerson said, sending the group into another awkward silence.

Olivia felt a weight settle onto her chest again. She did not want to force him to lie to spare her feelings. For surely that was the only answer.

"I propose a game," Emerson said, catching her off guard. His tone was still serious but in no way matching the possible fun inherent in his suggestion.

"What?" Arabella replied in shock.

Mr. Bradbury's eyes lit up, a devil-may-care grin spreading across his face. "I'm listening."

Olivia stood frozen to the spot, her eyelids fluttering as if the action could help her mind catch up with what was happening.

"Tag, to be precise." For the first time in a long time, Emerson smiled. His broad grin erased some of the shadows from his eyes.

"Are you serious?" Arabella voiced, her tone skeptical at best.

"Very. We could all use a momentary reprieve from life's expectations. Myself included." He paused, studying the small group, before his eyes settled on Olivia once more. "The game can be kept discreet enough that we can all enjoy ourselves while still playing the part society expects of us at functions such as these."

"How would it work?" Olivia asked, knowing she should not. Her attention should be on finding a titled gentleman who would have her and her connections, not on some silly, distracting children's game.

"Easily. Someone will start out as *it*, and throughout the evening the title will change hands, unbeknownst to the majority of us, thus keeping us in suspense. A tag requires you touch someone while also saying the words 'You are it,' to avoid any confusion. Then, the person who is *it* at the end of the evening shall start as *it* for the next ball." Everyone in the circle appeared to be considering his words. "What do you say?"

"You had me at suspense," Mr. Bradbury answered with another confident smile. "This might make attending these dreadful evenings enjoyable for a change."

Lord Northcott nodded his acceptance, his stoic face unreadable as to his true level of enjoyment regarding the idea. Arabella was all too eager to join in something so different and secretive.

Olivia was torn with indecision. Emerson said it would be easy enough to play, and her father and mother need not know. Certainly she could play *while* looking for a suitor. Besides, it could be just what she needed to remain in the ballroom long enough to be noticed. But was the risk of her parents' discovery worth the reward of a little fun?

"What do you say, Liv? Are you in?" Emerson asked, that rare hint of a smile returning to his lips.

"What did you call me?" she asked, caught off guard by his new use of her name.

"Liv," he answered. "I think it would suit you." His lips twitched in amusement.

Was he teasing her? *Liv Wilde*? She might have enjoyed such a name once, but it had no place in a London ballroom. Not with so many expectations set upon her.

Yet look where following society's expectations had got her. Alone in a corner.

Could playing the game really be possible?

She desperately wanted it to be.

Perhaps she should grant herself this one chance to *live*— as Emerson had put it—before she would have to settle down and marry a gentleman of her parents' choosing. One who would require her to act a certain way, be a certain way. One who would certainly not approve of games in ballrooms. Perhaps this moment of fun might help her accept whatever her future held.

"I will play." The words jumped from her lips, and her heart beat rapidly inside her chest. She hoped she would not come to regret it.

THREE

Emerson stood in front of the familiar Portland stone structure of Brooks's gentlemen's club, the frigid March wind biting at the exposed skin of his nose and cheeks. It was well into the night, the streets barren and dark except for the flickering light coming from the surrounding windows. The once-familiar haunt stood tall and imposing like a shadow from his past.

He had not stepped foot inside the place since before his father's death; it had not felt right to do so. He still would not have, if it had not been for the figurative blow to the chest Liv had dealt him during the Grishams' ball. How had he been so wrong? All this time, and she never thought he had been attempting to court her.

Grief and the pressures of responsibility had turned him into someone he no longer recognized—and neither, apparently, had she.

His father's final words stirred inside his head, setting the rhythm of his heart into a frantic, anxious beat.

What is it you want from life, Emerson? And how do you plan to obtain it?

Emerson had put into motion a game, one that if it were successful, would change the course of his life. A change he would have put off for years had it not been for the questions asked by his dying father—and even now he feared he might be too late.

Taking a fortifying breath, Emerson entered his club, his hands shaking in anticipation as he handed his hat, gloves, and winter coat to the waiting footman. His feet carried him as if from memory toward the cardroom, where he was confident he would find his two friends. Bradbury could be found anywhere there was a game to be had, and Northcott preferred places where he could fade into the background, unnoticed and unbothered.

Emerson entered the opulent cardroom, the heels of his boots sinking slightly into the red carpet as he scanned the long room. Opposite the window-lined wall sat three, large half-circular gaming tables with several gilded chairs around them. Almost every chair had an occupant, and Emerson was unsurprised to find Bradbury seated at the most boisterous table of all. A sizable crowd stood around him as he put ink to what Emerson feared to be the betting book.

Many gentlemen had won and lost their fortunes by the wagers they inscribed inside that infamous book. It was a ledger where anything and everything could be wagered upon, from the date in which the Americans would come crawling back to England to when a man with a high penchant for drink would draw his last breath. But Emerson and Bradbury used it most often to make wagers regarding all manner of daring feats they vowed to accomplish.

He used to consider himself to be the adventurous type, but Bradbury was a step above that. Emerson would even go as far as to say Bradbury was reckless when it came to having a good time. And ever since Emerson's father had died, Bradbury had been relentless in his attempts to get Emerson back into their old ways.

"The prodigal son returns!" Bradbury's voice called out over the din of the crowd. Arms stretched out wide, he moved through the crowd toward Emerson with an ease that would put most royalty to shame. "I knew this would be the night. Come, let us toast your return!" Bradbury shouted to the crowd as he slapped Emerson's back.

Bradbury belonged in this kind of atmosphere; he was boastful and confident, which always drew in a crowd, at ease even when the stakes piled high against him, and he always appeared collected even when a wager did not go entirely as planned.

"Perhaps later, my friend," Emerson said, turning to spare himself from any more overly enthusiastic blows to his back. "Where is Northcott?" He scanned the room, ignoring Bradbury's groan at his mention of the baron.

He spotted Northcott seated alone at one of the smaller, private gaming tables farther down the room, an open book in his hands.

"Continuing to take in the brooding beast will not guarantee you sainthood," Bradbury grumbled, though he kept pace with Emerson as he made his way toward Northcott.

"Northcott is as much your friend as he is mine," Emerson said, not fooled by Bradbury's facade.

"We can only afford to have one saint in the Brooks's Brotherhood," Bradbury drawled. His use of the term *brotherhood* did not go unnoticed.

"Then what would you say is your role?" Emerson asked.

"You mean besides being the dashing one?" Bradbury beamed. "Why, I am the entertaining one. Which is a good thing, considering how boring old Northcott tends to be. Look at him—who reads a book when there is coin to be had?" Bradbury waved his arm in the direction of the bustling gaming tables.

"He is barely a year older than we are." Emerson shook his head and chuckled. "And as I remember it, you were the one who initially wagered with me to go over and talk to him."

"How was I to know the buffoon would take that as an open invitation to join us? The man was a reputed recluse, for heaven's sake."

"You've enjoyed having him as part of the brotherhood, admit it," Emerson stated, using Bradbury's own choice of words against him.

Bradbury scoffed.

"I watched you this evening depart the Grishams' ball in his carriage," Emerson pointed out. "If you dislike him as you say, why would you willingly spend more time with him?"

"To save from having to pay for a hackney, of course."

"For one who wins as many wagers as you do, Bradbury, you certainly are a miser." Emerson raised a challenging brow.

"You are lucky I like you enough to overlook such an

erroneous statement. Why, because of my sacrifice, I was able to put a stop to the most far-fetched tales Northcott was lamenting on about."

Emerson had a hard time believing Northcott spoke enough words to qualify as lamenting, let alone that he would be a source for gossip. Bradbury, on the other hand, could inadvertently be a real possibility.

"Why do I fear this has something to do with whatever you wrote in the betting book?" Emerson asked, his chest tightening at the thought of his personal game being known by others outside their small group.

"No, no." Bradbury shook his head. "Though we will speak on the matter of the betting book later. I have come up with the perfect plan to celebrate your return to Brooks's." He leaned toward Emerson and brought a hand up to the side of his mouth as if he were about to reveal some great secret. "What I will tell you about the wager is that we shall soon be in the market for a pig."

"A pig?" Emerson stopped, blinking rapidly. Bradbury had not wasted any time in throwing himself back into their old ways, but Emerson was not ready to do the same.

"No need to worry about it right now, Latham," Bradbury said in slightly more subdued tones. His eyes were watching Emerson closely, and his arm eventually came up to wrap around Emerson's shoulders. Bradbury propelled him forward in a brotherly embrace. "Enjoy your first evening back, and tomorrow I shall inform you of all the fun yet to be had."

Emerson nodded, forcing a smile, wondering if they had

the same idea of fun anymore. He hoped they did, but only time would tell.

Northcott sat in his chair, a book shielding most of his face. Bradbury helped himself to a seat at the table. Dropping down, he dangled one leg over an armrest while leaning his body back, his chin resting comfortably in the palm of his hand.

"I believe Latham has something to discuss with us, Beasty," Bradbury said in a tone designed to provoke.

"I know," Northcott replied, watching them over the top of his book. He never seemed bothered by Bradbury's many names for him, making Emerson question the many rumors and stories told about the Brooding Baron's past, all of which seemed a better fit for gothic novels or nightmares.

"Oh, come off it. You cannot seriously believe your earlier speculation to be the reason for Latham's return of spirits, can you?" Bradbury balked.

"Ask him." Northcott nodded in Emerson's direction.

Bradbury scowled before addressing Emerson. "Northcott believes you are up to something with this whole tag business. I reassured him that you were merely settling back into your old ways. It is unfortunate that you had to involve the ladies, but—"

"I am up to something," Emerson said, interrupting his friend.

Bradbury's mouth closed as his body tensed. Slowly, he swung his leg from the armrest and sat upright, his feet resting on the floor.

Emerson met his friends' eyes, willing them to understand

something he himself had only recently come to believe. "And I need your help."

"Miss Wilde?" Northcott asked without looking up from his book.

Emerson nodded with a smile born from deep inside his chest. "Miss Wilde."

He wanted Liv. He wanted the spitfire he had grown up with, not the subdued debutante he witnessed at balls. Her lack of spirit was soul-crushing, and he could not take much more of it.

Was it love? He did not know. Having never been in love before, it was difficult to say, but there was something. Unfortunately, time was against him. Olivia's father had made it clear what he wanted from his daughter's marriage, and after the cold realization of how unaware Liv was of Emerson's feelings for her, this game was his only chance to get her to see him as something more.

"What in blazes are you two going on about?" Bradbury's voice snapped Emerson back to the present moment. His panicked eyes darted between Emerson and Northcott while a muscle in his jaw clenched.

"I am going to propose to Miss Wilde," Emerson said. It would be cruel not to be upfront and honest with him.

"You cannot be serious?" Bradbury asked, his tone spiking from incredulity to anger.

"I am." Emerson squared his shoulders for what he was certain would follow next.

A chilling laugh fell from Bradbury's lips, his usual levity extinguished and replaced by something altogether feral. "You cannot actually be foolish enough to join that institution."

"Whoever said marriage was an institution?" Emerson asked, holding his ground.

"Every male member of the Church of England, that's who." He leaned forward, agitated, in his chair. "Have you not heard the vows they force you to make? 'Til death do you part' is the very definition of a life sentence." Bradbury clenched the arms of his chair, the color draining from his knuckles.

Emerson opened his mouth to argue, but closed it, stunned by Bradbury's frantic assertions. He had heard his friend's feelings on the matter before, but never to this extreme. Instead of expressing his usual dislike, Bradbury seemed plagued by fear.

Sliding forward to the edge of his chair, Bradbury shifted as if he would bolt at any moment. "I am telling you there is a reason why every high ecclesiastical station does not wed. They are wise to what they force the rest of us to do."

"Bradbury, that is not—"

"And what's worse," Bradbury interrupted, "are the Scots. Do you know they quite literally tie the couple's arms together at the church so you cannot run away if by some miracle you come to your senses?"

"You seem to have put a great deal of thought into this," Emerson said, trying and failing to make sense of any of it.

"Can you blame me?" Bradbury recoiled, running his fingers through his well-kept hair. Different sections stood on end, giving him the look of a man who had not slept in days. "I am going for a walk." He bolted from his chair and was across the room before Emerson could even blink.

Neither he nor Northcott spoke until Bradbury had left the room.

"Would you have expected such a reaction from him?" Emerson asked Northcott, his eyes still fixed on the doorway.

"It's Bradbury, one never knows what to expect," was Northcott's impassive reply. "You have been friends long enough; he will come around."

Emerson nodded, but for the first time in his friendship, he was not so certain. "What are your feelings about my decision?" he asked.

"Do you think it wise?"

Emerson sighed. Northcott answering his question with another question gave away none of his feelings. Emerson returned with a question of his own. "What is life if not a fated adventure?"

"Not every story's hero succeeds," Northcott said, an unmistakable warning in his tone.

Emerson knew Northcott spoke from a place of concern, proving his steadfastness. Neither Northcott nor Bradbury had thought twice about accompanying Emerson to Bedfordshire the moment the news of his father's sudden illness had reached him. They had remained with him through the worst of it, even staying long after the funeral.

Which was more than likely why Northcott was questioning Emerson's decisions now. Suggesting marriage so soon after losing so much would seem rash to most people, but if Northcott had been part of the discussions Emerson had had with his father, he would understand. His father had opened his eyes to the greatest gift and legacy God could give a man—a wife and children of his own. Emerson would be a fool to ignore that one gleam of grace amidst all his loss.

"This hero will succeed." Emerson's conviction burned inside his chest.

"Her father is known to be seeking a certain type of match—one with a vital quality you do not possess."

"Which is why I need this game to work. I should have known courting Miss Wilde in the typical manner would be wasted on her. I need for her to see me in a different light, but also as familiar, safe. This is the only way I can see of accomplishing that."

"It will be difficult for her to go against her parents. If she does not deliver a title for her father, they could very well cut her from their lives. Can you live with knowing you are the reason for a family's rift?"

"I know I cannot sit back and do nothing," Emerson admitted, tilting his head back against his chair and closing his eyes for a breath. He was almost certain there would be no love lost between Olivia and her father if she were to wed someone like Emerson. But he did fear that possibility with her mother.

"What is it you need me to do?" Northcott's steady voice asked.

"Help me get as much time with her as I possibly can. I cannot risk her parents' suspicion. If they cut me off from her, I do not stand a chance."

Northcott nodded, seeming to have met his limit for talking.

Emerson scrubbed at his eyes and released a heavy breath as the day's events weighed upon his mind. "What am I to do with Bradbury?" he whispered to the black abyss behind his eyes. The thought that he might lose his friend was unsettling and new to him.

Northcott surprised him by answering, "Give him time. He will come around."

Emerson dropped his hand from his eyes. "And if he does not?"

"I hear he will be in the market for a pig. Perhaps you could tempt him with that." He flashed the faintest of smiles.

A burst of laughter escaped from Emerson's lips. Apparently he was not the only one capable of change.

FOUR

Olivia slowly made her way toward the drawing room, her excitement for morning callers about as thrilling as watching milk curdle. The never-ending days of sitting, waiting, and needlepoint were enough to make one desperate. Or reckless. In her case, it was hard to tell the difference.

Having spent almost two Seasons trapped among a society that judged her on everything down to the very cut and color of her gowns—which were never as flattering as she would have hoped for—Olivia longed for the simple days of her childhood, when she, Arabella, and Emerson were free to go just about anywhere their feet and imaginations could carry them.

It all seemed so far away now that life's expectations had caught up with her. Which was why, after she indulged herself with this one last moment of frivolity and fun, she would resign herself to the future her father had planned for her. Surely nothing bad could come from playing a harmless child's game.

Olivia took a seat on the sofa across from her mother.

"Your father wants us to revisit the modiste before the end of the week," her mother said, looking up from her needle-point.

"Whatever for?" Olivia groaned. Why must everything always be about gowns or dresses? This morning, her dress was the most unflattering shade of green, a color she was certain made even her skin appear sickly—the "cast up her accounts at any moment" shade of green. "Father need not purchase any more gowns for me. I already have more than enough to clothe all of London." It was an exaggeration, but not by much.

Her mother's back stiffened, and her hands pulled down at the lace-trimmed hems of her long sleeves. It was a reaction Olivia had often seen her mother make, and the large, finger-shaped bruises around her mother's arms were something they never discussed.

"Your father feels you are not standing out enough to be noticed."

"I stand out well enough. The *ton* looks at me as though I were a piece of silver the butler neglected to polish." She shuddered as she thought back to the shimmering gray satin gown she had worn to the theater earlier in the week. She had felt like a giant spoon next to the other girls' gowns.

"And it is up to us to prove them otherwise," her mother said with a firm but sympathetic tone, before giving away to a reluctant sigh. "You know there is no point in arguing against your father. But if you would like, we could have Bess select some of your old gowns and have the material donated to the Foundling Hospital."

"It would serve a greater purpose if we took the money

and had clothes specifically made for the children. Father would never know the difference. He would get his bill, and I could continue to wear the gowns already purchased but have not yet worn."

Her mother tilted her head and held Olivia's gaze. "He would know." She said each word slowly, her eyes imploring Olivia to understand the importance of their meaning.

And she did. It was a thinly veiled warning that her father had already threatened to be more involved in securing Olivia's future. Olivia was only surprised it had taken him this long. He was a man of results, and she had certainly supplied him none.

Nodding her understanding, Olivia clutched at the skirts of her morning dress, believing she might very well be ill. Her time to find a match on her own had run out, and it chilled her to think of her father watching her every move.

She thought of the balls her father had so far neglected to attend. He much preferred his club or the more private gentlemen's parties where drinks and gambling could be easily had.

She cleared her throat and asked hoarsely, "Will he be joining us from now on?"

"To some events, yes," her mother replied softly.

Closing her eyes, Olivia concentrated on her shallow breaths. Her heart threatened to beat right out of her chest. She had to withdraw from Emerson's proposed game. There was no question. If her father ever discovered what she had almost done . . .

The repercussions were too frightening to contemplate.

He was like a fuse permanently set to a keg of gunpowder.

Only she never knew how much powder was inside, ready to ignite at the first spark.

Driven by that terror, Olivia offered her mother a blank smile. She would do well to remember that her and her mother's futures were one and the same. If her mother could marry a man for her family's gain then Olivia could do the same. No matter how disappointed she felt at having to turn down Emerson's game.

It was difficult to keep her attention on their first few morning callers until Arabella and her mother walked through the door.

"You look *in a pickle*," Arabella said. Her tone was teasing but her eyes were worried as they greeted and hugged one another.

"*The Tempest*," Olivia easily supplied for Arabella's game of quotes. "And it is probably because of the color of this dress." Olivia held out her skirts, a half-smile barely curving her lips.

Arabella cringed as she focused more on Olivia's dress. "My apologies, I did not think that one through."

"No apology necessary. It is fitting, actually." She managed to maintain a small degree of normalcy, before they both gave in to a somewhat awkward laugh.

"Is something the matter?" Arabella whispered, glancing back and forth between Olivia's mother and her own, who conversed together on the opposite sofa.

Not wanting to have this discussion where their mothers might overhear, Olivia offered her friend tea. Arabella nodded, following her to the silver serving tray placed behind their sofa.

With hot tea in hand, they walked to the front-facing window.

"You are frightening me," Arabella said as soon as their backs were turned to their mothers.

Olivia focused on the busy Mayfair street. "I have to withdraw from Emerson's game."

"What?" Arabella practically shouted, then quickly looked over her shoulder.

"Is everything all right?" Mrs. Latham asked, her eyes chiding her daughter for her outburst.

"Olivia says she has never read *Twelfth Night*." Arabella was quick with a response, while Olivia struggled to even put together a complete sentence. A telling sign that she would be foolish to think she could try to hide Emerson's game from her parents.

Arabella's mother looked to the ceiling as if seeking divine help for her outspoken daughter before settling back into conversation with Olivia's mother.

"You see," Arabella grinned, nudging Olivia with her shoulder, "Shakespeare is *always* the answer."

A smile Olivia felt down to the tips of her toes rose to her lips. Where would her life be without her dearest friend?

With a reciprocating smile, Arabella continued her inquiry, this time with a more appropriate tone for secrecy. "What do you mean you have to withdraw from the game?"

Olivia turned apologetic eyes to her friend. "I do not have a choice. My father has decided to accompany my mother and me to social events. If he should discover—"

"Do you truly believe we would be so careless?" Arabella

cut her off, her tone turning to annoyance. "Do you trust Emerson and me so little?"

She did trust Arabella, that answer was easy enough. But trust Emerson? Was it strange that she had never thought about it before? He was no enemy, nor was he a confidant to her as Arabella was. He was Emerson. Her closest friend's teasing older brother. The boy she had grown up with. She did not *not* trust him, if that meant anything.

"Of course I trust you," Olivia said, choosing her words carefully and hoping to reassure her friend.

"Then at least agree to play one game. Please. This is the most fun Emerson has been since—" She stopped, swallowing hard.

Olivia reached out and took Arabella's hand in hers, giving it a supportive squeeze.

Arabella squeezed back. "We all need this," she said, her voice soft.

Olivia agreed. She wanted to bring her friend a moment of happiness after so much grief. If only her father could be so easily overlooked. She offered a half smile and gave the only answer she could. "I shall consider it."

Arabella inclined her head. Slipping her hand from Olivia's, she returned her attention to the Mayfair street and released a heavy breath. "We should go for a walk in the park," she said to the windowpane.

"I will ask for our cloaks," Olivia replied with a smile, trying to set the tone between them to rights.

Securing their mothers' permission, they bundled up in their fur-lined cloaks, shawls, scarves, kid gloves, and bonnets in preparation to face the unseasonably cold London air.

With a maid as chaperone, Olivia and Arabella hastened across the busy cobblestone street to Hyde Park. They chose a simple footpath off the main thoroughfare, keeping to the outer edges of the park. Snow piled along the edges of the path, clinging to the bare shrubberies and trees. It was not Hyde Park at its best, the coal dust turning what had started out as a crisp white to gray.

"Is your nose as frozen as mine feels?" Olivia asked, burrowing further into her scarf.

"You do wear the shade of red rather well," Arabella said with a teasing sideways glance, huddling deeper into her own garment.

Olivia bumped her friend with her hip, only reaching Arabella's upper leg due to the differences in their height. Arabella released a laugh.

"I do not understand why you have to be so tall," Olivia teased. "We were once of a similar height, and now either you have grown or I have shrunk."

"Consider your height a blessing," Arabella said with a grin. "I stand at a similar height as most gentlemen, which for some reason, makes them uncomfortable. It is not as if I am going to challenge them or something—my mother would never allow it."

Olivia burst out laughing, shaking her head at Arabella's boldness. "Could you imagine the look on Emerson's face if—"

"If what?" Emerson's deep, teasing tone cut in.

Olivia jumped, her hand clutching Arabella's arm. They spun around together, where they found a grinning Emerson and the forever stoic Lord Northcott.

Her cheeks warmed, thawing the chill that had frozen much of her face. Was it too much to hope that he would not notice the sudden rise in her color and that he had somehow not overheard her talking about him? Which, now that she thought about it, her sudden blush was a strange reaction to be having. He was, after all, just Emerson. All those times he had asked her to dance must have gone to her head.

"You were saying, Liv?" Emerson pressed, his knowing smile telling her that he had heard everything.

Not wanting to give him the satisfaction of catching her talking about him, but unable to think of one thing to say instead, she stammered on for far too long. "Um—that is to say—we were—Arabella and I—the fact of the matter is—"

"No need to tie yourself up in knots about it," Emerson said with a chuckle, managing to close the distance between them with a few of his confident strides. "I shall resign myself to being flattered that you think of me even while we are apart."

He watched her with a quiet smolder in his eyes that would have many ladies swooning, which was why she found it rather unnerving when she felt her breath catch. Again, he was *just* Emerson.

She tried to swallow against the rising tightness in her throat, and Emerson's eyes darted down to the slip of exposed skin not covered by her scarf. A pleased and sly smile slowly spread upon his lips. The smile of a man who knew what he wanted and would stop at almost nothing to get it.

He was trying to provoke her. The odious bounder.

With a lift of her chin, she took a defiant step back, which only seemed to please him further.

Arabella had been right. The game would be good for Arabella and her brother. Which only made it more difficult to choose what she should do.

Or did it?

She knew she wanted to play the game for her friends as much as for herself—maybe even more for herself. Her future was already determined for her, and all that remained was the matter of whether she would accept it now or later.

"Were you spying on me?" Arabella asked her brother, pulling Olivia back to the present.

Arabella's nose wrinkled as she stared down her brother.

"Will it matter if I answer you or not?" Emerson countered, giving his sister a contested stare. "Either way, you will not accept it." He held out his arm to Olivia. "Shall we?"

It was not the cold that froze Olivia to the spot, but the shock of witnessing Emerson concede to Arabella. In the past, both parties would have battled to their last breaths. Perhaps, he was not the Emerson of old.

"Liv?" he prodded, a curious grin crossing his lips as he watched her.

Embarrassed by her slow response, Olivia quickly tucked her fingers into the crook of his arm. He guided them farther down the path, leaving his sister and Lord Northcott to catch up.

Olivia glanced over her shoulder to see Lord Northcott offer his arm to Arabella. They walked behind them at a slower pace, while the girls' maid followed even farther behind.

Just before she returned her attention to Emerson, she paused, her eyes catching on the strangest thing. Lord

Northcott held the faintest of smiles on his lips as he stared down at a chattering Arabella. Had she just witnessed a crack in the Brooding Baron's armor?

Could there be interest on the baron's part, instead of a call to duty as Arabella believed? Was Emerson being the protective older brother, wanting to see his sister properly secured in a marriage to one of his good friends? As Arabella's closest friend, it was Olivia's responsibility to find out.

"Are you trying to arrange a match between Lord Northcott and your sister?"

"What?" Emerson chuckled in disbelief. He looked behind them and then back to Olivia a few times. His grin only grew wider with every glance. "I believe it is safe to say that would be a foolish match to press on my part." He nodded back toward their friends, and Olivia followed his gaze.

Lord Northcott and Arabella were still walking arm in arm, only this time the baron did not appear amused by Arabella's constant chatter. In fact, he looked rather indifferent.

"Who said two people had to be similar to be married?" Olivia asked, not certain why it even mattered, other than not wanting Emerson to win. Arabella had never admitted to any interest in the baron.

"Are you against a married couple being similar?" His eyes watched her closely.

"I can see the benefits and the disadvantages." She shrugged; the subject of marriage was not one she was interested in discussing.

Emerson slowly nodded, returning his attention to the

path in front of them. "What led you to think I was playing matchmaker?"

They came upon a half-frozen puddle covering nearly the entire width of the path. Cracked ice lined the edges and the jagged points melted into a thawed center.

Emerson took Olivia's hand from the crook of his arm and held it inside his own, using it to guide her in front of him along the narrow path around the slick ice. He followed so close his chest brushed up against her shoulder and back. The warmth and tenderness from his touch spread flutters and heat from the tips of her toes to her frozen nose.

"Liv?" The rumble of his baritone at her ear jolted her from—whatever silly things she was feeling. Olivia shivered. What a strange sensation to be having; *it was Emerson*, for goodness' sake. Not some hero from one of her novels.

Once past any danger, Emerson guided her back to his side, replacing her hand in the crook of his arm. Setting them back to rights with the needed distance, Olivia returned to her previous point.

"Arabella mentioned that she thought you had asked Lord Northcott to dance with her as a favor, but then here you are, making sure they have a private moment together."

Emerson shook his head slowly, another deep chuckle rolling from his chest. "No, I can assure you that was not my intent." He paused a long moment, then asked quietly, "What if I told you that I wanted to have a private moment with you?"

Olivia burst out laughing at the ridiculous idea. Expecting Emerson to join her in the joke, she was taken by surprise at his deep, furrowed brow and the serious set of his mouth. Had she wounded his pride with her reaction? If so, it was not her fault that he misunderstood.

"The only time you have ever wanted a *private* moment with me, Emerson Latham, was when you wanted to further torment me after a victory."

"Torment?" His expression went from bewilderment to frustration.

"Yes. Torment," she repeated. "What else would you call your relentless teasing and the games we played over the years?"

Emerson scoffed. "If my memory serves, you were no innocent when it came to tormenting *me* on the very odd chances *you* won. I also recollect you freely joining in on all those games."

The staggering truth shot straight from his lips to her ears, and Olivia's chest tightened at his reminder that what she did with her life was no longer her choice. Not if she wanted to please her father and spare both her mother and herself from her father's temper. "I have grown up since then." She sounded pitiful even to her own ears.

"Do you mean since the Grishams' ball? You agreed to play my game then," Emerson said, his arm growing tense beneath her touch, but from disappointment or anger, it was hard to tell. His facial expression revealed nothing, his lips pressed into a thin line.

"I should never have done so," she replied, hanging her head in order to avoid his eyes.

"But you did," Emerson challenged, tugging back on her arm and stopping their progress.

She felt his eyes boring into her, and like the coward she

was proving to be, Olivia slipped her hand free and quickened her pace along the path. She hated disappointing him and Arabella, but she feared disappointing her father even more.

Emerson's boots crunched on the frozen gravel behind her as he closed the gap between them far quicker than she had wanted. Tugging at her arm, he turned her around to face him. From the hard set of his features, she expected him to list all the ways she had disappointed him, but instead he simply stood there, studying her, a prominent muscle in his jaw flexing until he finally broke the silence. "Will you at least promise me something?"

"What?" Her voice shook, uncertain if she wanted to hear his request, let alone fulfill it.

"Promise me that you will give this game a chance." His grip on her arm tightened, not out of anger or a desire to control her, but as if he were holding on to something he feared he might lose. As if her answer truly did mean something to him.

Her gaze caught on Arabella and Lord Northcott in the far distance.

We all need this. Arabella's words filtered through Olivia's mind.

Emerson's pleading stare told her the same. He had already lost so much; could she truly deny him this respite?

"One game," she whispered, the sound disappearing almost as quickly as the cloud her frozen breath made. She would play one game for him and pray her father was not in attendance.

FIVE

Having narrowly avoided losing Liv before the game had even begun, and having waited for Bradbury to show himself for more than five days, Emerson was a man driven into action. He had one opportunity to convince Liv to give him a chance, and if he was going to take the biggest gamble of his life, he needed to know that the one friend who would go to any length to win was going to be on his side, despite their difference of opinions.

Suspecting he would find his friend in the one place Bradbury called home more than his actual home, Emerson marched up the steps to Brooks's gentlemen's club.

It was early morning, and the club was in its rare form of quiet. Emerson heard a soft murmur coming from the coffee room, so he decided to start his search there. Scattered about the three small rows of rectangular, linen-covered tables sat a few of the club's members, none of them Bradbury. Emerson was not discouraged, however, as there was still plenty of the two-story building to search.

Returning to the corridor, he found himself detained by Lord Digby, one of the club's more difficult members.

"Ah, Latham," Lord Digby called as he made his way toward Emerson, his steps were tipsy for only half past eleven, which was not that uncommon for the well-known drunkard. "I was just discussing with our Mr. Bradbury your sudden disappearance from vice."

Emerson suspected that not only had Lord Digby forgotten the fact that Emerson's father had died a little more than a year ago, but that he was also unaware that Emerson had returned to society a new man with new responsibilities. After all, it was likely Lord Digby would remember none of *this* conversation once he sobered.

"Might I be the first to suggest, Lord Digby, that perhaps you should try to practice some restraint in vice." Emerson forced a smile.

Lord Digby stumbled another step forward, his head slopped back in laughter, which threw off what little balance he had and propelled him toward a nearby wall.

Emerson closed the space between them in an instant, his conscience forcing him to prevent the gentleman from colliding with an unforgiving wall followed by the marble floor. "Steady on, my lord," he grunted from underneath the drunkard's weighted paunch.

A footman appeared, and together they assisted Lord Digby into the club's morning room. Lord Digby slouched into the wingback chair, his eyes sagging as much as the cushion did beneath his substantial backside. Mumbling and grunting his thanks, Lord Digby slipped into a disheveled sleep.

Emerson reached into the chest pocket of the lord's wrinkled jacket and pulled out a few of his coins. Handing them to the waiting footman, he ordered, "See to it that his lordship has something close by to cast up his accounts when he awakes, and then give him *only* water. When he is steady on his feet, call for his carriage to deliver him home."

"As always, sir," the footman replied, pocketing the coins.

With his conscience met, Emerson turned his attention toward the cardroom. If one could trust the ramblings of a drunkard—and in the habitual case of Lord Digby, Emerson believed he could—he should find Bradbury already in the cardroom.

The moment he stepped through the doorway, Emerson knew he had found his friend before even having to lay eyes on him. The long, rectangular room was filled with boisterous laughter, all centered around the only gaming table in use. Bradbury looked the very picture of carefree ease as he laid a set of cards upon the table, which was met with a round of applause.

Aggravation boiled Emerson's stomach, heating his skin. It was clear that the gentleman he considered more brother than friend had so easily removed himself from their bond— and over something Emerson did not fully understand—and his pride wanted to know why.

Not caring what others thought, Emerson pushed his way through to the table, soundlessly dropping the butcher's bill for one live pig in front of his friend. He had intended the purchase as a peace offering, a way to resume conversation as friends. He did not want to lose Bradbury, but neither would he sacrifice his chance at winning Liv.

The crowd hushed, and Bradbury's gaze settled upon the bill, his expression placid and unconcerned. Emerson waited one breath, then two, for any semblance of a reaction.

With slow, almost studied movements, Bradbury turned his head, his eyes tilting up to meet Emerson's. "Latham."

"Bradbury." It was the shortest conversation they had ever shared, and yet the two words spoke volumes about where their friendship now stood.

Turning away, Emerson left the room, his neck and shoulders prickling from both indignation and a room of watchful eyes.

Bradbury's reaction—or lack thereof—to Emerson's offering changed its intention. What had been meant for peace now felt like a gauntlet. He had made the first move, now it was up to Bradbury to make the next.

Emerson entered the large dining hall, a stack of white plates next to the sideboard glistening under the reflected lights from two chandeliers. An array of foods, presented on polished silver trays stood before him, and yet Emerson barely had the stomach for any of it. Selecting some eggs and a few pieces of bacon, he sat at a private table.

Fake, that was what Emerson thought of his friend's demeanor. No person could have such an intense reaction one moment, and then appear to be uninterested the next. Emerson wanted answers, and he was not about to let Bradbury continue as if nothing had happened.

Emerson did not have to wait long before Bradbury entered, accompanied by a group of merrymaking gentlemen. They were all laughing, the noise cutting into the quiet of the dining hall, as Bradbury tucked a stack of banknotes into his inside jacket pocket.

The other gentlemen headed for the sideboard, and then to one of the larger dining tables, but Bradbury broke away, moving at an unfamiliar and subdued pace toward Emerson. He was stopped by a few of the club's patrons along the way, his smile stretching to the point of falseness—a gesture Emerson was sure only he recognized.

Reaching the table, Bradbury stopped behind the chair opposite Emerson, an air of caution surrounding him.

"You certainly know how to make an entrance," Emerson drawled.

"One could say the same about you," Bradbury replied as he pulled out the chair and took a seat at the table. "Shall we draw cutlery next? Will that suffice for whatever temper you are in?"

Emerson scoffed, shaking his head. "Temper *I* am in? *I* was not the one who stormed out on an important conversation and then disappeared for days at a time."

"I did not disappear."

Emerson raised a brow.

"Just yesterday I saw Northcott in this very place."

Emerson pressed his lips together to keep from shouting. "It is not Northcott whom you are avoiding."

"Who said I was avoiding anyone? You obviously knew where to find me." Bradbury held his arms out, gesturing to the room at large.

They were at a standstill, neither allowing the other to gain any ground. If they were going to be able to move past their differences of opinions, he needed to say something that would bring them to equal ground. After losing the foundation of his father in his life, he did not want to lose the support of his long-time friend as well.

"You are right," Emerson said, taking the first step. "I did know where to find you, and I had brought the bill for the pig as a peace offering. Only, imagine my frustration when I find my friend—whom I have not seen nor heard from in days—going about his life as if it did not matter whether I was a part of it or not."

A stiff silence stretched between them.

"I do care," Bradbury spoke to the cream-colored linen covering the table, his voice humble but firm. He looked as if he might have more to say, his eyes hesitating to meet Emerson's.

"Bradbury, if you need—" He stopped short as Bradbury took the folded serviette placed before him and shook it out with two flicks of his wrists.

As if he were seated at his own table at home, he tucked it into his cravat then reached forward, pulling Emerson's plate of half-eaten eggs and bacon across the table. Picking up his fork, he stabbed at the light-yellow egg yolks and brought them to his mouth. He took three more bites before picking up his knife and cutting into the bacon.

Emerson watched, speechless.

"This is good," Bradbury offered between bites, looking at Emerson with a satisfied smile. He stabbed at another roasted piece and popped it into his mouth. "We should think about contributing our pig to the club after the wager is finished. I could see a pair of complimentary dining vouchers in our future." Bradbury waggled his eyebrows at the prospect.

Shaking his head, Emerson chuckled. Leave it to Bradbury to find a way to get something for free.

"We should talk about this wager of yours," Emerson said, giving up hope of seeing his plate returned to him.

"*Ours*," Bradbury corrected between bites of bacon. "And it's going to be our greatest one yet. The number of bets in the betting book that say we cannot pull this off are astonishing—and they are going to be more than enjoyable to collect."

The devil-may-care grin on Bradbury's face did nothing to assuage the growing unease in Emerson's stomach. He was not even certain he wanted to resume these daring feats. He had more than himself to look after now, and hearing that so many people doubted the wager's success made his hesitancy all the more justified.

"What are the requirements for this wager?" Emerson asked.

Bradbury's smile grew. "We are sneaking into White's."

Emerson's eyes widened. "With a pig?"

"Dressed in Beau Brummell's waistcoat, yes. But as you took care of procuring the pig, I shall see to the waistcoat," Bradbury said, waving the matter off as if obtaining an article of the legendary dandy's clothing was a simple task.

"How courteous of you," Emerson said, dumbfounded.

"It's the least I can do." Bradbury smiled, and untucked the serviette from his cravat. "Can you forgive my earlier reaction, friend?" Bradbury asked, that newfound humility returning to his tone. "And my silence?"

Nodding, Emerson asked the question he had intended before Bradbury had taken his food. "Would you care to talk about it?"

Bradbury shook his head. "It is nothing to concern yourself with. Besides, soon you will have your hands full with a wife and a carriage full of children wailing and screeching. You will soon have no time for my irresponsible behaviors."

Recognizing his friend's diversion, Emerson let the matter drop for the time being. Every man had his secrets, and it was up to them to choose the time of their unveiling.

"You will always be welcome at my table, friend," Emerson said as a peace offering. Bradbury looked as if he wanted to squirm his way out of his chair, so he added, "You can even have your own plate." He gestured to the now-shared plate between them, where only a few specks of egg and some bacon grease remained.

"I doubt Miss Wilde will keep as good a table," Bradbury teased with a wink.

Emerson raised a pointed brow in challenge.

"Look at me that way all you like, my friend. I have heard about enough of your exploits with the lady, and I would not be surprised to find that she had deliberately tricked you by placing the salt in the sugar dish and the sugar in the salt."

Emerson chuckled, imagining the very likely scenario. The thought of sharing his life with such a remarkable woman by his side was sweet. There would be nothing simple about marriage to Liv. And he wanted to experience that more than anything.

"What is your plan?" Bradbury asked, his forefinger nervously rubbing the dip in his spoon lying on the table.

"I need her to see me as more than just Arabella's older brother," Emerson replied, leaning forward until his elbows rested on the table.

Bradbury handed Emerson's empty plate to a passing footman. Awkwardly, he smoothed out some of the lines in the table linen. "And you believe playing this game will do that?"

"Courting her in the customary way has not worked," Emerson replied, sighing in frustration.

Bradbury's eyes bulged as he looked up at Emerson. "All that dancing? That was you attempting to court Miss Wilde?" He blinked in bewilderment. "I thought you were playing some stuffy old nursemaid to your sister and her friend."

Closing his eyes, Emerson pinched the bridge of his nose. Had he truthfully appeared that way? Had his attempts at subtle wooing fallen so far short of his mark? It was no wonder Liv had not a hint of what he was trying to do.

"Are you certain you want to marry this woman?" Bradbury asked, intruding into Emerson's bleak thoughts.

Emerson opened his eyes, the truth of the answer setting his heart alight in his chest. "As certain as I shall ever be."

"Well, then," Bradbury paused, taking a fortifying breath, "guess I better see to it that you do not mess it up."

SIX

Olivia gripped the banister, struggling to maintain an outward appearance of calm. Her father stood with her mother in the entrance hall. His black, double-breasted dress coat pressed, and his cravat intricately tied for an evening among the *ton*. He was making good on his threat of attending more events, and for a brief moment, Olivia contemplated risking a stumble down the stairs to spare her from the catastrophe that was sure to unfold that evening. Why had she been so foolish to promise Emerson a single game?

"Save your grace for the aristocracy, daughter. If you move any slower, we will miss out on all the prime stock," her father called up to her. He chuckled to himself as if he had said something clever and not cringeworthy.

How appealing to hear one's suitors talked about as if they were nothing more than horses to be purchased at Tattersalls, she thought sarcastically. She might not be able to marry for love, but she still hoped for a connection with the man who would one day be her husband.

"Yes, Father," she replied, trying to keep her nerves out of her voice.

Picking up her skirts, Olivia quickened her pace down the stairs. The color of her dress was the most beautiful shade of lavender, and she would have been excited to wear it had it not been for the triple layers of lace at the waist, neckline, and hem, each row a garish shade of dark purple, green, and pink. The gown reminded her of Cook's famous layered confections she baked for special occasions. Only this dress was anything but delightful and far too sugared to be palatable.

"Your hair looks lovely, Olivia," her mother said, reaching out to squeeze Olivia's hands. She swallowed with visible difficulty.

Concerned by her mother's discomfort, Olivia studied her, then glanced at her father, relieved that he did not appear to be in one of his darker moods.

Her mother's usual lithe form stood stiff in a golden silk gown, drawing Olivia's attention to the ostentatious ruby necklace that lay snug around her neck. No doubt the necklace had been acquired by her father from some ancient family line of a now-impoverished duke or earl. Her mother would never have selected such a piece; she preferred jewelry that was more elegant and simple.

"Thank you, Mama. Is that a new necklace?" Olivia asked, offering a soft smile of commiseration. Her father's tastes in fashion were a burden they both had to bear.

"Yes, yes," her father grumbled. "Enough talking. We have a viscount to impress." Ripping his beaver hat from a footman's hands, he shoved it on his head, and briskly exited their home.

Olivia jerked her head toward her mother, panic threatening to claw out of her chest. "Viscount?"

Her mother adjusted her necklace, the flesh hidden beneath its larger gold pieces already marred by its weight. "Your father has made a new acquaintance," she managed to say before an army of liveried footmen descended upon them with their winter cloaks.

Dread flooded over Olivia, washing away all her earlier panic. Any new acquaintance of her father's was never good. Money was always involved, and a beholden aristocrat did not a favorable connection make.

Entering the Stansburys' ballroom, Olivia's father walked with the confidence of a man who knew his position among the *ton* was as real as the currency he put in their diminished coffers. There was no eye he did not dare to meet, nor any acquaintance he did not hesitate to exploit.

Finding Viscount Trenor, Olivia's father greeted the lord with a booming voice and a familiarity that would make any member of the gentry sputter. The indignation on the viscount's face was undeniable, and the way his flat, dark eyes scanned the onlookers told Olivia he would have liked to give her father the cut direct. But poverty was real, and her father was the only thing keeping the gentleman and his family from it.

"Mr. Wilde," Lord Trenor finally acknowledged, though his aristocratic nose remained high in the air as if he were afraid her father still carried the stench of the docks.

Olivia had to admire her father in that moment. He held himself as a man who knew he had labored hard and was proud of his elevation into society, unlike Lord Trenor, who simply had been born to it.

"My wife, Charlotte. My daughter, Olivia," her father said.

Olivia's admiration vanished at her father's less-than-formal introductions, but she followed her mother's example and curtsied to the viscount.

Lord Trenor gave a stiff bow. "A pleasure," he replied, though his manner and tone suggested otherwise. Turning to his own wife, he offered, "My wife, the Viscountess Trenor."

Lady Trenor curtsied, the slightest of bobs. Olivia would have missed it had she blinked.

"And my sons, the Honorable John Trenor and the Honorable Edward Trenor."

The sons, who looked nothing alike, save for their height, stiffly bowed. The eldest Mr. Trenor barely gave Olivia and her mother his notice, while the second watched them, his brow deeply furrowed.

Olivia shifted on her feet. The whole experience felt as awkward as a pig wearing a corset, which Olivia knew all about, thanks to a long-ago experience with a young and mischievous Emerson.

Arabella had overheard her family's cook mention that the pig was finally fat enough to be eaten, and on a silly whim of heroics spurred on by Emerson, Arabella and Olivia had stolen one of Mrs. Latham's corsets, believing that if they could hide the pig's size, they might save the poor animal's life.

Mr. Latham had found Olivia and Arabella covered in mud, along with their half laced-up pig. He had laughed uproariously and helped them dispose of the soiled corset.

A giggle escaped her at the memory, and Olivia quickly bit her bottom lip. Locking eyes with the viscount's family, she was met with unpleasant stares and a heavy frown from Lady Trenor.

"My apologies," Olivia said, avoiding her parents' eyes. She dared not guess what they thought of her outburst.

Lord Trenor merely nodded, his attention returning to Olivia's parents. Never before had she been so grateful to be ignored.

"Miss Wilde?"

Olivia jumped, surprised to hear Mr. Edward Trenor addressing her.

"My apologies," he added in a flat tone.

She felt flustered and out of place. She did not belong here. She did not want to *be* here.

You did when Emerson proposed the game.

"Miss Wilde—"

Olivia fought against that annoying little thought.

"—to dance?" Mr. Trenor finished, about the same time Olivia realized she had not been listening to half of what he said.

Latching on to the last word, and noticing Mr. Trenor's extended arm, Olivia surmised the gentleman wanted to dance—though "want" was likely the wrong choice of word.

He was as duty bound to his parents as she was to hers. Only, he could be rid of her the moment the music struck its last note. Olivia's father, on the other hand, would believe this offer to be the start of a courtship. Olivia saw it for the slight it truly was. The entire *ton* would see her dancing with the *second* son and not the first.

"Yes, thank you," Olivia replied, taking his arm. The opening chords for the next set had begun, and she could not wait to be done with the farce.

Joining the other couples on the dance floor, Olivia took a page out of Mr. Trenor's book and feigned an interest in the room around them as they danced.

Hanging in a row from the oval-shaped dome ceiling were three great, cascading chandeliers that lit up the room with a sparkling splendor as the colors illuminated from the crystals reflected onto the lavish gold-and-cream-covered walls. It was a breathtaking sight, and she would have continued to enjoy admiring it if her eyes had not caught on a watchful Emerson at the edge of the dance floor.

Olivia swallowed, suddenly shaky and feeling almost ill. Her promise to Emerson weighed on her mind, twisting her stomach into anxious knots. Had he noticed her father's presence? Did he still intend to hold her to her promise?

Trust him. Arabella's encouraging words found their way through Olivia's fears, followed by the most absurd image of a corseted pig. A smile played out upon her lips. Life had been so happy then.

Could she trust Emerson?

As soon as the music and dancing for the set came to an end, Mr. Trenor quickly escorted Olivia from the dance floor, which she was most grateful for. She wanted to be around Mr. Trenor as much as he wanted to be around her. The only folly was that, in their haste, Olivia lost sight of Emerson.

He had to be *it*, she was certain. Why else would he have watched her so intently if it were not for the game?

She and Mr. Trenor were halfway through the crush of people before Emerson appeared directly in her and Mr. Trenor's path.

"If you will allow me, Mr. Trenor, I believe Miss Wilde's next dance belongs to me," Emerson said, uncharacteristically formal, and his eyes seeming darker than she remembered as they locked with Mr. Trenor.

Tension crackled in the silence between the two gentlemen as they stared the other down. Olivia did not understand it, but she knew if she stayed she'd be at risk of being tagged in Emerson's game.

She smiled at Mr. Trenor and offered, "I thank you for the dance, Mr. Trenor. Give my good wishes to your family." Slipping her arm from his, Olivia curtsied and quickly stepped away.

Emerson was by her side within four steps, his hand wrapping around hers as he pulled her, without her permission, toward a less-crowded spot at the edge of the room.

He turned Olivia so her back was to the wall. "What was that about?" he demanded, towering above her and blocking her from the view of the bustling ballroom. His heavy-handedness striking Olivia's ire.

"Forgive me," she began, not bothering to hide the sarcasm in her tone. "I was unaware that you did not understand the fashionable custom of dancing while at a ball."

He leveled her with a hard stare. "You have never cared about what is fashionable. And you know that was not what I meant."

Not caring to soothe his wounded pride after he had come for hers, Olivia held out her ridiculous, over-confectioned skirts. "Are you accusing me of not being fashionable?" She had intended her words to make him uncomfortable, though Olivia found herself struggling to get them out. Her gowns were utterly terrible, and she hated every one of them.

"Look me in the eye and tell me that if you had the choice you would have picked out all that lace"—he waved his hand about the colorful monstrosity—"and I shall bend down on both knees in this very ballroom to beg your for-giveness."

Unable to resist his dare, she jutted her chin and met his heated gaze. "I love this dress."

He smiled a broad and triumphant smile that told Olivia her trick had not worked. "How did those words taste?"

"Like vinegar mixed with salt," she replied, flexing her tongue in disgust.

He chuckled. "I wonder if I should be flattered or in-sulted that lying to me causes such a reaction in you," he teased, restoring the last bit of familiarity between them.

"Neither. I would feel the same if I lied to anyone." That itself was somewhat of a lie. She could, in fact, think of a few choice lies told during her life that she would never feel poorly about, but Emerson did not need to be privy to all her flaws.

"I am glad to hear it," he said. "I was beginning to won-der if you had done so when you made your promise to me." He took a step closer to her, no doubt to intimidate her into a confession. This was Emerson, after all; he was always about a game.

"I can assure you I had no intention of going back on my promise. But my father—"

"Is in the cardroom with Lord Trenor," Emerson said, cutting her off. "He went in about halfway through your dance."

Trust him. The words seemed to have taken up residence in her mind, only this time she felt inclined to believe them. Emerson was already watching out for her, without her even having to explain or ask.

"Is there something between you and Mr. Trenor?"

Olivia blinked in surprise. "I—I beg your pardon?"

"I simply noticed your father is playing cards with Lord Trenor, and you were dancing with his son. All would suggest some sort of connection between your two families."

His condescending assumption provoked her ire once again. "If the evidence before you was so *simple*, I wonder why you bothered to ask." She picked up her skirts, ready to shoulder her way past if need be, but she was halted by his hand grasping her arm.

His jaw flexed, and his lips pressed into a thin line. "Answer my questions, Liv. Please."

Baffled. Bothered. Resigned. She did not know what she felt, but against her better judgment she answered him honestly, regardless of how it might expose her failings. "There is *nothing* between Mr. Trenor and me, at least not outside of my father's business dealings with the gentleman's family. They receive sound investments in order to refill their coffers, and my father gets to believe his daughter could end up on the arm of a viscount. So you may rest assured that your game is safe for at least one evening."

He studied her a moment before slowly releasing her arm. "Dance with me?" he asked in a suspiciously gentle tone.

"Out of pity?" She hated having to ask the question, and how his answer had the power to upset her. He was her best friend's older brother, but for some strange reason, she found his answer truly mattered to her.

He shook his head, never breaking her gaze.

Olivia's breath quickened, and she found she had to look away.

"Come on," he said, playfully nudging her underneath her chin until she looked back at him. The intimate touch caused her to blush. She was making far too much of the connection, but his touch was pleasant. "It was why I came to find you in the first place."

The blood rushed from her cheeks, and she felt the fool. Of course his attentions meant nothing; this was all for the game.

Not wanting Emerson to suspect her tumultuous emotions, Olivia took his arm, her mind racing on how to free herself before he could tag her.

They reached the dance floor just as the music began and joined the end of the line. Emerson guided her across from him, and they watched as the lead couple made their way down the center.

It was a spirited dance, and Olivia struggled to remain cautious of her captor. Emerson must have sensed her emotions softening, for he wasted no time in finding opportunities to tease her. Holding on to her hand at one of the crosses, he made her late in partnering with another gentleman, who was taking the dance far too seriously with his straight face and exacting moves.

The gentleman glowered at Olivia for her tardiness, and as soon as his back was turned, Olivia shot Emerson a glare that promised retribution at the first opportunity. He merely laughed, clearly enjoying the prospect of the added sport during the evening.

She quickly settled upon a plan that would require a brief bend in the rules of etiquette, but if successful, would thwart Emerson of his victory. Taking a fortifying breath, she sent up a prayer that her father would remain in the cardroom and that her mother would be kept distracted by good friends.

Waiting until they returned to the end of the line, and with the music nearing its conclusion, Olivia gave Emerson her most beaming smile. He smiled in return, a lightness reaching his eyes.

It was the perfect time to strike. Without a backward glance, she dashed into the surrounding crowd. The press of people would make it difficult for Emerson to follow—assuming it would take him a moment to fully comprehend what she had done.

She held her breath as she wove through the moving crowd, fearing she was only delaying his opportunity to officially tag her as *it*.

Those were his rules. A tag only counted when contact was made *and* the words were spoken.

As more seconds passed and the distance between her and the dance floor grew, Olivia thrilled at the rush of excitement—though she would never admit to Emerson that it was all because of him.

SEVEN

Emerson watched Liv bolt from the dance floor. Her sudden rebellious spirit made him grin from ear to ear, and he felt utterly and completely transfixed. He could search the world over and never find another who called to him like she did.

Even now, his body twitched to chase after her as she disappeared into the crowd. But he forced himself in the opposite direction. He could not run the risk of being too obvious too soon in his attentions.

The fact that she was playing with him proved his plan was working. He prayed he had enough time to see it all the way through.

The moment he had seen Olivia's father enter the ballroom with his family, Emerson's heart had nearly stopped. Then having to watch as Mr. Wilde directed them to converse with Lord Trenor and the sight of Liv standing up with one of the sons had been akin to torture.

He had felt the same way he had when his father had

been on his deathbed. He never wanted to feel so helpless when it came to someone he lov—

Emerson froze midstride, his breath seizing in his lungs as his heart pounded hard. Someone in the crowd knocked into his back, and yet he did not move. Had he truly just thought what he believed he did?

Yes! His mind practically shouted.

He was a man in love.

He needed air. He needed a drink. He needed to win her love.

Emerson pressed forward toward the cardroom where Bradbury had been keeping watch over Liv's father. It had been a task his friend had been more than willing to take—better than dancing with Arabella, he said, to which Northcott then agreed to escort Emerson's sister to the dance floor.

In the cardroom, Bradbury sat with his customary group of gentlemen onlookers, laughing at something his friend had said—no doubt outlandish—as he threw down his last card onto the table.

Not wanting to draw attention to himself, Emerson walked along the outer wall until he found a spot directly in Bradbury's line of sight.

When Bradbury looked up, he tipped his head toward his left.

Emerson glanced over and saw Olivia's father seated at another table in the far corner of the room. He was engrossed in a high-stakes game, judging by the stacks of banknotes and possessions piled on top of his table.

Relieved that Mr. Wilde remained unaware of Olivia's

whereabouts, but still needing to speak with Bradbury, Emerson tried to regain his friend's attention. His attempt was noticed—but by the wrong gentleman.

"Ah, there you are, Latham." A soused Lord Digby nearly toppled over in his endeavor to reach him. "Finally come back to your senses to join me in the delights of vice?" The lord hiccupped, an empty crystal glass slipping from his unsteady hand.

Lunging, Emerson caught the glass before it could shatter. Handing it to an approaching footman, he reached for Lord Digby before he could follow his glass to the floor.

"Allow me, my lord," Emerson said, assisting him to the nearest chair. The humor of having played out almost this exact interaction a few days before was not lost on him; Lord Digby, on the other hand, likely held little recollection of it.

The portly lord crashed into his seat, the wood creaking beneath the sheer force of the drunkard.

"You are a good"—Lord Digby belched—"lad. Unlike that friend of yours—Bradbury." He slurred his words, swaying slightly in his seat. "That man has been trying to goad me into betting more of my coin by claiming that wager of yours in the betting book is as good as done." He scoffed. "Inconceivable, is what I told him. I know Brummell well enough to know he has his boots polished with champagne. A dandy like that would never let one of his pristine waistcoats out of his sight. And I am so confident, I wagered him another ten pounds saying it will never be done."

Emerson's shoulders quaked as he held back the burst of laughter threatening to break free from his lips. "From what you have just told me, Lord Digby, it sounds as if my friend has accomplished his purpose."

Lord Digby chuckled, clearly not comprehending Emerson's words, then, when the realization settled upon him, his eyes bulged and his laughter died upon his lips.

Shooting to his unsteady feet, Lord Digby stumbled forward, his rounded gut catching the closest table, causing him to stumble backward.

Emerson caught him before he could fall back into his former chair.

"Well, see here—that scoundrel—" Lord Digby sputtered in shock.

"Do not let it trouble you, my lord," Emerson said, hoping to calm him before he could make any more of a scene. He dared not draw Mr. Wilde's attention. "My friend and I have only gone so far as to procure the pig. There is still much more to accomplish before our time is up. You may very well be seeing that money returned to you."

The group of gentlemen around them, all of whom Emerson recognized from their club, broke into private clusters of conversation, no doubt discussing the time that remained for Bradbury and Emerson to fulfill their wager and whether they should follow Digby's example and stake more against Bradbury's claim.

With Lord Digby settled, Emerson left him in the care of a footman. Securing the notice of Bradbury, he signaled with a nod to meet at a more private corner of the room.

Bradbury nodded and excused himself from his game.

"I could not have done that better myself," Bradbury said as soon as they came together, a pleased smile on his lips. They leaned back against one of the outer walls, arms crossed over their chests as they surveyed the part of the room buzzing about the words Lord Digby and Emerson had exchanged. "I would say there is at least another fifty pounds to be won, if any of them fall for your artifice."

"Who says it was artifice?" Emerson replied as he eyed his friend. "We still have yet to collect one of Brummell's waistcoats."

"As I said earlier, leave that to me."

"I wish I could share in your confidence," Emerson drawled. He had serious doubts about the wager he'd had no part in making but had somehow become caught up in.

Neither one of them was personally acquainted with the dandy Beau Brummell, though his reputation as the singular authority of men's fashion was well known. He had been a close, personal friend of the Prince Regent, until a few years ago when the two had had a falling out at a ball at Watier's. While Brummell remained a popular figure among fashionable society, where he held his own court in the bow street window at White's, the odds of Emerson or Bradbury procuring an item of his clothing was narrow at best.

Bradbury's green eyes flickered with mischief. "I never make a wager I cannot win."

"What about when we were at Eton and you said you could knock Fredrick's hat from his head by throwing an apple from the first-floor window as he walked through the courtyard?" Emerson asked.

"Your only argument is to recall a wager from when we were boys?" Bradbury scoffed. "Besides, I would have won if the dunderhead had not pulled his attention from his book at the last minute. Honestly, who is afraid of a few squawking birds?" He threw his hands up in exasperation.

Knowing of several more instances when Bradbury had lost wagers, Emerson continued. "Last year, you wagered—"

"Do we not have better things to be doing?" Bradbury cut him off, his annoyance hard to mistake.

"You are right. One problem at a time." Emerson was grateful for the perfect transition to ask for what he needed from his friend.

A wolfish grin spread across Bradbury's face. "So you agree. I am always in the right."

Emerson looked to the heavens for patience. "I believe the argument was not about how you are always right, but whether you always *win*."

"Right, win—they are practically one and the same." He waved a dismissive hand. "Now, what is it you need from me? By the looks of it, Mr. Wilde has no intention of leaving the cardroom." They both glanced to where Liv's father sat, his attention still focused at his table.

Emerson nodded. "We can keep a more casual eye on him for now. But I would appreciate it if you could search for Miss Wilde. I suspect you will find her somewhere near my sister."

"Oh, good, your sister is always easy enough to find. One needs only to follow the trail of annoyed groans from the gentlemen she has driven mad with her incessant chatter," Bradbury said with a raised eyebrow.

Emerson felt he should defend his sister with at least a scowl directed to Bradbury—though his friend's assumption was likely correct. "Will you go?"

"So you are saying that I am *it*, then?" Bradbury asked, thankfully steering the conversation in its intended direction.

Emerson patted him on the shoulder with an easy smile. "You are *it*."

"It is about time," he drawled. "I was beginning to fear you had tagged that bore of a baron."

"You know I have asked Northcott to keep an eye on my sister."

"Trust me, I am well aware, and I am grateful you did not ask me."

Emerson glared at Bradbury, who held up his hands in mock protest.

"I am merely stating that the pair of them would be a good idea. He is better for listening, while she is good for talking." He touched his fingers to his thumb, opening and closing them in the form of a mouth as if that would help further prove his point.

Emerson eyed Bradbury, wanting his friend to see the hypocrisy of his own words and gestures, but he either did not notice or did not care. "Are you going to play or not?"

Bradbury huffed as if Emerson's request was suddenly a burden. "There is no rest for the wickedly handsome." He tugged at his lapels. "The devilishly charming." He dusted a speck of nonexistent fluff from his jacket sleeve. "The dashingly sophisticated. The—"

"Ridiculously pigheaded," Emerson finished, before shoving him in the direction of the ballroom.

Bradbury turned back, his hand pressed to his chest as if he had been stabbed. "You wound me, sir."

"Will you just go?" Emerson practically begged, trying to hold back his laughter.

"How can I deny an encore?" Bradbury grinned, offering an exaggerated bow, complete with a flourish, before exiting the room.

Emerson shook his head fondly, laughing. He should be envious of Bradbury's carefree life, but he found he could not. He would not trade a life of hardship for a life of ease, because he knew his struggle could earn him a lifetime with Liv.

EIGHT

Olivia knew she was acting foolishly. As the dutiful daughter, she should have returned to her mother's side the moment she left Emerson. But the thought of smiling, simpering, and practically begging any gentleman with a title to notice her forced her to continue weaving her way through the crowded ballroom. Her small taste of rebellion was pulling her elsewhere.

She needed to find Arabella. Olivia was not so foolish as to think she could play this game all on her own. And Arabella would know what to do about the entire herd of elephants running wild inside her stomach.

Cheeks flushed, heart stampeding, she tried to maintain her composure as she felt more and more eyes shooting questioning glances in her direction.

Was she making a terrible mistake? Was her attempt at deception written all over her face?

Olivia tried to draw in a few calming breaths but the air felt thick in her lungs. She swallowed hard, suddenly panicking that she might be choking. Her skin felt cool, almost clammy, and she could not shake the urge to sit down. She changed her course, moving toward the nearest corner where there was a group of empty chairs. She just needed a moment to catch her breath, then maybe she would not feel she might faint. She just needed—

Her vision immediately went dark. She heard a voice whisper from behind her.

"Knock. Knock." Arabella's voice held a laugh, and Olivia realized her friend had covered her eyes with her hands.

"Macbeth," Olivia replied with a sigh of relief. She removed Arabella's hands and turned around to hug her. "I am so relieved to see you. You will not believe what I just—"

Arabella cut her off with a laugh and freed herself from Olivia's embrace. "No, no, wait. You are supposed to say, 'Who's there?'"

Olivia's lips twitched, but she did her best not to laugh, though she desperately wanted to. Arabella loved playing her word games. "My apologies. *Who's there?*"

"Faith, *an English*"—she paused, as if thinking through something—"lady, *come hither for stealing* you away for an evening of fun: *come in*—so that I *may roast your goose.*"

"What?" Olivia's laugh could no longer be contained. From what she could make of it, only bits and pieces of Arabella's words had actually been from Shakespeare, but other parts appeared to be completely made up.

Arabella huffed with feigned annoyance. "In other words, I have come to see to it that you have an evening of fun." Excitement danced in her eyes.

"But that is what I was trying to tell you," Olivia said, shaking her head. "I have already crossed paths with your brother, and oh, Arabella, it was thrilling. I narrowly managed to get away before he could tag me. If only I could have seen the look on his face." This time there were no stampeding elephants inside her stomach, but rather the spreading of a peacock's magnificent tail, its feathers fanning a spark into a flame.

"I imagine you will know soon enough," Arabella said as she took Olivia by the shoulders and turned her to face the refreshment table.

At first, Olivia felt almost frozen in shock, thinking Emerson had caught up to her. But it was not Emerson standing at the refreshment table, but Mr. Bradbury. He looked rather pleased with himself, and he raised a glass of punch in her direction.

"This is what I meant earlier," Arabella said, giggling in her ear. "It appears that after you escaped my brother, he tagged Mr. Bradbury, and then Mr. Bradbury tagged me."

Olivia's head snapped around to stare at Arabella. Both her hands were still on Olivia's shoulders, holding her in place.

Arabella grinned. "As I said—your goose is cooked, Olivia. Tag. You are *it*."

Within the blink of an eye, Arabella bolted from Olivia's side, leaving her stunned, realization slowly dawning about what had happened.

She was *it*. And tagged by Arabella, whom she had believed would stand loyally on her side. Olivia waited for her earlier panic and fear to take over, but instead, the faintest of giggles burst from her lips, which she quickly smothered behind her fingertips. This was the most fun she'd had at a ball in months.

Knowing she had to start somewhere if she was going to

free herself from the role of being *it*, Olivia turned toward the refreshment table. She truly did not expect to find Mr. Bradbury still standing there, but there he remained, a sly, smug smile upon his lips. Only now he had changed his position at the table—he had moved to the other side, using its long slender length as a veritable moat. She would have to find a way over or around the table if she was going to be able to tag him.

Rising to Mr. Bradbury's challenge, Olivia approached as if merely a lady in need of refreshment. She stopped directly in front of him, the large crystal bowl of lemonade at the center of the table between them.

"Was the punch not to your liking, Mr. Bradbury?" Olivia asked, choosing her words carefully to avoid raising suspicion to anyone who might be listening. She hoped Mr. Bradbury alone would hear her teasing him for hiding on the other side of the table.

"On the contrary, Miss Wilde, I found the *drink* quite satisfying and sweet." His wolfish grin told Olivia that he knew very well what she had meant.

"I am sure Lady Stansbury would be delighted to hear such a compliment," Olivia replied, her mind racing to find a way to get to the other side of the table. And then the answer came to her, and she smiled both at its simplicity and practically. "Perhaps, Mr. Bradbury, you would be so kind as to hand me a lemonade?"

Her smile grew into a triumphant grin. When he handed her the glass of lemonade, Olivia would be able to brush her fingers across his, thus tagging him as *it*.

Mr. Bradbury's eyes widened as he realized her scheme.

He looked to the right and the left, but the two footmen assigned to the table were occupied assisting others elsewhere along the table.

"Mr. Bradbury?" she prompted with a teasing tone. He was as good as trapped.

He cleared his throat. "Uh, yes. Of course."

His movements were slow, as if he were holding out for a miracle. His hand had barely reached the ladle when he froze. His gaze moved beyond Olivia's shoulder just as she felt the presence of someone coming to stand beside her.

"—And then I took him for twenty pounds," the gentleman boasted to another man beside him.

As the newcomer reached for one of the cups, Mr. Bradbury smiled in relief. "Ah, Lord Emsworth," he said. "How convenient we should meet outside the cardroom."

The gentleman snatched back his hand as if it had been slapped, then he awkwardly cleared his throat and looked around, which only appeared to please Mr. Bradbury further.

Lord Emsworth's companion scuttled away as fast as decorum would allow.

"Yes, Mr. Bradbury. I was—That is to say, how fortunate." Lord Emsworth swallowed, a line of sweat beading across his brow. "I shall be able to pay my promissory note much sooner than I had previously thought."

"I am glad to hear it." Mr. Bradbury's smile grew exponentially as he looked from Lord Emsworth to Olivia, and then back to the lord. "Have you had the pleasure of making the acquaintance of Miss Wilde?"

"I have not had the pleasure," Lord Emsworth said,

forcing a thin smile as he offered her a slight bow, barely enough to bend his neck in a nod.

Olivia did not know if the gentleman owed her father money, but clearly he at least knew *of* her father. Lord Emsworth's visible distaste was all too familiar to Olivia.

She demurely smiled while offering him a proper curtsey. "Lord Emsworth." The new acquaintance would not last long, but with any luck, her father would at least see or hear that she had spoken with the gentleman.

"I was just offering Miss Wilde some lemonade as a sort of consolation," Mr. Bradbury began. "You see, I promised the beautiful lady a dance, but my accursed knee has been acting up tonight." He leaned forward and patted his leg, giving a dramatic, pained hiss at the touch.

"How unfortunate," Lord Emsworth said, either not understanding Mr. Bradbury's intent to pawn Olivia off on him or simply not wanting to take the bait.

Mr. Bradbury looked to the ceiling. "I say . . ." he said slowly, as if an idea had just then struck him. He tapped a finger to his chin. "Why do you not ask the lady to dance?" Lord Emsworth made to object, but Mr. Bradbury cut him off. "As a *favor* among friends."

Olivia's cheeks warmed, hating being the main—and unwanted—topic of their conversation. "Thank you, Mr. Bradbury, but I would not want to be—"

"I would be happy to step in. For a *friend*," Lord Emsworth replied, nodding once to Mr. Bradbury before turning to offer Olivia his arm. "Shall we, Miss Wilde?"

Olivia could only offer him the barest of smiles as she slipped her hand into the crook of his arm. No matter how many times she had danced with a gentleman who had been forced—or in this case—blackmailed into standing up with her, the sting of the degradation never seemed to ease.

Dropping her gaze, she turned and followed Lord Emsworth toward the dance floor.

"Miss Wilde?" Mr. Bradbury called out to her in a gentle tone, stopping Olivia's retreat. His amused smile had faded, replaced by one of compassion and regret.

"Yes, Mr. Bradbury?"

He cleared his throat. "At another time, I would be honored to stand up with you."

A friendly warmth settled in her chest, and she knew Mr. Bradbury saw her as his equal. "Thank you, Mr. Bradbury," she said with a quiet dignity that she rarely felt. She straightened her back, held her head high, and stepped onto the dance floor with Lord Emsworth.

The dance was a reel, which Olivia appreciated because it gave her ample amount of time to search the surrounding ballroom while the other couple in their group performed their part of the alternating dance.

About halfway through the dance, Olivia spotted Lord Northcott standing alone toward the side of the room. The baron was known to be a private man, the whispers about his family's dark past no doubt a reason why he preferred to keep to himself. She had never known him to be anything other than a gentleman, which was why she made up her mind to try to tag him as soon as the dance was done.

Her plan would require her to tell a few small lies, but as they would only be to Lord Emsworth, she felt confident she would be spared the taste of salt and vinegar.

As soon as the music ended, Olivia wasted very little time smiling at the other couple and clapping for the musicians. She needed to move quickly before Lord Northcott could disappear into the crowd.

Taking Lord Emsworth's arm before he had even offered it, she asked, "I wonder, my lord, if you would be so kind as to escort me to Lord Northcott? My next dance is promised to him."

Lord Emsworth was more than happy to oblige her. Clearly his "friendship" with Mr. Bradbury did not extend to insisting on a second dance.

"He is right over there," she said, gesturing toward Lord Northcott.

"I see him, Miss Wilde," Lord Emsworth said with annoyance. "No need to point."

Olivia's mother would have also been displeased at seeing her daughter perform such an uncultivated gesture in the middle of a ballroom, but Olivia's plan required swiftness and precision.

When they found their way to Lord Northcott, Lord Emsworth did not bother to engage in small talk.

"Here you are, Lord Northcott," he said, offering Olivia over to him. It was not the most polite of ways to make the exchange, but Olivia was not about to object. She had no plans to ever encounter Lord Emsworth again.

Lord Northcott studied them both and then raised a single brow—which was a shocking display of emotion from the Brooding Baron—but Olivia held firm. She was grateful he did not question Lord Emsworth. Now, she hoped Lord

Northcott would show mercy on her for the sake of the game and play along.

"Lord Emsworth was kind enough to escort me to you for our dance," Olivia said with enough sugar in her smile to rival her over-confectioned gown.

Lord Northcott studied her for another long, agonizing moment. Each passing second tightened the pressure in her chest until she thought her lungs might seize. A real panic began to weigh like a stone upon her chest.

Please understand, she begged him with her eyes.

"Yes." Lord Northcott nodded an unspoken dismissal of the other man, who quickly made his excuses and left.

Olivia blinked, not sure at all as to how she had managed to pull off her plan. She stared at Lord Northcott for a moment. Never before had they been together without one of the others from their social group, and it was proving to be rather awkward.

"I wanted to thank you, Lord Northcott, for playing along in my little—my little ruse," she said, taking the coward's way out and not admitting to her lie.

Lord Northcott simply nodded.

Goodness, this is proving to be rather difficult.

"What is this I see?" Emerson stepped up beside Lord Northcott with far too much smugness, proving his arrival was anything but coincidence.

Olivia had to believe Emerson was completely aware that she was *it*, but she found it too enticing to not try to get back at him for attempting to catch her earlier during the ball. She prayed Lord Northcott would forgive her for one last ruse.

"Lord Northcott was kind enough to ask me to dance," she said with the confidence of any actress on stage.

Emerson looked to Lord Northcott with a questioning eyebrow. Perhaps it was too contrived of a lie to say Lord Northcott had actually said anything at all.

She slyly shot Lord Northcott another begging glance.

Lord Northcott cleared his throat and then spoke to Emerson. "Indeed."

Sweet victory and relief flooded through her as she reached for Lord Northcott's arm. She would apologize and thank him as soon as they were away from Emerson.

Before she actually made contact with Lord Northcott's extended arm, however, she turned to Emerson, noting that his eyes were fixed on the gap between his friend's arm and her hand. "I wanted to apologize for my flight from the dance floor earlier this evening. I hope you were not too embarrassed being left there all alone."

Emerson finally met her eyes, but instead of looking annoyed as she had hoped, she thought he almost looked delighted. "Quite the contrary, I can assure you."

His answer caught Olivia off guard, but she would not allow him to rob her of her victory. Moving her hand from where it still hung over Lord Northcott's arm, she delicately clasped Emerson's forearm.

She leaned forward, so close that she could smell a rather stirring scent of leather and winter from his skin. With a smile she was sure met her eyes, she whispered, "What a relief. For now, I must inform you that you are *it*."

NINE

Emerson could not have hoped for a better start to his game. Even now, days after the Stansburys' ball, he could still picture the twin flames of mischief and amusement in Liv's eyes as she leaned forward and whispered to him that he was *it*. The feel of her breath upon his skin had sent a jolt of pleasure directly through him, and he had wanted nothing more in that moment than to lean forward and kiss her firmly upon the lips.

He would be chasing after her now, in Major General Cromwell's ballroom, which was lavishly decorated in the new and budding style of the Egyptian revival, if only Liv's father could somehow be removed from her side. Mr. Wilde appeared determined to throw Liv in the way of any gentleman with a title. Watching him parade Liv around the room made Emerson sick.

"What the devil is this?" Bradbury asked with both horror and disgust.

Emerson dragged his eyes away from Liv to find his friend poking at a robust, black marble statue of a man holding a gold flail in his left hand and wearing a gold ribbon around his neck. His head was that of a jackal, complete with a long, canine nose and pointed ears.

"It is the Egyptian god Anubis," Emerson said in a wry tone.

Bradbury was nearly eye level with the statue and regarded it with distrust.

"You need not look so alarmed," Emerson continued. "He will not bite—unless, as god of the underworld, he decides to come back from the afterlife."

Bradbury jerked his hand back and shot Emerson a scowl. "Why on earth would someone want something like that in their home? Daft mad, if you ask me." He frowned, a wrinkle forming down the middle of his brow as he scanned the rest of the Egyptian statues and artwork around the ballroom.

It was a sight to behold. Every table and every chair was made of black beechwood and gold. Several gold columns stood sentinel along the edge of the ballroom, each supporting a statue of an Egyptian god or pharaoh.

"How do you know about all this . . . ?" Bradbury waved his hand toward the other statues.

"I have an aunt in Bath who is an admirer of Thomas Hope and shares his love of Egyptian furniture and antiquities. She delights in treating me as a credulous boy of seven and tries to frighten me with ancient stories of mummies and the afterlife," Emerson said, his lips twitched with amusement.

Bradbury shot him an annoyed glance and tugged at his lapels. "Smirk all you want, but I have no interest in entertaining anything to do with curses or bad luck."

"You and your imagination, Bradbury," Emerson said with a laugh. "I was only goading you before. They're not cursed. They are simply statues. They cannot hurt you."

Bradbury grumbled something under his breath, still refusing to lay another finger on the statue.

Out of the corner of his eye, Emerson caught Liv and her father moving around the ballroom, ending up in the company of the ancient, and thrice-widowed, Lord Beckwith. The gentleman did not appear at all interested in the conversation, but Emerson could not stop his mind and stomach from roiling at the thought of Liv having to be subjected to such a match.

"Have you figured out a way to extract Miss Wilde?" Bradbury asked.

Emerson let out a heavy sigh. "Ideas? Yes. Ones that will not draw unwanted attention? None."

"Well, then," Bradbury said, clapping him on the back, "you are lucky to have me. I, for one, love attention. What must I do?"

Emerson shook his head and chuckled at his friend. "I must warn you, it will require you to ask her to dance."

Bradbury grimaced, then nodded like a soldier preparing for battle. "Very well. I am indebted to her for one dance, after all."

"What?" Emerson asked, his mind bristling with unreasonable jealousy. Why would Bradbury owe Liv a dance?

Bradbury grinned without remorse, as if pleased to have kept a secret from Emerson. "Never worry—your lady is yours. I merely foisted her onto another man's arm at the

Stansburys' ball to avoid being tagged. I promised her a dance to make amends."

Emerson scowled, but Bradbury continued as if not seeing it.

"Your Miss Wilde is a remarkable woman. One forlorn look and even I was brought to contrition. Are you sure you want to pursue her? One flutter of her eyes, and she will be directing your willing heart about like a babe in leading strings."

The thought brought a grin to Emerson's face. To have Liv as his wife, he would gladly sew the straps to his breeches himself.

Bradbury groaned. "Would you wipe that lovestruck look from your face? We have a game to play." Shaking his head, Bradbury headed toward Liv and Mr. Wilde.

Knowing his friend could talk his way into anything, Emerson did not wait around to witness his success. Instead, he went in search of his mother and sister.

He had been neglecting his duty to them almost the entire evening, which was something his father would never have done. His father's memory weighed heavily upon Emerson's shoulders, and at times, he felt as if he would never be able to carry the burden of so much responsibility as well as his father once did.

His mother and sister were easy enough to find, thanks to the towering, dark pillar Lord Northcott proved to be. He stood to one side of Emerson's mother, no doubt using her as a screen from Arabella. Though, now that his own eyes had wandered to Arabella, she looked rather cross, which did not bode well for him.

"There you are," his mother said, offering him a hesitant smile. A further sign that Arabella was in one of her moods due to boredom. "I was wondering where you had gone off to."

"Forgive me, Mother," he said, using all his willpower to ignore the sudden stabbing pain of guilt buried deep inside his chest. "I was somewhat detained. Are you well?"

Though his father's death had happened well over a year ago, Emerson still worried about his mother's fragile sensibilities. She did her best to look the picture of health to all in society for Arabella's sake, but Emerson could see her struggle in the dimness of her eyes and the small steadying breaths she sometimes took.

"I am well." She cleared her throat and darted her eyes toward Arabella, who was tapping her feet beneath her skirts as she stretched her neck to try to look over the crowd.

He held back a groan. He needed to do something for his sister before she began to vocalize her boredom or, worse, do something on her own to fix it. "Lord Northcott, would you be so kind as to escort my mother to the refreshment table? I believe she is looking a bit parched."

Northcott nodded and held out his arm to Emerson's mother.

She hesitated before taking it, looking to Emerson with concern. She had recently spoken with him regarding how she and his father had learned that a heavy-handed approach with Arabella never worked. She no doubt feared he would continue his old ways despite her advice, not knowing that her words only added to his guilt.

He had known that about his sister, which proved to

him yet again how he was falling short in his responsibilities. Where most girls were calm, Arabella was curious, and any attempt to hold her back only sparked her resistance. Which was why involving her in the game had done much to quell the majority of their quarreling.

With Northcott and his mother away, he turned to Arabella. "Is—"

"Are you *it*?" she asked with excitement, grabbing hold of his arm. "Oh, please tell me you are. If I have to dance with another indifferent dandy I am bound to lose all sense."

"I am sure Lord Northcott would be displeased to hear that you refer to him as a dandy." He was not sure why he did not give her a straightforward answer, but some part of him wanted to tease her as her brother—and not as her guardian.

"Seeing as he has not asked me to dance this evening, I doubt he will take offense," she replied with a triumphant tilt of her chin.

The sudden feeling to call out his friend for such a slight to his sister flooded over him, and then he realized the wisdom in it. The ever-observant Northcott would not wish to have society see him ask Arabella to dance at every ball. Such behavior would only provide fodder for the insatiable gossips. Emerson would do well to remember such actions when it came to Liv.

"So, are you *it*?" Arabella repeated, bringing Emerson back to the present.

Emerson hesitated with his answer. He was indeed *it*, but he had been hoping to use it as a means to pursue Liv. If he tagged his sister, he would be at the mercy of whenever she could tag someone else. And if Arabella tagged Liv, what were the odds she would come after him? He was not sure he was patient enough to find out.

Ready to deny her, Emerson stopped short, his sister's wide fawn-colored eyes staring up at him.

Your father knew when to indulge her spirit and when to guide it back. His mother's counseling words filled his head, and his duty to his father's memory won out.

Reaching out to pat her hand, which was still tugging on his forearm, Emerson forced a smile. "Never say I do nothing for you, little sister. Tag, you are *it.*"

"Yes!" Arabella hissed with excitement, her eyes already scanning the dance floor for her next victim.

But Emerson was not quite willing to let her go just yet. "Only promise me that you will behave yourself. Nothing rash, and nothing that could risk getting back to our mother."

Arabella scoffed. "It is like you do not know me at all. I am the epitome of discretion. Why only yesterday, I switched the large mantel clock in our sitting room with the small one in our library, and neither you nor Mother has mentioned anything about it."

Emerson shook his head and chuckled to himself. He truly had not noticed her activities. "What would possess you to do something like that?"

"Shakespeare, of course." She grinned. *"Make use of time, let not advantage slip; beauty within itself should not be wasted: Fair flowers that are not gather'd in their prime rot and consume themselves in little time."*

Emerson wanted to question her on how that passage had inspired her to switch around the clocks, but his mind had snagged on one part of the verse: *"let not advantage slip."* He had no intention of doing so when it came to Liv.

Giving his sister her freedom, Emerson went in search of Bradbury and Liv. A dance had just concluded, and it took him several minutes to spot Bradbury in the crowd of people surrounding the dance floor. He was alone, and a wave of disappointment hit Emerson. What had Bradbury done with Liv?

"Where is she?" Emerson asked, the moment they came together.

Bradbury gazed over the crowd in satisfaction. "You can wipe that scowl off your face, my friend. Your lady is free of her captor."

Emerson scanned the crowd, but still he found nothing. "What did you do with her?"

"I danced with her and then tagged her." Bradbury beamed as if he had done something remarkable.

"You did what?" Emerson did his best not to shout. His heart pounded in his chest, and his body tensed. Both Arabella and Liv were somewhere in the ballroom under the impression that they were *it*.

"I tagged her." Bradbury frowned in incomprehension.

"What possessed you to do that?" Emerson asked as cold sweat beaded the back of his neck. Should Liv and his sister attempt to tag one another and discover that both of them had been tagged *it*, they would both come in search of him demanding answers. He would then be forced to admit in front of Liv that mistakes had been made.

Mistakes he could not afford to make. Not when her tentative agreement to play was held on the promise that he had made the game foolproof and that he could keep it safe enough for her to play.

She could decide to withdraw from the game before more mistakes could be made.

He could not let that happen.

A look of panic washed over Bradbury's face. He glanced to the nearby marble statue of the Egyptian god Horus and swallowed.

"Would you stop being so suspicious and help me figure out what to do?"

"Why? What does it matter if I tagged her or you? Either way she is out there somewhere playing the game."

"Because I also tagged my sister," Emerson said in exasperation. "I never told you that you were *it*. I only asked you to get her away from her father."

"Oh," Bradbury replied, looking contrite and serious. "What are you going to do now?"

"*I* am going to look for Liv. *You* are going to go look for my sister, so that you can throw yourself in front of her and beg to be tagged as *it*. And then you are going to do nothing."

Bradbury's jaw flexed, his lips tight and turned down. "I was hopeful that I would no longer have to tell you this, but you, sir, are proving to be even less fun than Northcott."

"That may be, but I have responsibilities I cannot ignore." Emerson tried to take in a calming breath, his chest heaving from his agitation.

Bradbury fell silent, which was a rarity for him. His breathing grew long and heavy, and he looked as if he were trying to make a decision. "Very well. I will find your sister." He began to walk away, but paused after the third step.

Turning back to face Emerson, he said, "And just so you are aware, I was also able to convince Mr. Wilde to meet me in the cardroom so that you could more freely go after Miss Wilde." Not waiting for a response, Bradbury turned and left.

Feeling guilty and like a terrible friend, Emerson scrubbed his hands over his eyes and went in search of Liv, even though he was no longer in a mood for fun and games. He would set the situation to rights and be grateful that no damage had been done. Then he would attend to his mother and see to her comfort for the remainder of the evening.

He had walked nearly the entire length of the ballroom before he spotted Liv near the winged statue of the Egyptian goddess Isis. She appeared caught in the snare set by Lady Bixbee and her circle of matrons, all of whom were whispering and pointing at whichever guest walked by. By the anxious look on Liv's face as she continually broke from the conversation and scanned the crowd, he would guess she was looking for a way out. How fortunate that he was prepared to do exactly that.

"Good evening to you, ladies," he said, stepping into the lion's den with a bow.

"Mr. Latham," a stout Lady Bixbee said as she took his measure behind the flicking of her fan. "I wonder at your joining us?" The other matrons around him hummed their agreement to the great lady's question, their eyes glancing from Lady Bixbee to him and then to Liv.

Emerson did not mind. With any luck, the matchmaking matrons would help move the needed outcome along. But he would have to work to not make it too obvious.

"I came in search of a lovely dance partner."

The other matrons were eating out of the palm of his hand as they smiled and flicked their fans faster, looking between him and Liv.

"What say you, Lady Bixbee? Would you care to dance?"

Some of the other matrons gasped, while Lady Bixbee raised a rather large, skeptical, gray brow. The old matron had never danced as long as he had known her, and he was gambling on the fact that she would continue the tradition.

The longer she watched him, the more unease he felt. Lud, this evening was not going at all as he had planned.

"I believe we would both rather not," Lady Bixbee replied as she continued to stare him down, which was an odd feeling as he was the taller of the two. "But, as we are both well aware of that fact, I will assume you came in search of this young lady." She pointed her fan at Liv, whose cheeks turned crimson.

"You are forever wise, Lady Bixbee," Emerson said, knowing the next best thing would be to flatter her pride.

"And do not forget it." Lady Bixbee smirked. "Now, properly ask the girl."

Emerson nodded and stood as rigid as a soldier. "May I have this dance, Miss Wilde?"

"I am afraid that is not possible," Liv replied, knocking him off balance.

"Whyever not?" His panicked mind began to run away with questions. Why would she not want to take advantage of the opportunity to tag him *it*? Had she already found Arabella? Had she come to Lady Bixbee to hide from him after discovering his deception?

"Well, Mr. Latham, dancing has adjourned at present,"

Liv replied, a slow smile cresting her lips. "You see, sir, this last set was the supper set."

Emerson jerked his attention to the nearly empty dance floor.

Many of the matrons giggled behind their fans, though Lady Bixbee did nothing to hide her boastful grin.

He had made an utter fool of himself and, for some reason, all he could do was laugh. "I see you are correct, Miss Wilde. Perhaps, you will allow me to change my request and offer you a tour through Egypt as we make our way to join the others at supper?"

Liv did her best to hide her grin, but the levity in her eyes was unmistakable. "A tour through Egypt? How exciting." The moment her fingers touched his arm, he was thinking the very same thing.

Emerson made their excuses, and then he made sure to walk at a much slower pace. No doubt her mother or father would claim her the moment they stepped into the dining room.

"You made a gallant attempt at my rescue, Emerson," Liv said with a giggle as soon as they were out of the gossipy matrons' reach. "Though, I do wonder what was behind such a decision?"

"Oh?" Emerson raised a brow, tempting her to tag him.

Her grip on his arm tightened, as if she feared he might try to run away. If only she knew he wished to be forever bound to her.

"Yes, Liv?" He teased her further, liking the way her breath suddenly quickened.

"You knew?" she gasped, slapping his arm with her free hand.

Emerson chuckled. "I knew."

"Then why would you approach me, knowing I am *it*?" She shook her head and laughed.

"To tempt you," he said, stopping their progress and looking deep into her eyes.

Liv swallowed as her cheeks reddened, and she looked elsewhere. "What is that?" She pointed to the statue of a man with the head of a falcon and crowned with a round sun.

"That is the Egyptian god Ra," he replied, never taking his eyes from her, though she kept her eyes on the statue. "It is said the Egyptians celebrated each sunrise because that meant Ra had risen victorious after traveling through the underworld every night."

"How comforting," she said, raising her hand to gently run a finger across the rounded edge of the golden sun. "To know that hope lay on the other side."

Emerson wanted to reach out to her, pull her into his arms and offer her comfort. Offer her hope for a brighter future.

Someday, he told himself, *someday when the timing is right, I will not hesitate.*

TEN

With a sense of over-indulged recklessness, Olivia surveyed the empty foyer below her. Satisfied she would not be seen, she hiked up her skirts to her knees and did something she had not done since she was a child. Sitting sidesaddle on the wide, marble banister, Olivia lifted her feet, intending to slide only a few yards of the way down. What she had not anticipated was how quickly she slid toward the giant gold orb at the end of the banister. Barreling down at a speed she could not alter, Olivia did the only thing she could to save herself from a surely disastrous ending.

With an internal cry, she launched herself off the banister, stumbling the moment her feet made contact with the steps. Unbalanced, her feet slipped down step after step. Reaching her arms forward, she grabbed for the opposite banister, her heart pounding in her ears as she anticipated a crash in her near future.

But a crash never came. Her slippered feet finally stopped, and her hands gripped the cold marble banister, helping her to stabilize the rest of her body.

"That was close," she said aloud, the words slipping from her lips unbidden.

"I couldn'a agree more, miss." A male voice, heavily laced with an East End Cockney accent, chuckled from nearby.

Olivia swirled to face the foyer, her feet nearly slipping one last time as she saw Jenson, her family's butler smiling at her. Keeping a proper English butler to serve a man like Joshua Wilde had proven difficult, which was how they had come to have a man like Jenson serving in such a high position.

Growing up, Olivia had found Jenson to be more secret protector to her mischief than servant.

Smiling back, Olivia brushed at her skirts. "I merely stumbled."

"Oh, aye, miss." Jenson shot her a half grin as he nodded. "I'll make certain the maids hold back on the polish. Wouldn' want to see ya go a stumblin' so fast the next time." Another chuckle rumbled from deep within his chest.

"That will not be necessary," Olivia began, wishing she could rub out the pain shooting up her legs. "I shall simply watch my *steps* from now on."

Perhaps she was a little too old for some of her childhood games.

Jenson's smile widened as he nodded once more. "Mistress Wilde informed me to tell ya, she will be out shortly."

Olivia thanked Jenson, who then excused himself to see to the carriage Olivia and her mother had requested for their visit to the Lathams.

Left alone in the large open foyer, Olivia sat in one of the ornately carved chairs placed against the wall to wait for her mother. Her mind pleasantly slipped back to the evening of the Cromwell's ball—or rather, her tour of Egypt.

A secret smile tugged upon her lips, and her stomach fluttered beneath the press of her hand. Something about Emerson seemed changed. He teased more than tormented, and she could not help but notice how often he sought her out. Of course, the easy explanation for all of it was because of the game, but some silly part of her warmed at the thought of receiving such attentions from a gentleman.

Her mother stepped out from her sitting room, followed by the housekeeper. "Forgive me," her mother said as she approached Olivia. "A wife and mother's tasks are never done. Shall we be on our way?"

"Yes," Olivia replied, jumping up from her seat. It had been enjoyable to think of Emerson for a time, but she knew such feelings were ridiculous. Though he might be the one man who made her smile, he was also the one man she could not have. She pushed aside the thought and turned to her mother, determined not to let a few dark thoughts cloud such a lovely day.

"I am glad to see you in such good spirits. Could a mother hope that it is because of what has transpired over the last two balls?" Her mother asked, arching a soft brow and smiling proudly.

Olivia knew her mother referred to the sudden increase in Olivia's dance partners, and she was happy to let her mother continue to believe that they were because Olivia's prospects were changing and not due to a child's game.

"One may hope." She offered a shy smile, hoping her mother would recognize the response and leave it at that. It was hard enough hiding the game from her mother; she did not want to add lying to her growing list of transgressions.

Jenson, along with a footman, entered the foyer, ending the conversation.

"A bit cold out there, Mistress," Jenson said, lowering her mother's cloak over her shoulders, followed by an additional cashmere shawl. The footman did the same for Olivia.

"Thank you, Jenson," Olivia's mother said, her kind heart was something Olivia admired.

"My pleasure, Mistress," he replied. "Your carriage is ready."

Stepping out of the house and into the cold, Olivia huddled inside her shawl. Her eyes caught on the groomsmen and coachman in their thick greatcoats waiting for them at the carriage.

Her mother slipped her arm through Olivia's, helping to guide her forward. "I made sure they each had a foot warmer as well," her mother leaned in to whisper. "Another benefit to your father's need for opulence." She winked as she tugged on Olivia's arm. "Now, come. We should hurry for their sake as well as for our own."

Olivia could not agree with her mother more. They had only been out in the chill for a few moments and already her gloved fingers were stinging.

They had just reached the bottom step when her mother stopped, her eyes locking on an approaching carriage. With its abundance of gold trimming and the way the black lac-quering still glistened in a city so filled with smoke, there could be no mistaking Olivia's father's carriage.

Before the conveyance could come to a full stop in front

of their home, the door flew open, and Olivia's father stepped out onto the pavement. In his haste, he trod directly upon the poor groomsman who had been rushing to lower the step.

"Move quicker, lad. Time is money," her father barked, not even sparing the groomsman a glance as he strode toward Olivia and her mother. "Ah, just who I intended to speak with." Without slowing his stride, he took Oliva's mother by the elbow and pulled her back inside the house. "Come along, Olivia," he ordered over his shoulder before crossing the threshold.

Olivia followed, but not before instructing the groomsmen and the coachman to seek warmth. There was no knowing how long her father would be. Time was money, and the money only belonged to him.

Once inside, Olivia followed the sound of her father's booming voice and made her way into his study. She was not surprised to find Jenson retrieving her father's coat, hat, and gloves from the floor, where her father had so carelessly discarded them. Crass manners, as Arabella had called it, was unfortunately putting it lightly in regards to her father.

Olivia offered Jenson a grateful smile, which he returned after retrieving the last item.

Her mother stood in front of her father's large palmalatta desk. The African wood with its striking contrast between the gold and brown streaks in the grain made it a statement piece in an already loud room. Books he would never read filled the shelves that spanned an entire wall. Paintings he purchased for their value alone regardless of what they portrayed covered the opposite wall. And furniture that was rumored to be a particular favorite of the Prince Regent was placed throughout the room. It was all so much, and yet Olivia doubted her father would ever be satisfied.

He took a seat behind his desk, his attention focusing on a stack of papers before he seemed to recall they were even in the room.

"You were on your way out?" he asked, briefly looking up at them under thick and furrowed eyebrows.

"We were going to call upon the Lathams," her mother replied, both her posture and her words equally formal.

Her father grunted with annoyance. "You would find more benefit in visiting a church. At least there you would have a better chance of meeting someone of importance."

"The Lathams are a good and well-respected family," Olivia blurted out before she could stop herself.

Exploding to his feet, Olivia's father grabbed the crystal ink decanter from his desk and flung it across the room. The glass shattered into a hundred tiny pieces as black ink dripped down the wall. Olivia jumped at the crashing sound.

"What good is the son of a second son of an earl?" he snarled, his voice shaking as he leaned forward on his desk with two clenched fists.

Despite her frustration with her father's words, Olivia's heart clenched in fear. Her father's temper was volatile and swift, and it would be to her detriment to argue that when the Wildes had been new to society, the second son of an earl had meant everything to her father. Emerson's father had shown them a kindness in befriending a man and his family not born to the station they currently enjoyed.

Her father glared at her with dark, hooded eyes and did not return to his seat until several minutes of silence had passed. "Now," he said with a satisfying sneer meant for Olivia, "the son of a viscount—that is a connection I would put my money behind."

Olivia understood her father's meaning clearly. He still hoped for the connection with the Trenors. Though, unlike her father, Olivia knew it was a lost cause.

"Of course, Father," Olivia said, another lie that would not taste of salt and vinegar. What good would speaking the truth do? He would come to the realization himself soon enough. She only hoped she was not close by when he did.

"I am pleased to hear it, because I have plans for you and Lord Trenor's eldest son. Has the gentleman called?"

Dread filled Olivia's insides. She never should have wished to be spared this moment. "He has not."

Her father scowled, and in that moment, Olivia did not know who should fear her father's temper more, her and her mother or the Trenors.

With one quick sweep of his large hand, her father knocked a stack of ledgers and a golden model of a ship from his desk. Olivia flinched, her hands fisting her muslin skirts as everything crashed to the ground. The last thump from the gold ship as it sunk into the Aubusson carpet echoed like the final blast from a cannon in the near-silent room. Loose ledger papers flicked through the air like white flags as they surrendered to the floor.

Her father seethed, his broad shoulders heaving with every breath. "If that good-for-nothing nobleman thinks he can—"

"I am certain there is no slight intended, Joshua." Olivia's mother cautiously stepped in, her tone wavering only a moment. "It is still too early to be discouraged." Her mother knew the temper of Joshua Wilde better than anyone, and how detrimental it would be for Olivia's chances if he reacted too strongly against a member of the aristocracy.

Olivia stood amazed. Everything her mother said had merit, and yet it did not. If either of the viscount's sons had wanted to court Olivia, they would have called before now. But Joshua Wilde, the boy from the docks turned profitable shipping merchant, knew very little when it came to the finer ways of the gentry.

Her father fell silent, and Olivia wondered if it was to frighten them or simply so he might consider her mother's words. Returning to his seat, her father pushed the sleeves of his white shirt up to his elbows and leaned forward on his desk. His attention turned to Olivia. "I want you and your mother to call upon the Trenors. Today. Enough time has been wasted. The Lathams will wait."

Olivia swallowed, feeling as though she might be ill. She could not argue with her father, but neither could she show her face at the Trenors, uninvited. Such a breach of etiquette would surely have their butler turn her away at the door. Her visit would then be whispered about among the *ton*, and any chance she had at securing a husband with a title would be gone.

Numb, Olivia nodded, knowing there could be no other response.

"Very good," he replied, turning to her mother. "See to it she does right, Charlotte. I want to see good proof that my investments are turning a profit."

"Yes, Joshua," her mother replied, as if accepting her

marching orders. It was obvious her parents' marriage was no love affair but only business, which was all her father was capable of.

Once excused from the house, Olivia and her mother settled into their carriage where the footwarmers did nothing against the chill that gripped her.

"We are to go to the Trenors, then?" Olivia asked, holding out hope that the disaster could be avoided.

"To the Lathams," her mother replied, her eyes focused on the ice- and fogged-covered window.

"What about Father?" She swallowed against the lump in her throat.

"I shall tell him they were not at home, and we shall hope he becomes distracted by other business matters."

Olivia nodded, wondering if there was a limit to how much one could hope for. She seemed to be doing quite a lot of it lately. Hope that she might be able to enjoy herself and play the game unnoticed. Hope that she might be able to find a husband and please her parents. If only they could somehow be one and the same.

ELEVEN

The carriage stopped in front of the Lathams' home in Kensington, and though it was not as prestigious as Mayfair, where Olivia's father had purchased a house, it was still respectable. In fact, she would say she preferred it. She did not care for the pretentiousness that came along with just the word Mayfair.

As soon as Olivia and her mother were permitted into the home, they were taken directly back to the family's private parlor. Olivia easily recognized Arabella's mother's voice before they even entered the room, and the tension between her shoulders and neck began to ease. Mrs. Latham had always been good to her in that motherly sort of way that comforted and also disciplined whenever the time arose.

Mrs. Latham, though still in mourning gray, sat upon the sofa closest to the roaring fire, her eyes on her needlepoint. Arabella sat on the sofa opposite her mother, a book—no doubt one of Shakespeare's—open upon her lap.

To Olivia's surprise, she saw Emerson standing next to the fireplace, his elbow leaning casually on top of the mantel. His tall, fit form turned toward her, and his rich, coffee-colored eyes watched her closely. She wondered if it were the flames that accounted for the intensity that burned behind those dark depths.

Her body shivered beneath his continued gaze, which was odd because her neck and cheeks felt overly heated. Looking away, she turned her attention to the mothers, who greeted each other more like sisters than friends. Without hesitation, they sat down and started their own private conversation.

Looking to Arabella, Olivia was surprised to see her friend sitting in a completely different position than she had been before. Her comfortable position had turned awkward. The book had slid to one side of her lap, and her arm was stretched out, reaching for the armrest on the other side of the couch. Arabella's eyes continued to dart between her mother and Emerson.

Olivia followed her friend's gaze, only to see Emerson was also in a completely different position. His elbow no longer rested upon the mantle, as he had now folded his arms across his chest. And rather than leaning, he now stood upright with his legs braced farther apart.

"What is going on?" Olivia whispered as she took her seat next to Arabella.

Arabella's attention remained focused on something her mother was saying. "We are playing Emerson's version of 'change seats,'" she whispered back. Her body slid into a new position—she no longer leaned to the side, but sat up straight. She picked up her book and held it against her chest as some sort of a shield.

"How is it played?" Olivia asked.

Arabella slowly changed positions once more. Lowering the book, she turned toward Olivia. "Every time Mama mentions something about a ball, we must change positions. The first person Mother catches moving loses."

Olivia giggled but quickly covered it up with a cough. It was a silly game, but at the same time so much better than talking about who was wearing what, and who was seen with whom. She had worried about that all last Season, and look where that had got her.

"May I join you?" Olivia asked.

"Of course. Just gain Emerson's attention so he is also aware." Arabella shifted her position once more.

Not wanting to miss out on the fun, Olivia turned toward Emerson, wondering the best way to gain his attention, only to find she did not need to. He was already watching her, his position in the room a few steps closer toward her and Arabella. Looking him straight in the eye, Olivia tried to communicate that she was joining the game by looking to him, then Arabella, and then at the two mothers several times.

Emerson stealthily nodded and smiled mischievously. This time, when he changed positions, he came to stand directly behind the sofa where she and Arabella currently sat.

Arabella changed positions next, and Olivia moved to do the same.

Subtly shifting her hips, she adjusted her seat and crossed her feet at her ankles. It was not the most apparent of changes as no one could see her ankles beneath her skirts, but she had moved at least. She was nervous and did not want to risk too much her first few times. Her mother was observant, a skill she had developed to survive so many years moving among the *ton* while being married to a man like Joshua Wilde.

"You can do much better than that," Emerson leaned down to whisper, his voice tickling her ear and causing her breath to catch.

Her mother's eyes suddenly looked in her direction and then rose upward until they rested on Emerson. Fighting the deep urge to fidget in her seat, Olivia pasted on a pleasant smile until her mother turned back to Mrs. Latham.

"You have grown cowardly since last I saw you," Emerson whispered again, only this time, his breath ignited a new sensation inside Olivia.

"Not cowardly," she said, subtly turning to better face him. "Only wise enough to know how to play a game and win."

"Yes, Emerson," Arabella said, cutting in with a harsh whisper. "You run the risk of Mother noticing all of us by standing so close. Now move away." Arabella was a competitive soul, and it was more than likely a good thing she was born a lady. Who knew how many duels she would have found herself in had she been born a man.

Emerson, however, did not move away. Instead, at the very next opportunity, he leaned forward even further, resting his forearms across the back of the sofa directly behind Olivia. His fingers grazed Olivia's shoulders, and she stiffened, startled by the sudden heat brought on by his touch. He was no doubt trying to unsettle her by towering over them.

"Are you afraid of taking a risk, Liv?" he asked, his breath hot against her ear and cheek. "As I recall, you were willing to take some risks when you fled, leaving me alone on the Stansburys' dance floor."

It took much longer than she would have liked to regain her nerves. Everything either felt hot or unsettled, but most of all she wanted to say something clever to him. He was trying to rile her, and she refused to let him. "I did not flee. I outsmarted you," she said, turning her head slightly to meet his eyes.

"Perhaps I let you get away," he said, with a confident smirk.

She flicked a look at him, their old competitiveness sparking a familiar determination in her. He always had to win, and that fact always made her want to make sure he lost all the more. She knew it was petty and childish, and it made Olivia wonder if she would ever be fit for a demure London life.

A life like her mother's. A life without love, where her choices would always be made for her.

Not realizing she had slipped into another one of her looming pits of despair, Olivia startled at the clanking sound of the tea service as it was brought in by a maid. Arabella's mother asked her daughter to pour, and their game was suspended.

"Walk with me?" Emerson asked Olivia, the teasing in his tone gone, replaced with a rich baritone that both unsettled and soothed her.

"Why?" Olivia asked, still trying to find her bearing. Why should being near Emerson cause her to feel this way?

"Would you stop being so stubborn and walk with me?" he stated rather bluntly before extending his hand to her over her shoulder. Their mothers briefly looked in their direction, but Arabella stepped in front of them and offered them tea.

"Would you stop being so demanding and answer my question?" Olivia replied.

He gave no reply, only stared at her with a seriousness that made her squirm in her seat. When she tried to ignore him by turning away, she could still feel his eyes boring into the back of her head. Finally giving in, if only to avoid drawing their mothers' attention, Olivia stood and walked around the sofa to join him.

"Lead the way," she said, stubbornly not taking hold of his outstretched arm. She could not entertain the feelings that were growing inside her. Emerson was all the things her father had forbidden in a match.

He motioned for her to walk toward one of the windows. She expected him to walk behind her, but it did not take more than a few steps before Olivia felt the warmth of his palm pressed against her lower back. It was not forceful, nor was it a barely-there touch. It felt possessive, strong, and clearly not from the ungainly boy he'd been in their childhood. This Emerson who walked beside her was a man full grown and exuding confidence.

Olivia, not quite knowing how to react, stumbled a step, and Emerson's hand immediately slid from her back and caught her hand that hung in between them as they walked. She felt a tremor run through his palm to hers as he threaded his fingers with hers.

He changed his course, pulling her deeper into the room and toward another window that overlooked the Lathams' small, frozen garden. It was not much for a view, and Olivia wondered why he had decided to bring her there.

They stood a while in silence.

"I have been able to stand on my own for some time now," Olivia said, before glancing down at their interconnected hands.

Emerson jerked his hand away as if he had been burned, his attention shooting over his shoulder to where their mothers still sat in deep conversation.

"You may rest easy," Olivia said, the strange spell over Emerson—and somewhat over her—seemingly broken. "My mother would never force you to marry me. You are not what my father wants." She offered a teasing smile she could no longer feel. A growing part of her was foolishly beginning to hope for such a rescue from her father's demands.

Emerson's eyes stared down at her without a hint of humor.

Surely he would not take that as an insult. Practically the entire *ton* knew what type of gentleman Joshua Wilde wanted for his only daughter.

"That was not my concern," he said, his mouth pressed into a firm line before he turned to stare out the window. She waited for him to continue, but he remained silent.

"Then what is your concern?" she pressed, confused by his reaction.

He let out a deep breath. "That what you think of me is not true."

"I beg your pardon?" she asked.

"It is like when you believed I asked you to dance out of

obligation or pity. You could not have been further from the truth."

Olivia felt like a fish out of water, her eyes wide and round with the shock of being on unfamiliar ground.

Turning away from the window to face her, he looked into her eyes. "Just like now, I asked you to walk with me, because I *want* to walk with you."

Her heart pounded in her chest, her thoughts stumbling one over the other as she tried to make sense of his words. The Emerson who stood before her felt unfamiliar. Where was the teasing and taunting? When had he started to look at her with such intensity?

She did not know how to respond, so she reverted to a teasing remark to get them back to common ground. "If you continue to speak in such a way," she began, wishing her voice sounded steadier, "I might believe you actually like me."

He shook his head and softly chuckled, offering her a slow grin. "Would thinking of me that way make such a difference between us?"

Emerson took a subtle step toward her, his eyes darting down toward her mouth. Suddenly her lips felt parched and dry.

She jerked her gaze toward where they had left the others. Where was Arabella with that tea? She needed to calm her senses. He was playing with her, there could be no other explanation. "I—We should—"

Why could she not seem to get any words out?

"Liv?" He stepped even closer, his tone low and deep.

The atmosphere in the room became still and charged, as if lightning could strike at any moment. Her breaths grew short and fast, and she no longer felt sure of anything. Panicked, she quickly turned on her heel to run away, but her slipper caught on the long window drape. She spun around to try to free herself, which merely ensnared her foot even further in the dark green-velvet trap. The drape tightened, and Olivia's leg slipped out from underneath her. She fell backward, and she reached her arms behind her to soften her imminent fall.

Emerson was behind her in an instant, his steady arms catching her and pulling her to his chest. She could feel the heat from his solid form against her back, his heart beating almost as fast as her own.

"Olivia, what on earth?" Her mother's shocked gasp filled the room, washing over her like a bucket of cold water.

She was wrapped in Emerson's arms for all the room to see. She pitched forward but misjudged how much force it took to untangle her foot from the drape. She stumbled and again fell forward, unbalanced. Emerson's large, steady hands gripped both sides of her waist, and he held her tight as she kicked at the fabric until she was free.

Every eye in the room was upon her. She knew that without even having to look. Which left her with only one thing to do.

Extracting herself from Emerson's hold, she took a deep, calming breath, smoothed down the front of her skirts, and with a grace that would make any aristocratic mother proud, she walked with her head held high toward a giggling Arabella as if nothing had even occurred.

TWELVE

Emerson entered his study shortly after Liv and her mother had taken their leave, and he could not stop himself from smiling. His words had unsettled her—quite literally.

Her reaction was proof enough that he had been very much in her thoughts as of late, and not in a "tormenting older brother of my friend" sort of way as she had once described him. She was becoming aware of him, as a woman becomes aware of a man, and the idea pleased him.

Taking a seat at his father's desk—for that was how it still felt to him—Emerson leaned forward, resting his forearms on top of it. His gaze moved to the portrait of his young father and mother that hung above the fireplace mantel. It was yet another thing about the room he had not the heart to change, and for good reason. He wanted a reminder of what life could be like if he but strove for it.

"The true making of a man is not measured by what he can physically obtain, but by his love for the woman he would give up all else for."

Emerson's chest tightened as he remembered his father's

words, and he reflexively moved a hand to rub at the spot. At the time, he had thought his father's words poetic, but now that he himself was working for that opportunity, he felt them—believed them—for the truth that they were.

"Emerson? Do you have a moment?" his mother asked, stepping halfway through the door. Her hands were clasped tightly in front of her, her fingers pale even against the cold, gray color of her dress. She kept her eyes trained forward, and somehow Emerson knew it was because she was avoiding the portrait he had just been studying.

He clenched his fists together hard on the desk, almost to the point of pain, needing to distract himself from the tears that threatened. He needed to remain strong for her as she struggled to find her way through her grief.

"Of"—his voice caught, forcing him to clear his throat— "of course. What can I do for you, Mother?" he asked, forcing himself to remain steady and calm as he rose from his seat. "Would you like to sit by the fire?" He flinched, regretting bringing up the very space where the portrait hung. He had only wanted to see to her comfort.

She glanced at him, perplexed, before her subdued appearance faded, replaced by the strong and capable woman he remembered her being before his father's death.

"Do not try to mother me, Emerson Samuel Latham," she began, taking quick, purposeful strides into the room. "If anyone is in need of mothering, it is you." With the grace of a queen, she sat down in one of the two chairs in front of his desk, her back turned so the portrait was not easily in her view.

"My apologies, Mother," he replied, holding back a faint smile as he retook his seat. "What may I do for you?"

Once more she eyed him in that way only a mother could possess. "Word from belowstairs has reached me about a most peculiar delivery." She paused, as if awaiting his answer.

He did indeed know the answer, but his curiosity to see how she would handle the conversation won out.

"And?" he prompted after another moment of silence.

The lines above her brow deepened. "And it appears that we have a live pig taking up residence in our mews. Have you all of a sudden taken up pig farming?"

Chuckling at the formidable opponent his mother was turning out to be, Emerson answered, "No, I have not taken up pig farming. And it shall only be in residence a few nights more."

She gave him a searching look as if she did not believe it to be that simple. "What are you doing with that pig, Emerson?"

"Nothing to worry yourself over." He smiled wide to reassure her.

She tilted her head in that knowing, disbelieving way of hers. "You are up to something."

His lips twitched in amusement. It felt good to banter with her again. "What makes you think I am up to something?"

"You are always up to something," she challenged.

Emerson laughed. "Then you should know not to worry."

"A mother always worries." No statement could have been more true.

"As I said, the pig will be here for only a few days more,

and then you need never worry about it again." In truth, he was fairly certain that the pig would either be consumed by the patrons at White's or Brooks's by the end of Bradbury's ridiculous wager.

She pursed her lips, considering his words a moment. "Very well. But I do have one more matter I would speak to you about."

"Yes, of course," he replied. He would much rather visit with his mother than see to the overwhelming pile of letters from his steward and solicitor.

"What are your intentions with Olivia Wilde?" she asked, causing Emerson to choke, wheeze, and cough on his quickly inhaled spit.

"Devil take it, Mother." He struggled to get the words out, pounding his chest with his fist in order to find some relief. "What would make you ask such a question?" He had been so careful. What had given him away? His entire future depended on keeping his peculiar courtship a secret.

"Call it a mother's intuition," she replied, watching him as closely as Bradbury did playing cards.

"We are friends," Emerson said, not wanting to get her hopes up. She was already grieving the loss of a husband, and she did not need to be weighed down by his loss should he fail.

She nodded slowly. "That is all?"

"That is all." He kept his tone detached and neutral, though an unsettling twist of guilt turned in his stomach.

She nodded again, her studied movements twisting like daggers in his gut. "I always thought you two would be good for each other," she said distantly. "I even told your"—her

voice wavered as tears gathered at the corners of her eyes—
"your father this, when he talked to me about his and your
discussions."

Emerson swallowed hard. "He told you about our talks?"

"He did." She slid forward to the edge of her chair, her
hand extending across the expanse of the desk and resting on
his twitching fingers.

"It's not for certain," he said through a hoarse throat.

"Nothing in life is," she whispered. She squeezed his
hand, then she looked for the first time to the painting of her
and her husband.

Emerson's heart broke again for her. Standing, he moved
around the desk to wrap his arm around her shoulders. He
held her as she leaned into him and released a few gentle
tears.

After a time, she pulled away, her eyes red. "Your father
and I could not be more proud," she began, a warm smile
cresting her lips.

He nodded, the lump of emotions stuck in his throat cutting off any words.

"Tell me one more thing?" she asked.

He nodded, not sure if he could get any words out.

"Please tell me your way of courting her has nothing
to do with the pig?" She appeared genuinely anxious, and
Emerson could do nothing but shake his head and laugh.

THIRTEEN

Olivia stood inside the Earl of Banbridge's gold-trimmed and surprisingly open gallery. There was no labyrinth of marble sculptures to hide inside. Nor a collection of antiquities or furnishings to hide behind. Gold-framed portraits lined the walls, and a single row of benches ran down the center of the red carpets. Large golden curtains cascaded over every darkened, arched window, while golden sconces reflected their light across the cream-colored walls of the narrow room.

It was no wonder why Olivia's family had been invited to the ball. The earl's family had already sold anything of value, and her father was their last resort.

Curious the family would want to cover the extravagant expenses of a ball. But Olivia had never claimed to understand the ways of the aristocracy. Appearances were everything, and apparently nothing looked better than a ball.

Knowing she had been spotted by Lady Bixbee and her gaggle of matrons, Olivia continued into the room not wanting to be trapped in their circle once again. If Lady Bixbee was not matchmaking, she was gossiping, and Olivia wanted no part of either one.

She stopped in front of a large portrait of a man holding a musket and surrounded by a ridiculous number of hunting dogs. It was the best place to take up her watch as it was to-ward the center of the room, which gave her the advantage of being able to see both doors, should anyone playing the game enter. In truth, she was hiding from one person in particular who seemed to be haunting her figuratively as well as literally.

Emerson.

She had not spoken to him since that morning in his family's sitting room, and when she saw him enter the Banbridges' ballroom, she bolted.

He was behaving so strangely. Everywhere Olivia turned, there he was, watching her, approaching her, teasing her, saying such perplexing things to her. It was unsettling to say the least, and overwhelming to say the most. The game was clearly playing tricks with her mind. This was Emerson, for pity's sake. Up until his father's death, he had lived for a game. He was merely settling back into his old ways.

"It does not bode well for the success of a ball when a lady would rather stare at paintings than dance." Emerson's familiar voice drawled in her ear.

Olivia gasped, snapping her head around so quickly that a pain shot up her neck.

Emerson stood just behind her, an unrepentant grin on his face.

"You are horrid, Emerson Latham," she hissed, rubbing the back of her neck as she turned to face him. Her eyes shot over his shoulder to where Lady Bixbee and her gossiping geese were huddled together. Because of their talents for fluttering their fans over their faces, Olivia was hard-pressed to say if they had witnessed the entire scene.

"Horrid?" Emerson guffawed, acting insulted, though the teasing spark in his eyes told Olivia otherwise. "First, you accuse me of being a tormentor and now horrid? What other accusations should I be anticipating, I wonder?"

Annoyed at him for startling her and annoyed at herself for being caught unawares, Olivia shot him a withering look. "How about—"

And then he moved. It was the slightest shift in her direction, something so small no one else would have paid it any notice. But because he had been in her thoughts more often than not, she noticed. And she froze. She could not speak. She could not move. She could not look away.

Emerson gently nudged her chin with his finger, and then pointed to the painting over her shoulder. "Dog got your tongue?" He looked down at her with a warm, inquisitive smile, a soft chuckle rumbling from deep inside his chest.

A definite heat flooded her cheeks, and her heart sped up without her permission. It seemed to be doing that a lot whenever Emerson was near. Shaking herself, she struggled to form words.

His smile widened, and there could be no mistaking the gleam of satisfaction in his eyes. He was not here for her; he was here for the game.

She was a fool.

A complete and utter fool.

"What do you think of the painting?" he asked, the earlier awkwardness evaporating.

"Too many dogs," she replied, watching his hands from the corner of her eyes. Why did he always insist on waiting so long to tag her? Why couldn't he just be done with it?

"You like dogs," he said as he slowly and purposefully brought his arms to cross his chest. Had he seen her watching his hands?

Good. With any luck, he would remember how well she had outsmarted him that first time.

"I find I do not care for dogs anymore," she stubbornly argued, not wanting him to think he unnerved her by his presence.

He arched a single brow. "Anymore?"

"Yes. I am a proper miss now." She shook out her ridiculously rich, belongs-in-a-fruit-basket-lemon-colored skirts to emphasize her point. "We are only allowed to like the pianoforte, needlepoint, and tea." It was an absurd argument to be having, but he had been the one to push her.

A frown marred his lips. "You should not have to be someone you are not for anyone, Liv."

She scoffed. "Says the gentleman who came up with a silly game to play at balls."

"Who says I am playing a game at the moment?" he challenged, tilting his head as he held her heated stare.

"Are you not?" she challenged back, not caring that he could tag her as *it* at any moment.

"No. No games. We are simply talking." A flare of annoyance crossed his dark eyes.

"I would much rather be dancing," she said beneath her breath, wanting to be anywhere else. It was exhausting how he dragged out the moment. If he needed to have his fun, then she wished he would tag her and be done with it.

"Allow me to rectify that," he said, holding out his hand to her.

She startled, realizing that he had heard her muttered words. "You cannot be serious." Her eyes widened.

Deliberately, he turned his head toward Lady Bixbee, who was watching with her pack. He offered them his best gentlemanly smile before turning back to her, capturing her with a direct stare. "Dance with me, Liv."

Left with no other choice if she wished to avoid a scene, she took his hand. His fingers instantly wrapped around hers, bringing back those unnerving memories from the last time he'd held her hand.

He secured it in the crook of his arm. "That was not so painful," he teased, whispering into her ear as they passed a smiling Lady Bixbee and her studying eyeglass.

"Not for you. You got what you wanted," Olivia said.

"How so?" They continued out of the gallery and made their way to the ballroom.

"You have yourself as they say: a cooked goose. A pig to the slaughter. A hen surely plucked."

He chuckled. "So many references to cooked animals. Tell me, Liv, should I be escorting you to the refreshment room instead of the dance floor?"

Frustration heated her skin, boiling up her neck, and causing her forehead to crease. Pulling hard on his arm, Olivia stopped them in the corridor that led to the ballroom. "Why is everything a joke with you?"

His nostrils flared. "Not *everything* is a joke, I can assure you." He took a step toward her, and she took a step back. His eyes registered the forced distance between them, and he seemed to take a deep breath.

Something she had done or said had got to him. Which was ridiculous. Any attempt she had ever made to get under Emerson's skin when they were children only ever seemed to inspire him to torment her further.

He studied her a moment, his mouth opening as if he intended to speak, and then closing once more.

"Emerson?" she asked, needing for him to make sense of what was happening.

Subtly shaking his head, he held out his hand to her. "Come. Let's get you your dance." His words felt like a resignation through and through, and Olivia found she hated it. Hated the way it was happening, hated the way it was making her feel. But she did understand how to make it all go away.

Olivia retook his hand, and slowly they resumed their walk toward the ballroom, which for her was akin to walking the plank, all for the sake of the game.

The tension followed them into the ballroom, dulling her senses until she could only focus on the overwhelming number of people around them. Guilt over her words weighed heavily on her mind.

She had been too hard on him. He had recently lost his father and gained the responsibility for the well-being of his mother and sister. Who was she to judge if he wished to find enjoyment somewhere in his life? She owed it to him, and to Arabella, to see the game through—no matter how confusing his actions seemed to be.

She gently flexed her fingers to draw his attention. His pace slowed as he glanced down to meet her eyes.

"I wish to say something to you." She had to raise her voice to be heard over the din of the ballroom.

One of his brows raised, then he nodded and drew them to a less-crowded spot.

"I am sorry if what I said offended you," she began, relieved to have the ballroom to his back so she could have his full attention.

"There was nothing I took offense to," he stated, the usual life in his expression absent.

"Yes, there was. I wrongly judged you."

Half-heartedly he shook his head, and he released a heavy breath. "I only ever want your honesty, Liv." It was a simple statement, and yet it sounded like so much more.

Why did it feel like so much more?

"You have it," she said, knowing she meant every word. The realization surprised her, but not as much as the way he stared at her for what seemed to be an endless moment.

"And you shall have mine," he stated, his voice calm and soothing. His eyes dipped down to her mouth, and unconsciously, Olivia bit into her bottom lip. She needed to stop imagining things that could never be.

He faintly smiled, offering her a truce.

They returned to the dance floor, the music for a quadrille gradually filling her ears.

They were late in entering, but Emerson was able to transition them smoothly into another pairing. Dancing with lively steps, Olivia allowed the music to take over. Her renewed spirits lightened her steps as she crossed the square,

JENTRY FLINT

turned, curtseyed, and enjoyed the growing smile upon Emerson's lips.

"You look radiant," Emerson said as he took her hands and led them around the square.

"I am happy," she replied with all honesty.

"I am happy that you are happy, Liv." His gaze intensified, and Olivia was relieved when the steps of the dance forced a temporary separation from him.

His words stole her breath. He had not been teasing; he had been compelling. Which made her want to run from and lean into his touch all at the same time. In that moment, she felt she could have unburdened her deepest fears—of being married but feeling alone, unwanted, and afraid—upon his strong shoulders. But then he would feel compelled to do something to ease them, and she could not allow him to take such a risk. She knew more than anyone that Joshua Wilde was not a man to be challenged.

When they came together again, she said, "You really must stop calling me by that name. What if someone should overhear you?" She needed to stop her thoughts before they ran away with themselves—again.

"Then you are really not going to like what I am about to call you." Before Olivia could react, Emerson leaned down until his breath tickled her ear. "You are *it*, Liv."

FOURTEEN

"Would it not have been easier to put it on button-side up?" Emerson argued, struggling to keep the back of a frantically squirming and squealing pig to his chest.

"Already looking for the easy way out?" Bradbury replied, his eyes squinting as he worked on getting a satin, creamed-colored waistcoat buttoned onto the pig.

"Not easy," Emerson grunted as the pig thrashed its head back and forth, nearly connecting with his chin. "But doable."

"You used to be made of sterner stuff, my friend. It is a good thing I have taken it upon myself to—" Bradbury broke off with a curse as the pig squirmed right and he fought left, pulling out two of the already fastened buttons.

Abandoning his seat on the bench, Bradbury knelt on the floor of the carriage parked behind White's, his determination written in the creases along his forehead.

"Why does it matter which way the buttons are facing?" Emerson continued his argument. "The pig is wearing Brummell's waistcoat. That was the wager. The last thing the members of White's are going to notice is whether or not the pig was properly dressed as it runs through their morning room."

Emerson was ready to wipe his hands of the wager before it had even begun. He had a grieving mother to see to at home, a restless sister to see wed, and an estate and its tenants to care for during one of the coldest winters England could remember. Not to mention the insurmountable task of winning Olivia. Wrestling with a filthy pig, in his shirtsleeves, inside a carriage, in bitter cold weather, did not need to be added to his list of problems.

Bradbury remained silent until he finished the last button, then returned to his seat. "It will matter, once you see this." He grinned as if they had not been wrestling with a pig for the last twenty minutes. He reached inside his inner coat pocket and retrieved a piece of cloth wrapped around two sticks.

"What on earth is that?" Emerson asked. With Bradbury, it could be anything. He hoped it was not something to add to their growing list of requirements that needed to be completed in order for them to win the wager.

"Take it." Bradbury waved the objects at him, his grin growing.

Settling the pig onto the carriage floor, Emerson slid over a basket of table scraps which they had used to keep it occupied during the ride. He took the objects from Bradbury and unrolled the cloth to reveal black lettering painted across the white material.

"'Brummell's fat friend,'" Emerson read aloud. "You cannot be serious?" The *ton* was still gossiping about Brummel's infamous insult he had dealt in front of, and about, the Prince Regent to Lord Alvanley two years ago—the final cut that had severed any remaining friendship between the two men.

Bradbury nodded with a chuckle as he retrieved the items from Emerson. He leaned over the scrounging pig and slipped the two sticks into tiny pockets sewn on either side of the waistcoat, securing them so the cloth was stretched between them and the letters could easily be read.

"Oh, come now. I think it's brilliant. This is the perfect opportunity to turn that pompous dandy's judgments against him."

It was brilliant—risky, should Brummell discover it was them and want to retaliate, but brilliant.

"You do realize we will not be able to witness everyone's reactions?" Emerson asked. "It will not end well if we are apprehended."

"Your confidence in my intelligence is astounding," Bradbury said, annoyed.

"Perhaps I would feel more confident if you had shared any part of your plan on how we are to see this absurd wager through."

"I asked you to get the pig, did I not?" Bradbury argued.

Emerson was forced to nod; Bradbury had done that.

"I got the waistcoat, did I not?" He pointed at the world's best-dressed pig.

Emerson nodded again.

"We are here, are we not?" He held out his hands to encompass the carriage.

Emerson's shoulders slumped, his earlier fight snuffed out of him.

"I have been the one preparing to win, which is more than I can say about you." Bradbury glowered.

"You told me to leave everything to you," Emerson shot back, his anger returning.

"Then why are you arguing with me? Can you not see that I have done all this for you?" Bradbury said in exasperation.

"I did not ask you to do this. I have enough going on in my life to worry about."

"That is exactly *why* I did this." Bradbury threw his hands up in disbelief. "You are not yourself. It is like you are trying to be someone you think your father wanted you to be. What you think your mother and sister need you to be. What grief *made* you to be." Bradbury paused, letting out a deep breath before running a hand through his usually well-groomed hair. "I thought doing something like this would help you find your way again."

Bradbury's admission rendered Emerson speechless. He had been under the belief that he was going along with this wager for the sake of Bradbury and their friendship. When in fact, Bradbury had been doing it all for him. His friend had somehow seen Emerson's sense of loss, something he himself had only just begun to recognize.

"I think that is the most kind, unselfish thing I have ever heard you say," Emerson said, with both shock and awe in his tone.

Bradbury shifted in his seat, his hands tugging at his

sleeves and pulling at his coat. "Blazes, Emerson, why did you have to go and make it uncomfortable?"

"Me?" Emerson laughed in disbelief. "You were the one going on about—"

"I was merely stating facts," Bradbury said, cutting him off with an upheld hand.

"Very well," Emerson said, holding back his desire to say more out of respect for his friend's unease. Bradbury was a man of action, not words. If Emerson wished to show his gratitude, he knew exactly what to do. "What is the plan?"

Bradbury's eyes lit with a mischievous glint that Emerson had learned long ago promised trouble. "You will be so glad you asked." Sliding to the edge of his seat, he continued, "Now, grab that pig, shove this"—he bent over, grabbed an apple from the floor, and tossed it to Emerson—"in its snout, and let us squeal soundlessly into the night."

With a dramatic sweep of his arm, Bradbury dashed out into the alley, leaving Emerson with the unsurprising burden of collecting the pig.

"It is five in the afternoon," Emerson countered with a chuckle. He leaned over to retrieve the pig, ready with the apple-muzzle if it threatened to struggle.

Thankfully, the pig settled into the curl of Emerson's arms, no doubt ready to sleep off the feast it had just devoured. The prickly hair of its chin poked through the mud-stained white linen of Emerson's shirtsleeves, while the pig's hindquarters and swirly tail rested comfortably on his other arm. His shirt would have to be burned, but at least he'd had the foresight to remove his coat.

Emerson stepped out of the carriage, the chill that filled

the stone-covered back alley immediately prickling his bare forearms. Perhaps he should have kept his coat on after all.

The pig squirmed and grunted as it nuzzled itself even closer to his chest. He would smell of pig and whatever dead or rotting thing currently made the alley its final resting place. The row of stacked wooden crates lining the back wall of White's would be the perfect place for any scavenging rodents to call home.

Emerson was surprised to see Bradbury walking directly to the servants' entrance and knocking as if they were there to make a delivery and not about to pull off their absurd scheme.

"*This* is your plan?" Emerson hissed, sprinting up to join his far-too-casual, clean-coat-wearing, pig-free-smelling friend.

Looking over his shoulder, Bradbury grinned. "Trust me."

FIFTEEN

Emerson did not feel this was a matter of trust, but a matter of insanity. It seemed impossible that this prank could be pulled off so easily. Especially with the pig already dressed. Perhaps if it were a regular-looking pig, but then again, why would the servants at White's allow a live pig through their door?

The servants' door to the club opened, and Emerson braced himself for a scowling footman or other kitchen staff to be staring down at them.

"Oy." A young voice sounded from inside the empty frame. "I was begin'in ta wonder if you would show at all, Mr. Hood."

Bradbury stood in front of Emerson, blocking his view, but the voice was unmistakably a child's.

Mr. Hood?

Bewildered, Emerson leaned around Bradbury, meeting the filthy face of a boy no older than seven, smiling wide, his two front teeth missing. He stepped aside allowing Bradbury to enter, leaving Emerson no choice but to follow.

"'Mr. Hood'?" Emerson whispered to his friend as the boy secured the door latch.

Bradbury shot him a sly smile. "I always wanted to be Robin Hood. Stealing from the rich to feed the needy, and all that." Bradbury said as if the answer should have been obvious.

"First of all, we are not stealing anything." Emerson leveled his mischievous friend with a stare that would brook no argument. "And secondly, none of this has anything to do with the poor."

"I did not say the *poor*. I said the *needy*, which I am. And technically we shall be stealing from the rich—once we pull off this wager and fleece all those who doubted us."

Emerson looked to the heavens for patience or the understanding of how one could be a man grown and still live a life as Bradbury did.

"Now, thank Little John for allowing us in, and we shall be on our merry way."

Emerson raised a brow as he readjusted the awkward weight of the slumbering pig. "Is your name really John?"

"Aye, named after me pa, I was." The boy beamed, his hands going proudly to his hips. The boy's coat sleeves pulled away from his wrists, proving he had outgrown the tattered garment long ago. Emerson remembered his own parents lamenting on how quickly he too had grown out of his clothing.

"Do you work here with your father?" Emerson found himself asking, wishing he had taken more time to learn from his own.

"Nah. Me pa works over with the horses at Tattersalls."

The boy's toothless grin grew even wider. "Me gran works here in the kitchens, though, and she says I could let yous in as long as we gets a few coins. And your promise not to rat me out if yous gets caught."

"Your gran makes a good bargain." Emerson found it impossible not to smile at the proud lad. With the war dragging on, coin was growing harder and harder to come by. A challenge he knew all about as he struggled to turn a profit and provide a secure future for his mother and sister. Not to mention his responsibility to see that his tenants did not starve if this unseasonable winter never turned into spring in time for planting. Emerson found he could not blame the boy's family for taking advantage where they could.

"You got the blunt?" Little John asked, holding out his dirt-stained hand.

Bradbury chuckled from beside Emerson as he reached inside his coat and pulled out a few coins. "The last of your winnings from our last wager," he said, shooting a wink to Emerson.

"Last wager?" Emerson asked. "I have not made any wagers in months."

"Oh, did I forget to tell you?" Something about Bradbury's tone made Emerson believe he really had forgotten. "I took the liberty of making a few wagers for you using coins I borrowed from the top drawer of your desk. Congratulations—you won." Bradbury looked far too entertained to be repentant.

"It appears I have lost my coins once more," Emerson drawled as Little John snatched the money and stuffed it into his pocket.

"Of course not." Bradbury said. "Simply think of it as an investment."

"I am beginning to wonder what else I may have *invested* in," Emerson said, trying to remember how many spare coins he'd had in that drawer.

"A few of the servants at Brummell's house thank you." Bradbury's innocent expression belied his growing transgressions.

"You *bribed* the man's servants to give you one of his waistcoats?"

"Technically, *you* bribed them. It was your coin, after all."

Emerson shook his head and laughed. He never could stay angry at his friend. He was simply Bradbury, always looking for the next wager and the next win. Emerson was grateful he was always on his friend's winning side.

"You twos goin' to stand here much longer?" the boy asked.

Something crashed in the kitchen, and the pig jumped and snorted before burrowing back into Emerson's body.

"I believe that is our signal," Bradbury said as he patted the head of their finely dressed pig. "If you would be so good as to point us toward the morning room, Little John, we will be on our way."

"This way," Little John replied. He led them down a corridor that ended at a tight switchback of stairs. "Two floors up, then a left, and you'll come out by the main stairs."

Emerson's heart beat a nervous rhythm, and the boy must have sensed as much for he continued, "But I wouldn' worry. Gran says this be about the time Brummell holds his court at the bow window. Not many of those hoity-toity's do much else when he's 'round. The landing should be clear 'nough for you to run 'cross it and get to the morning room."

Emerson wished he felt relief at the boy's reassurances, but the words *main stairs* had twisted his gut in knots.

"Seems simple enough," Bradbury said with a slight hesitation. The knots in Emerson's stomach tightened. "By chance, what is the room to the right of the top of the stairs?"

"Billiards room," the boy replied, proud of his insider knowledge of the castle.

"Very good." Bradbury paused, his expression unreadable. "Well, then. Shall we be off?"

"After you," Emerson replied. His arms shook under the sheer weight of the still-slumbering pig. His hand, which clutched the apple they had not yet needed, had begun to cramp.

"My thanks for your assistance, Little John," Bradbury said, as he tousled the boy's long hair. "Might I suggest that you and the other staff make yourselves busy at the farthest end of the club for the time being?" He winked.

The boy nodded, pausing to stroke the bulbous belly of the pig before skipping his way back through the corridor.

Emerson followed Bradbury, the pig stirring with every jostling step he took up the narrow stairway. He tried to soften his steps, but it was proving rather difficult as he was climbing the stairs blind. He should not have purchased such a plump pig.

They had nearly reached the halfway mark when he misjudged the height of a step. His foot stopped short, while the rest of his body had already committed to going up. Instinctively, he tightened his arms, bracing himself for a fall.

The pig squealed at the sudden pressure, and Emerson's heart nearly burst from his chest.

Bradbury whirled around faster than Emerson could blink and snatched the apple from his grip, shoving the fruit into the pig's snout.

The pig bit down, splattering apple juice down Emerson's arm.

Bradbury held a finger to his lips as he scowled from his upper step. "Did you not hear the boy say 'main stairs'?" He pointed toward a door that was one short flight above them.

"I have the same amount of control over this pig as you do. Now move—the apple is almost gone."

Bradbury's eyes shot to the pig, who continued to happily slosh the disappearing apple around in its mouth. He picked up his pace, and Emerson did his best to match his stride.

Bradbury made it to the landing first and pressed his ear to the door that led to the club's main stairwell and hall.

"Do you hear anything?" Emerson asked as soon as he reached the landing, his arms and legs throbbing.

Bradbury shook his head. "Step back." He cracked the door open and peeked inside. Turning to Emerson, he whispered, "It's empty, but I can hear voices coming from the morning room across the main hall."

"What should we do?" Emerson whispered, though he could barely hear himself over the pounding of his heart. His throbbing arms now hummed with a familiar sense of nervous anticipation. But the possibility of actually pulling off the wager had grown into a temptation he could no longer ignore. They were too close to turn back now.

Bradbury tilted his head and shot him an exasperated

look. "Does the rest require a plan? We dart across the hall, shove the pig into the morning room, and run. Not much else is required."

"My concern was over how many people could be in that room. But by all means, after you," Emerson grumbled, ready to be free of the pig. With every one of its squirms, the banner, which was still pinned into the waistcoat, flicked closer and closer to sticking him in the face.

Bradbury stuck his head out the door from their current position inside the servants' stairwell, his hand raised behind him telling Emerson to wait. Eventually his fingers waved, signaling for Emerson to follow.

The first few steps into the main hall were the most daunting. His eyes continually darted toward the main stairway in fear of someone suddenly coming up them, and despite his resolve to see the wager through, a shiver of unease scraped down Emerson's spine. He took a shaky breath, his ears straining to make out anything that could be a threat. But when he heard the clear pontificating voice of the dandy Brummell and the murmurs of the sycophants who followed his every word, an anger Emerson had been battling against toward those who thought themselves superior because of their riches or titles sparked within him.

He moved with purpose, hoping to hear them squeal just as loud as the pig.

Reaching the open doorway to the morning room, Bradbury pressed his back against the adjacent wall and motioned for Emerson to get the pig into position.

Emerson knelt down, praying the pig would cooperate and remain silent until they were ready. Its hooves nicked against the wood floor, and it gave one quick snort as it began to sniff about. Trying to help it along, Emerson guided the pig with his hands toward the open doorway, but the portly beast seemed in no hurry to comply.

Bradbury let out a faint huff of frustration before bending down and swatting the pig on its backside. The slap of his hand against the pig's rump paled in comparison to the frantic squeals made by the animal as it charged into the room.

The sound of men shouting, furniture toppling, and glass shattering was all Emerson needed to hear to know he must be on his way.

For a nerve-racking moment, Bradbury remained by the door. Emerson feared his reckless friend intended to watch the commotion. A yank on the back of Bradbury's collar, and Emerson had them both sprinting across the main hall. The shouting behind them grew louder, and Emerson knew it was only a matter of seconds before they would be discovered.

Emerson wrenched open the door leading to the servants' stairs and slammed it shut the moment Bradbury came barreling through. He turned to take the stairs two at a time. The enraged shouting grew louder the closer the men got to the door.

"We will not have time," Bradbury shouted over the noise. Grabbing Emerson by the shirt collar, he dragged him toward the opposite door that Little John had identified as the billiards room.

By some miracle, they found the room empty, and together they moved a nearby mahogany sideboard to block the door. An ornately carved, wooden box slid from its top and crashed to the floor, releasing red and white ivory billiard balls in every direction, no doubt alerting their pursuers to their whereabouts. Soon, fists banged on the door and more shouting could be heard. Emerson wondered how long their barricade would hold.

Looking for more furniture to reinforce the sideboard, Emerson spotted another door on the far side of the room. "Come on," he said, pointing Bradbury toward a possible escape.

They sprinted across the room, only to be met by hurried voices coming from outside their escape route. Looking at one another, Bradbury let out a frustrated curse, and they each grabbed a stuffed wingback chair and used them to barricade the door.

"What do we do?" Emerson used his shoulder to push against the chairs when a force from the other side of the door managed to budge them.

Bradbury let out another curse and grabbed two more chairs to put in front of the door. With hurried steps, he cut between the two billiards tables to reach the only two windows in the room.

Emerson followed. He took one window while Bradbury took the other, and together they pulled them open and stuck their heads out. They stared down at the alley. There was nothing but wooden crates underneath Bradbury's window and dirty cobblestone below Emerson's. Their getaway carriage waited farther down the alley, near the mews.

"We could jump down," Bradbury offered with an unconvincing bravado. "I am sure the crates would break . . . most of our fall."

Emerson shook his head, the chill biting at his nose

and cheeks the longer he kept his head outside the window. Pulling his head back in, he looked around the room, searching for any other answer.

The pounding continued at both doors.

He spotted two woolen blankets spread between two wingback chairs in front of a fire. He ran for them and began to knot the corners together. It was as foolhardy of a plan as jumping, but as the banging persisted, he knew they had no other choice.

"What do you propose we tie them to?" Bradbury asked, examining the few pieces of furniture that were not being used in the two barricades.

"None of the chairs will hold either one of us, and the billiards tables are too far away," Emerson said, pulling tight at his last knot. "This should be enough to get you just above the crates, if I remain to hold the other end."

"How will you get down?" Bradbury asked, his eyes stark with apprehension.

Emerson did not have a definite answer, just a precarious and risk-filled thought, but it was their only option. "After I lower you down, run for my carriage. Have them move under the open window as close as possible, and I will make a jump for it."

The carriage would be much taller than the crates, and God willing, a much softer blow if he ended up crashing through the roof. At least when they won the wager, he would have the funds to repair the damage.

Bradbury hesitated.

The pounding and the shouting continued with more

fervor, and the furniture began to move inch by subtle inch. They were running out of time.

Grabbing Bradbury by the shoulders, Emerson pushed him toward the window. "Now is not the time to overthink. Just go."

Squaring his shoulders, Bradbury nodded. "Just like old times, is it not?" His grin was forced, but he grabbed the other end of the blanket-rope.

Emerson lowered him out the window, his hands burning as the woolen fabric tried to slip through his hands. He planted a foot behind him, using the other to press against the wall under the window for added leverage.

After what felt like several minutes, but was only a moment, Emerson felt the strain on his hands and arms cease as the rope became slack. Bradbury had made it to the crates.

Dropping his end of the rope, Emerson looked out the window. His friend was sprinting toward the carriage, for which Emerson was grateful. The pounding had stopped, but in its place was the shouted command to heave. Something heavy slammed against the door at slow, regular intervals, the furniture moving farther away from the door with every attempt.

Willing his mind to focus on what was happening outside the window, Emerson watched as the carriage pulled forward and the horses charged toward him. His coachman, along with Bradbury, who sat next to him, managed to pull the conveyance directly under the window, the horses nearly crashing into the wall of wooden crates. He would have to push hard away from the window to cross the gap that was left between the carriage and the building.

His mind set, Emerson climbed out the window, his hands clutching the frame, as the balls of his feet teetered over the edge. His heart raced, and he made the horrible—but necessary—mistake of looking down. The air seized in his chest, and for a moment, he debated returning to the room.

One of the doors burst open.

"Get him!" someone shouted, and Emerson jumped.

Arms out, knees bent, he aimed for the carriage roof. His feet hit first, the force of the blow buckling his knees until they were nearly at his ears. He grunted as pain shot from his toes to his head. He reached out to grab hold of something—anything—when, like a coiled spring pressed then released, he launched backward off the edge of the carriage.

Bradbury reached out, grabbing him by both wrists, and pulled him back onto the roof of the carriage.

"Go!" Bradbury shouted to the coachman.

The carriage jerked, and angry voices could be heard from above them, but Emerson did not look up. He needed all his concentration to hold tight to the carriage as it jostled in its hasty escape.

As soon as the carriage was safely away from the club, it stopped, and they climbed down and ducked into the concealment of the carriage. For several minutes, the dark interior was filled with the sound of their strained and rapid breaths.

"It will be difficult to ever top that," Bradbury chuckled, running a hand through his crazed hair.

"I give you a week," Emerson replied, rubbing his hands up and down his face as he laughed along with his friend.

"Care to place a wager on it?" Bradbury grinned.

Emerson shook his head. "How about an investment?"

Bradbury burst into a fit of laughter, his head rolling back to rest on the back of the seat.

It felt good to laugh once again with his friend. Emerson had indeed lost sight of himself in his grief, and now, having found that missing part of him, he needed only a striking pair of blue eyes and a pert pair of lips to set his world to rights.

SIXTEEN

It was yet another uneventful morning spent in her mother's drawing room. Olivia sat in her usual seat across from her mother, fighting to get her needle through a stubbornly combative hole. Why had society decided needlepoint was a refined and delicate pastime? With one wrong push, the tiny dagger could plunge into the sensitive flesh of one's finger, drawing blood that would mar anything in its path. Carnage, that was all Olivia saw as she looked down at the bloodstains dotting her needlepoint, handkerchief, and skirt. She could not concentrate to save her life—or, in this case, her now-throbbing finger.

No matter how hard she tried, she could not stop her mind from reliving every night since they had begun to play the game. Throughout it all, Emerson had been a whirlwind of teasing smiles, captivating glances, and confusing words. It had progressed to the point where she could no longer believe all of his actions and her reactions were only because of the game.

A new and growing part of her wanted to believe there

could be something more. He was familiar and safe, which was likely why she was being fooled by her reckless heart. She was reacting out of fear because she knew she must face a future without him.

Olivia stabbed her finger again, extracting a frustrated hiss from her lips. She tossed her bloodstained needlepoint to the side, then grabbed her blood-speckled handkerchief and pressed it to the crimson droplet forming on her fingertip.

Her mother looked across the room at Olivia with a questioning brow.

Knowing a lesson in etiquette would be forthcoming, Olivia wished she could toss her needlepoint into the fire, but she settled for the basket at her feet. She took in a calming breath and folded her hands demurely in her lap.

"If you are done with your . . . needlepoint"—her mother blatantly paused, gracefully setting aside her own work—"perhaps we should discuss the Banbridges' ball."

Olivia's heartbeat quickened and every muscle tensed. "Oh?"

For the love of Arabella's need for Shakespeare, please let it be nothing about the game.

"I could not help but notice that you stood up with Emerson Latham once again. He seems to be making a habit of asking you to dance." Her tone was soft, nothing angry or accusatory. "Olivia, if your father should somehow hear of his increased attentions . . ."

Her mother's voice faded, her silence saying more than her words.

"There is nothing to worry over, Mama," she said, wishing her voice was steadier. They both knew it was foolish for

Olivia to entertain Emerson's attentions; they both knew her father's expectations.

Her mother continued to stare, worry creasing her brow.

"Emerson and I are friends," she said for her mother's sake, but mostly for her own. Any feelings she might possibly have for Emerson would eventually come to naught. Her father wanted a title, and her mother's reminder of that fact could not have come at a better time. As painful to her heart as it might be.

"He is a good . . . friend," her mother said with great care, her gentle tone making Olivia feel worse. "You have been fortunate to experience such kindness and familiarity with a family like the Lathams. Not many families of the upper class are so accepting." Her mother paused, and Olivia braced herself for what she suspected would come next. "But, as daughters to fathers who seek to further their standing in society, you and I both know the roles we are meant to play. Advantageous marriages do have things to offer a woman, but unfortunately, love is rarely one of them."

Olivia took in a deep breath and nodded, unable to find any words willing to pass the growing lump in her throat. It felt cruel that she must choose between a life filled with the advantages of wealth and position and a life of true happiness.

The room slipped into an uncomfortable silence, the only sound coming from the street outside the double windows at Olivia's back. Silence was common in the Wilde household. And she feared it would not change even after she left to establish a house of her own.

Wanting to be alone to collect her thoughts before Arabella was due to arrive for their ride in Hyde Park, Olivia prepared to stand, intending to make some excuse to leave, when she heard the front door slam shut and her father's voice thunder through the household.

"Jenson! Where are they?"

Olivia's heart picked up its pace inside her chest, filling her with trepidation. Her father's heavy, determined steps echoed in the entrance hall, and she sent up a silent prayer that he would continue past the sitting room and onto his study as he always did.

"Are they in here?" He called out again, this time his voice closer.

Jenson replied, but his tone did not carry like her father's did.

Looking to her mother, Olivia found her posture had greatly stiffened. She pulled at the cuffs at her wrists, and then clenched her hands in her lap.

They waited in silence, her father's steps continuing to grow closer and louder. And then they stopped.

The door to the sitting room burst open, and Olivia held her breath as her ears registered the sound of a second pair of approaching footsteps. Her father loomed large in the doorway, blocking any hope she had of seeing whoever was behind him.

His eyes swept over the room, a calculated grin cresting his hard lips as his eyes settled upon Olivia's mother. "There you are, my dear," he said, his smile growing before turning to look back into the corridor. "This way," he called, waving the person in with his large and meaty hand.

Her mother cringed before standing and smoothing out the nonexistent creases in her morning dress. Olivia followed her mother's example, her shoulders tensing with her father's visitor's every step.

A man Olivia had never seen before entered the drawing room. He looked the part of a gentleman with his immaculate blond hair and expertly tailored clothes. He might have been a true dandy except for the square cut of his broad shoulders and jaw, giving him a more masculine appearance.

"Charlotte, Olivia, allow me to introduce Lord Valencourt, the eighth Baron of Brixton," her father said proudly.

Olivia's stomach dropped.

Her father had done it.

He had found favor with a titled gentleman, leaving Olivia with the task of securing the connection. She froze in place. She could not move, could not speak. She felt as if all eyes were upon her, waiting for her to initiate a conversation, and she was helpless to act.

"Would you care for some tea, Lord Valencourt?" her mother asked, stepping into the role of exemplary hostess, as well as giving Olivia time to breathe.

"Yes, I thank you," the baron replied, his voice confident, though he watched Olivia, as if unsure of his welcome.

Olivia remained trapped inside her own fears.

"And, Olivia," her mother continued, "perhaps you could see that our guest is comfortably situated while I call for a tray?"

Olivia could sense her father's displeasure at her unresponsiveness. Tension poured off him in waves, and his gaze felt as heavy as stones. Taking a shaky breath, she attempted to set herself free. "Yes. Forgive me, Lord Valencourt."

He offered her a smile. "No apology necessary, Miss Wilde." He moved to join Olivia on the sofa.

Her father's displeasure immediately eased. Out of the corner of her eye, she watched as he grinned and rubbed his hands together, pleased with the opportunity he had created. Olivia could only be pleased the baron appeared to be there willingly and not due to any sort of threat made by her father.

A maid arrived with the tea service, giving Olivia a few more minutes to collect herself while she and her mother saw to preparing everyone's tea. Her father moved to stand by the fireplace, one elbow resting on the mantel. With a proud and powerful tilt of his chin, he watched over the room like a king surveying his kingdom.

Lord Valencourt did not appear to be put off by her father's unconventional stance. Instead his attention remained on Olivia as she attended to the tea tray. He was in no way ogling her, he simply watched her, a genteel smile appearing at the corner of his lips as they made eye contact. Her unease about him was fading, though they had barely spoken more than a few words to one another. It was her father who was making her uncomfortable, his constant, heavy stare making Olivia feel pressured to make a wonderful first impression.

After handing Lord Valencourt his tea, while her mother did the same for her father, Olivia sat, her mind scrambling for a topic of conversation.

"Have you been in London long, Lord Valencourt?" It was the most mundane of questions, but it was all she could think of.

"I returned with the opening of Parliament," he replied with disinterest, raising his shoulders in an indolent shrug.

Olivia bit the insides of her cheeks, feeling foolish for not thinking her question through. As a peer, he had a duty to be in attendance at the House of Lords. Any woman expecting to be the wife of a baron would be aware of that fact.

"Of course." She pressed a smile to hide her frustration. "I hope you have been able to enjoy other entertainments that London has to offer. I read in the paper that the walls of Westminster can get rather stuffy." She added the little quip she had read from the front page of *The Morning Chronicle* so he would not think her a total lackwit.

Lord Valencourt turned in his seat to fully face her, their knees connecting for a split second before Olivia jerked away, caught off guard. He openly smiled at her, and the surprise appearance of a dimple in his left cheek made him seem more approachable than before. Which gave her some hope.

"If Parliament could have members as refreshing to look at as you, Miss Wilde, it would be a much more amiable atmosphere." Again he offered her a smile with a dimple, but this time the smile did not ease her mind. He had complimented her looks and not her knowledge. He was saying what he thought every lady wanted to hear, which meant he was not concerned about who she was, but what her dowry could bring him.

"You are too kind," Olivia replied with her brightest smile. She too knew how to say what gentlemen wanted to hear.

Lord Valencourt opened his mouth to say something more when Arabella burst into the room unannounced.

Olivia shot to her feet in panicked surprise.

"You will never guess what your butler just tried to tell

me," Arabella laughed, entering the room in a whirl of pink skirts. She reached out and took Olivia's hands in her own, but her laughter stopped as soon as she spied Lord Valencourt on the sofa.

"Oh, forgive me," she said, fully taking in the room. Her eyes widened when they reached Olivia's father, shock flowing over her features. "Perhaps I should have believed your butler," she said to Olivia in a low tone.

The surprises continued as Emerson's exasperated laugh came from just outside the doorway. "Arabella?" he called as he stepped into the room. His laughter ceased, and his mouth pressed shut the moment his eyes landed on Lord Valencourt.

Lord Valencourt slowly rose from his seat, his movements controlled, refined, exuding power and distinction.

Emerson straightened his shoulders, and he seemed to grow even taller due to his rigid posture.

Olivia had seen such behavior many times before when two gentlemen were first introduced. Each sizing up the other, as if they expected to be thrown into a gladiator ring to battle out the hierarchy between them.

She expected the standoff to last a few more moments, but then Emerson surprised her by looking away. But he did not just look anywhere, he looked directly to her. His eyes focused on her as if he couldn't care less about anything else happening in the room. Their dark-brown depths silently asked if she was all right.

Olivia desperately wanted to tell him she was not. That she wanted him to take her away, back to a more familiar time where she could put off life's expectations and play silly games with him. But those times were past. Life's expectations had caught up to her, and the sooner she accepted that fact, the better.

Meeting Emerson's eyes, she managed to force a smile with a small degree of normalcy, though her chest felt like it was caving in and the small knot at the base of her throat weighed as much as a boulder.

"Lord Valencourt," she began, turning away and thus severing her connection to Emerson. "May I introduce to you Mr. Emerson Latham and his sister, Miss Arabella Latham?"

"The Lathams are very close acquaintances of ours," Olivia's father quickly added. There was an unmistakable scheming glint in his eye as he stepped away from the fire and approached the group. He waved for Emerson to join him, and when Emerson complied, her father wrapped his arm around Emerson's shoulder and patted his arm as if they were as familiar as father and son. "Mr. Latham, here, is the nephew to the Earl of Adley."

Olivia cringed, sickened by the way her father could so easily pick and choose when a person was useful or not useful to him. As if they were goods to be bartered with and not a living, breathing person.

A muscle in Emerson's jaw ticked.

"A pleasure," Lord Valencourt said, his flat tone revealing his true emotion. The stiff tension between him and Emerson remained, neither seeming to want to be receptive of the other.

Arabella, however, was grace personified, stepping in when Emerson remained silent. "A pleasure to meet you as well, to be sure, Lord Valencourt." She executed an elegant curtsey along with a smile, using her dark beauty to its full advantage. "Our apologies for interrupting, I—we"—her eyes jumped to Emerson—"had plans to take Olivia for a ride through Hyde Park."

So Olivia was not mistaken in her memory that it was only supposed to be her and Arabella for their weekly outing. Why had Emerson come along?

Her body heated, and she did her best to stamp down the ill-advised flame before it could spark out of control and leave her heart nothing but ash.

"Perhaps you would care to join them, Lord Valencourt?" Olivia's mother asked, coming to stand next to Olivia.

She wished her mother had not made the suggestion, but knew she was doing her duty to please Olivia's father. The more time Olivia could spend with the baron, the better her chances were of receiving an offer.

Olivia pitied her mother for having no voice in whom her daughter would marry and for living with a husband who cared for his own wealth and status above his wife's happiness. But then Olivia's heart sank. Her fate was about to be similar to her mother's.

As if of their own volition, her eyes drifted to Emerson, seeking the comfort of his teasing eyes. What she had not expected was to find that he was already watching her, as if awaiting her gaze. Hoping for it.

Slowly she felt herself being pulled in. She did not stop it, though she knew she should. She only wanted a moment to dream that she could be his.

"I am afraid I must decline," Lord Valencourt said, cutting through her dream. "I have matters that need attending to."

"How unfortunate," her mother said. "Perhaps another time?"

Lord Valencourt smiled, turning to Olivia. "Your father tells me you will be in attendance at the Twickums' ball. Perhaps you would do me the honor of granting me two dances, so we may become better acquainted?"

The look the baron gave her did nothing to her. Not a spark or a missed breath. She should not be looking for such things. Their marriage—if their time together resulted in one—would be a marriage of convenience. Convenient for him because her father had a vast amount of money, and convenient for her father because Lord Valencourt had a title.

"I would like that very much," Olivia said, speaking the words with no feeling behind them. They were only to appease her father, and perhaps, to convince herself that she could follow through with her father's demands.

SEVENTEEN

Stepping up to his barouche, Emerson waved his grooms-man back, needing to take the responsibility of handing Liv and his sister up into the four-seater conveyance. There was a tumultuous storm brewing inside him, one that, if he did not take control of something, would rage until it left regrets in its wake.

Everything he had been working toward with Liv was threatened by the sudden appearance of a gentleman whose only recommendation was his good fortune of being born to a title. Of course he had known another suitor for Liv could eventually present himself. Joshua Wilde was not one to re-lent. But now that the eventuality had happened, Emerson felt anything but prepared.

Lord Valencourt had appeared every bit the part of an affluent dandy, from his outrageously knotted cravat to his fitted, expertly tailored clothing. How the man could even lift an arm or a leg high enough to mount a horse was beyond him. But it had been the second glance where Emerson had spotted his bluff. Behind the baron's dark, hooded eyes was the gaze of a predator—calculating and volatile.

At the very first opportunity, Emerson would have his solicitor look into who exactly Lord Valencourt was. And why he was making himself known to a man like Joshua Wilde.

Arabella approached the barouche first, her steps hurried. A more subdued version of Liv followed after. He longed to bring back the sparkling Liv who dared to play his game in the ballroom.

Handing his sister up, he offered his hand to Liv. She barely allowed her fingers to touch his. Heartbroken by her distance but not giving up, he closed his hand around hers and held her back. She glanced at him over her shoulder, her front foot already on the conveyance step.

"Are you well?" he asked in a soft tone, hoping his sister might not overhear.

"Of course she is well," Arabella answered before Liv could speak. "We managed to get her out of that house. I cannot remember the last time I sat in a room with your father, Olivia, but I can honestly say I am in no hurry to do so again. The way he gainfully brought up our uncle . . ." Arabella's nostrils flared. "It took everything I had to act pleasant."

"I am sorry," Olivia said in somber tones, looking to Arabella and then to him. "It was not right what he did."

"We do not blame you," Arabella said, cutting Emerson off before he could say the words. "Now, come—*the world is our oyster*. Let us get away and have a little fun." His sister held out her hand to Liv, offering her a bright, reassuring smile.

"*Merry Wives of Winsor*," Liv answered with a faint smile before she pulled free of Emerson's hand and took Arabella's.

He let out a frustrated breath. Arabella was proving to be more hindrance than help.

Stepping up into the barouche, he purposefully took the seat directly opposite Liv. She sat on the forward-facing bench next to Arabella, a shared sheepskin rug placed over both their laps. Her head was turned away from him, her back ramrod straight as she watched the busy Mayfair street.

The barouche jerked forward, the abrupt motion freeing a single, misbehaving curl from beneath Liv's dark blue bonnet. The golden strand played across her budding, rose-colored cheek. He longed to reach out and untuck a few more of those engaging strands. Liv reached up and confined the strand back into its place inside her bonnet.

Frustration burned inside his gut, rising up until it nearly choked him. He needed to find a way to speak with her. He needed to understand what the arrival of Lord Valencourt meant to her. If he were to judge by her low spirits, he feared he was not going to like her answer.

Catching Arabella watching him with a quizzical eye, he tore his gaze from Liv. He needed to think.

A frigid March had given way to a somewhat milder April, and many, if not most, Londoners appeared to be taking advantage of the change in weather. No doubt the park would be filled, making his task to gain and hold Liv's attention all the more difficult.

His other obstacle would be Arabella. Short of tossing her off the barouche, he would have to find a way to ask Liv his questions without Arabella interrupting him—again. He would also need to question Liv without sparking his sister's suspicion. If Arabella let it slip too soon that he was in love with Liv, he feared it would put his whole plan at risk.

The horses turned, and the barouche jostled from the steady clip-clop of the cobblestone streets to the crunching gravel of the Hyde Park roads. The park was indeed swarming with people, more than the busiest beehive. It would take a miracle to keep even one of the other conveyances from approaching their own.

Emerson instructed his coachman to turn down one of the private lanes along the Serpentine. He had an idea, a crazed one at best, but what other choice did he have?

"How about a game?" Emerson asked, taking advantage of their momentary seclusion.

"Oh, yes. This should be fun," Arabella said, practically bouncing in her seat.

Liv remained silent, though she did finally look at him.

"What game do you propose?" Arabella asked.

"Truth or command," Emerson replied.

Liv appeared to hesitate.

He did his best to appear unaffected by her silence, though his future was riding on her consent.

"Liv?" he pressed, hoping both women had missed the slight desperation in his tone.

"If Arabella wishes to," she replied, her tone detached and neutral.

He hated seeing her so listless. It was nothing like the girl he remembered, or the woman he knew her to truly be.

"Splendid." Arabella clapped her gloved hands together, the leather muffling most of the sound. "I will go first. Truth or command, Emerson?"

"Command," Emerson replied, not liking the way she had been watching him since they left Liv's house. Who knew what her clever mind might have suspected, and what question she might have asked him.

For a brief moment, she appeared disappointed in his choice, and then she grinned. "Very well. I command you, brother dearest, to tell us why you were so discourteous to Lord Valencourt."

"I was not discourteous," he replied before he could think better of it. Drawing more attention to his behavior would only bolster Arabella in her search for answers.

"You were. You did not say a single word to him, and I had to step in so he would not take offense." She raised a brow, daring him to contradict her.

If only he could. But Liv had been there, and if she had not noted his behavior then, she was thinking about it now. He was not ready to have a life-altering discussion with Liv yet. He needed her to be more confident in him, and more importantly, herself.

"Stop trying to get out of my command, brother," Arabella said.

Emerson grimaced. Perhaps he should ask the driver to slow down so he might toss his sister from the conveyance.

"Very well." He paused. His mind and honor warred over whether he could withhold the truth, and then he realized his sister had given him the perfect loophole. "The reason for my behavior was because I took a disliking to the color of his waistcoat."

"What? That is ridiculous!" Arabella snapped, throwing her hands in the air. "You have to answer my question."

"But I did, sister *dearest*," he taunted, unable to help himself. She had tried to trick him, and unfortunately for her, two could play at that game. "I chose 'command,' not 'truth.' Therefore, I am not compelled to answer truthfully." He spread his hands as though helpless in the face of such logic.

An enchanting burst of laughter bubbled from Liv's lips, and she made no effort to conceal her amusement at her friend's expense. It felt good to see her react so. It had to be the first genuine smile he had seen from her since his arrival in her mother's sitting room. He only wished he had the opportunity to elicit even more smiles from her today. But he had questions that needed answering, and he was uncertain what her reaction might be.

"I believe that makes it my turn," Emerson said, shooting Arabella a not-so-sly grin.

She glowered at him, her look promising retribution.

Emerson turned his attention to Liv. Her soft blue eyes were looking repentantly toward Arabella, though a corner of her mouth continued to twitch. What he would not give to have those eyes look to him in such a way.

Someday, he told himself. *Someday she will, and I will kiss the laughter from her teasing lips.*

"Truth or command, Liv?" he asked, jealous for her attention.

She turned toward him, the twitch vanishing from her lips. An unusual awkwardness settled between them as she acted as if she did not know where to look.

"Liv?" he pressed, frustrated by her reaction.

Timidly she met his gaze. "Truth."

It was the response he needed, but he still felt a small

pang of disappointment in her not wanting to take the risk of a command. He needed to remember, however, the future he could lose if he pushed her too far too soon.

He saw a flash of that future, filled with love and laughter, and all because of the beautiful and challenging woman sitting before him. He would have a carriage full—as Bradbury called it—of blue-eyed, spirited little daughters and sons. He longed to laugh and play with them and to teach them, just as his father had taught him, about what truly mattered in life. He was discovering that he was a family man, and he intended to build a legacy his father would be proud of. He wished his father had lived long enough to see it.

Clearing his throat, he spoke, "Since my sister seems fixated on the subject, perhaps we should hear your impression of your father's newest acquaintance?" He stubbornly refused to speak Lord Valencourt's name in front of Liv. "The truth, if you please."

Liv's shoulders tensed. "My father appears pleased by the acquaintance."

"That might be so, but I asked what *your* thoughts were, not your father's," Emerson said, trying to keep his tone gentle but direct.

She shifted in her seat, and this time Arabella seemed to take note of Liv's uneasy pause. "From first impressions, Lord Valencourt appears to be a complimentary sort of gentleman. And I am sure such impressions will improve upon closer acquaintance." Liv turned her face to the sunshine for a moment, then let her gaze fall to her lap. She distractedly smoothed over the sheepskin rug that covered her knees.

"Olivia," Arabella began, "if you do not—"

Emerson cut her off. He needed to be the one guiding the conversation, not his sister. "Do you believe your father has your best interests at heart?"

Emerson's heart pounded as he awaited her answer. If she was willing to trust her father, his plan was doomed to fail.

"You have asked two questions, which is against the rules of the game," Arabella argued, her fury rising with every word.

Emerson ignored the way his sister's eyes burned a hole through him. "Do you, Liv?" he asked her again.

She continued to study her hands in her lap.

Look up at me. He pleaded silently. He needed her to trust him in that moment more than he needed breath.

But she never moved.

"Do not let him cheat you, Olivia. It's your turn," Arabella said, her agitation toward him still apparent in her tone.

Liv turned to Arabella, forcing a soft smile while patting her arm to soothe her. "I was just trying to decide who to ask," she replied, though the way she avoided his gaze told Emerson it would not be him.

How could he get her to fully trust him? To see him and believe that he would do all in his power to make her happy and feel protected—something he doubted her father ever did.

The barouche reached the end of the secluded lane, then turned back onto the more populated Kings Road. They crossed paths with another conveyance carrying a mother and several daughters.

Arabella's eyes followed them closely, and she bit her bottom lip. She was contemplating something, and he wished he had focused more on the faces attached to the occupants instead of simply their number. There was no knowing what mischief his sister could be plotting.

Arabella leaned to the side and whispered something to Liv. Whatever she said, it made Liv quickly look at him before she turned back to their secret conversation.

"What are you two whispering about?" he asked, not liking the way Arabella's smile grew with every passing second.

For a moment, he thought they intended to ignore him entirely, but then Arabella looked to him with far too much confidence in her eyes. "Go on, Olivia, ask him."

Liv's eyes were slow to meet his. She opened her mouth, looking as if she might speak, but then closed it.

"Come on, Liv, let me have it." He encouraged her with one of his teasing grins, needing the comfort that only one of her smiles could give. "What shall it be this time? Stealing one of Cook's cream pies to satisfy your and Arabella's craving for sweets?"

Liv and Arabella exchanged mischievous looks. A challenge, if ever he'd seen one.

"I remember a time when you commanded me to ride the world's most stubborn mule, backward through town. To this day, half of Bedfordshire refuses to take me seriously."

A quick rush of giggles burst from Liv, propelling Emerson to continue.

"Perhaps worst of all was your outrageous idea to remove all of the chickens from the coop and replace them with the goose feathers from one of my mother's pillows. It looked like a complete massacre by the time I was finished. It took me a week to remove all the feathers and clean the coop to my parents' satisfaction. The gamekeeper still scowls at me every time our paths cross."

Liv couldn't contain her full, heartfelt laugh, and her shoulders shook with mirth.

"So go on, Liv, let's hear it. When have I ever refused you anything?" He held her smiling gaze, silently willing her to trust him.

But, even as he watched, the laughing smile that had lit the depths of her stunningly blue eyes faded, leaving behind the charred look of someone whose spirit had been doused.

Turning to Arabella, Liv asked, "Truth or command?"

"What?" Arabella gasped. "No. You were supposed to ask him, not me." She glared heavenward.

Emerson felt a stab of disappointment at Liv's choice to take the easier way out. But he would not allow himself to dwell on it. He had time, not much, but there was still time.

"Truth or command?" Liv asked Arabella again, a hint of annoyance in her tone. She was back to avoiding his gaze.

Arabella huffed her resignation. "Fine. Truth." She shot Emerson a side glance, letting him know his time was coming.

"Have you truly read all the works of Shakespeare?" Olivia asked, shocking Emerson into choking on his suddenly inhaled spit. Perhaps she had not lost her fire after all. Not even he would think to challenge his sister's devotion to the Bard.

Arabella jerked back as if she had been struck, her mouth flapping open and closed like a caught fish. He expected his sister to answer wholeheartedly in the affirmative, but after her continued stutter and inability to answer he was beginning to have doubts.

After one last huff, she said, "Truth? All right, no, there is one I have not been able to finish. Are you happy?" Arabella threw her hands up in exasperation. "I have, at least, read *Much Ado About Nothing*, which I find to be ridiculous. And you, Liv, would do well to read it yourself. For the life of me, I cannot stomach a world where so much trickery and games have to be played just to get two people to tell the other how they feel. If you feel something, say it!"

Emerson started choking for a whole other reason. Had she figured him out? Was this her not-so-subtle way of calling him out?

Of course it was, nothing about Arabella was subtle. And she was brilliant—most of the time—when it came to her use of Shakespeare, though he prayed she would leave voicing her suspicions regarding his own feelings at that.

"I knew it!" Liv gave a little bounce in triumph. Her grin spread as the creases along the bridge of Arabella's nose deepened.

Emerson sighed in relief that Liv had overlooked Arabella's intended message in her celebration.

Arabella turned her anger on Emerson, which held a high possibility of not ending well for him. "Truth or command, brother?"

"Mr. Latham!"

Emerson had never been so relieved to hear the scolding tones of Lady Bixbee.

He turned toward the lady as she approached. She sat inside an exquisitely polished conveyance, an astonishing amount of fur rugs covering her and her gaggle of friends.

"Lady Bixbee." He tipped his hat in greeting. "What may I do for you on this fine afternoon?"

The matron ordered both conveyances to stop, and, like a queen inspecting her subjects, she took her time to look at every one of them.

"Good afternoon, Lady Bixbee," Arabella called out with a friendly smile.

Lady Bixbee smiled in return, which was more than she had ever offered Emerson. "I must talk with you and your mother soon, Miss Latham. I have a nephew I wish to introduce you to."

The color in Arabella's complexion fled, and she offered Lady Bixbee a forced smile.

Lady Bixbee turned serious eyes on Emerson. "The most curious information has reached my ears that requires your explanation, Mr. Latham. Lady Masdon's"—she gestured to one of her companions—"grandson told her that he is indebted to you for thirty pounds. All because of some ridiculous tale of a pig taking tea at White's?"

Emerson held back a chuckle. It hadn't taken long for the gossips to learn of his and Bradbury's actions. He would deny the tale, of course. Anonymity was still key in keeping himself and Bradbury from any serious repercussions, but that did not mean he could not have a little fun with the tale.

"While I cannot currently recollect why Lady Masdon's grandson owes me a debt, I can tell you that I have heard that story rather differently."

As one, the matrons in Lady Bixbee's conveyance leaned forward, their accusations turned into anticipation.

"What I heard happened was this . . ."

EIGHTEEN

Olivia was supposed to be at the Cartwrights' ball. At least, that was where Arabella and the others were expecting her to be. Instead, she found herself seated next to Lord Valencourt at a dinner party held by Mr. Yardley and his sister. They were close acquaintances of the baron's, and Olivia had never felt more out of place.

From the moment she had been introduced, Olivia had noted the Yardley siblings' taste for appearances. Miss Yardley, who could not be but a few years older than she, wore a gold-colored turban with white feathers atop her head. Mr. Yardley, whose burgundy coat and pantaloons were so fitted he moved with a stiff gait, also boasted an immaculately knotted cravat. Olivia thought it looked to be devouring the gentleman's throat, rather than adorning it.

She even felt outdone by their table setting, which rested upon the most pristine, white tablecloth trimmed with a wide lace around its edges. With every pass of her fork or spoon, she feared leaving behind a single crumb or droplet. Two silver, six-candlestick candelabras were positioned along the center of the table; two silver-tiered platters overflowing with fruits sat on either side of them. Placed at the center of the table was a crystal bowl, filled with a delicious-looking pudding and a decoratively spun sugar creation balanced on top.

Everything about the Yardleys spoke of the height of fashion, and Olivia's father could not appear more pleased.

She knew she should feel pleased—relieved, really—that everything was happening as her father wanted. A titled gentleman wanted to court her. He had sent her roses, claiming the yellow petals reminded him of her hair. It was all the stuff of romance novels, and she should have been swept off her feet. And yet . . .

Her mind was full of a pair of dark brown eyes that had only days before looked across a barouche at her as if she were more vital to him than the very air he breathed.

"Do you not agree, Miss Wilde?" Miss Yardley asked, pulling Olivia back to the present. She was watching her from the head of the table, her eyes sharp and inquisitive, her golden turban with goose feathers shining in the candlelight.

Olivia did not know Miss Yardley well, but, upon seeing that look, she felt confident that the woman enjoyed having a little fun at someone else's expense.

"Forgive me," Olivia said, setting down the spoon she had not realized was in her hand. She could feel her father's angry stare from across the table. "My mind was elsewhere." She forced a repentant smile, a newfound caution for Miss Yardley forming in its wake.

"No forgiveness necessary, Miss Wilde," Miss Yardley replied with a far-too-sweet smile. "Especially if your thoughts were on a more pleasing subject"—her eyes flashed to Lord

Valencourt and then back to Olivia—"than this droll conversation my brother is insistent upon having."

Heat ran up Olivia's neck and cheeks, just not for the reasons everyone was now suspect to believe. She had been distracted by thoughts of a certain gentleman, only he was decidedly not seated at the table. Luckily for her, Mr. Yardley spoke first, sparing her from having to reply.

"Droll conversation?" he scoffed, snatching the serviette from his lap and tossing it down on what was left of his pudding. He was seated at the foot of the table and turned to address Olivia's mother, seated to his right. "Surely you do not agree with my prejudiced sister, Mrs. Wilde?"

Dabbing at her lips with a serviette, Olivia's mother paused before offering Mr. Yardley a delicate smile. "One cannot help but feel for some of your arguments, Mr. Yardley."

Her response was flawless, safely navigating between their two warring hosts, and Olivia could not be more envious. Her mother always seemed to fit into society no matter the circumstance. It was an ability Olivia doubted she would ever possess. She was far too pensive in social settings, constantly fearful she might say or do the wrong thing. If only her thoughts could be reined in from their wanderings.

An image of Emerson, teasing her about the silly tales of their past, brought her some comfort. Times had been much simpler then. Before life and responsibility had caught up with them.

"You should ask *Miss* Wilde what she thinks of your argument, brother," Miss Yardley spoke in that sly tone again, proving to have a real talent for catching Olivia off guard. "I am certain that once she hears your side of the tale, she will undoubtedly side with mine." Her smile was that of a lady, though her eyes were those of an instigator.

"Are you sure you wish for me to do so, sister? I would hate to best you twice in one evening, and in front of our guests no less," Mr. Yardley said with a mocking grin.

Olivia's father snorted as he scooped himself another large serving of pudding.

"I would not go so far as to say one of us has already been bested this evening, brother," Miss Yardley began with a wry smile, "but I will say that one of us *will* be bested, and I am fairly confident it will not be me."

Olivia did her best not to laugh, though Lord Valencourt and her father were not so successful.

"Go on, Yardley," Lord Valencourt said, pressing his friend. "Put her in her place."

Shooting a glare at his sister, Mr. Yardley tugged at the cuffs of his jacket before turning to Olivia. "Miss Wilde, what do you have to say about this detestable buffoonery done against Brummell's character?"

A corner of Olivia's mouth twitched. "Are you referring to the incident with the pig?" she asked, knowing there could be no other notable event that he could be referring to. It had been grist for the gossip mill for days.

"Incident?" Mr. Yardley reeled back in outrage, while his sister made no effort to hide her growing smile. "That was no mere incident. The man's belongings were stolen and then publicly defaced. The criminals responsible should be thrown into Newgate."

A swell of laughter built inside Olivia's chest, forcing her to cough into her shoulder to hide her response. Emerson had spoken to Lady Bixbee about the incident and claimed it had not been him. Olivia thought otherwise, having judged the proud glint in his eyes.

He is so handsome when he smiles.

Her cheeks flushed, and she glanced up through her lashes to see if anyone was watching her at the table. To her dismay, Mr. Yardley was, while Miss Yardley continued to argue her point that it had been nothing more than what Mr. Brummell deserved.

Knowing she could not get away with such a strong opinion as Miss Yardley did, Olivia attempted to follow her mother's example, though on the inside she loathed always having to accommodate.

"Forgive me, Mr. Yardley. I must add I have heard only a little of what took place." She offered the gentleman the sweetest smile she could manage.

"You make a very good point, Miss Wilde," Lord Valencourt said, turning in his chair. The space between them seemed to vanish, and Olivia felt suddenly uncomfortable with such close attention. "It is not a lady's place to concern herself with such difficult matters as the law. The subject is more suited for a gentleman, who would promise her a home and security."

"Here, here," Olivia's father echoed, slapping his hand twice upon the table.

Lord Valencourt made a show of looking deep into Olivia's eyes, but she recognized it as the false mask of sentiment performed for the benefit of everyone else in the room. He merely wanted a good and obedient wife—and her father's money—and she was finding it more and more difficult to believe she could tolerate such a life.

Ignoring the pleading voice inside her head that sounded a lot like her mother, Olivia turned from Lord Valencourt and looked directly to Mr. Yardley.

"I did hear, however, that the words painted onto the banner the pig carried referenced the very words Mr. Brummell had spoken in regards to our Prince Regent. Some might argue Mr. Brummell's actions could be far more treasonous than those who wrote them on a pig."

Her mother gasped, her father growled, and Lord Valencourt and Mr. Yardley both scoffed in outrage. But it was Miss Yardley's reaction that stood out from the rest. A bell-like laughter flitted from her rose-colored lips, and, with a smile that could mesmerize any gentleman, she rose with ease and confidence. The room slipped into silence as she made her way to Olivia's chair.

"I can see, Miss Wilde," Miss Yardley said, taking Olivia by the hand and lifting her from her seat, "that you and I are going to be very good friends." She shot a telling smile to her brother. "Now, let us retire to the drawing room and leave the gentlemen to their ever-serious discussions and port."

None of the gentlemen attempted to argue with Miss Yardley's decision, and Olivia was grateful for the escape. Lord Valencourt and Mr. Yardley politely rose from their seats as Miss Yardley led Olivia and her mother out of the room. The anger radiating from her father's eyes followed Olivia until she reached the safety of the corridor.

Suspecting she had traded one trouble for another, Olivia

felt uneasy at how easily Miss Yardley had latched herself to her arm.

They entered the drawing room, and instead of being allowed to join her mother on one of the sofas, Olivia was directed to follow Miss Yardley to take a turn about the room.

"I must tell you, Miss Wilde," Miss Yardley leaned in to whisper, "that I am absolutely in raptures over your spirit."

Olivia forced a smile, not sure why such a conversation needed to be conducted in private. Her mother had been present for Olivia's show of spirit.

"But, if I may offer you a small piece of advice?"

Olivia nodded, though she doubted she would ever use Miss Yardley's advice.

"When you are Lord Valencourt's wife—"

Olivia stumbled, and Miss Yardley shot her a guileless smile and reestablished her grip around Olivia's arm.

"It would be best to keep such witty remarks for when we are spared the gentlemen's company. I have known the baron for some time, and he is not one who responds well when challenged."

"Lord Valencourt has made me no offer of marriage," Olivia said, quick to correct her. The thought of him doing so sent a wave of icy chills through her.

"Oh, it is inevitable." Miss Yardley waved her free hand, dismissing any doubt. "Why else do you think we are all here? This dinner was merely a formality. The *ton* expects a courtship, and when that expectation has been met, you shall be the next Baroness Valencourt." Her smile grew, and she patted Olivia's arm as if congratulating her on winning a great prize.

Only Olivia did not feel as if she had won anything. Could it truly be that easy? Why was it so easy? She had expected to do much more smiling and simpering—possibly even begging—before Lord Valencourt would settle for asking for her hand. This sort of urgency went far beyond what the baron would financially gain from her dowry. There had to be something more.

"Has Lord Valencourt confided in you?" Olivia asked, playing the part of a blushing potential bride to gain more information.

"Not in so many words," Miss Yardley said with another one of her sly smiles. "All you need to know is that your futures will be secured."

Futures? Was Lord Valencourt in some sort of financial trouble?

"I shall take comfort in your reassurance," Olivia said, though it was the complete opposite. She needed more answers. "I only wish I knew more about him. Everything is happening so fast."

"Lucky for you, I am always up for a bit of gossip," Miss Yardley whispered as they passed directly behind Olivia's mother for what felt like the twenty-third time. "What would you like to know?"

"How long have you known Baron Valencourt?" Olivia asked, needing to know just how far back her questions could go.

"Long before he was even a baron," Miss Yardley replied, as if she had told Olivia how she preferred her tea and not just made everything all the more confusing.

"I beg your pardon? Are you referring to when he was a child and his father held the title?"

"Oh, his father was never a baron."

Olivia blinked in utter confusion.

"Did you not know this?" Miss Yardley laughed, seeming to enjoy Olivia's shock. "Lord Valencourt has only held the barony these past few months. He inherited it after the deaths of both his father's ancient uncle and the uncle's drunkard son. Apparently, Lord Valencourt was the next in line to inherit—though there is some trouble about another gentleman trying to prove his legitimacy as the son and heir."

Olivia could barely breathe. Miss Yardley had listed off a series of life-changing events as if they were nothing more than items on a housekeeper's shopping list. And if what she said was true, then Lord Valencourt's title stood under a serious threat of being taken away.

Did her father know anything of this? Or was he blinded by the fact that there was a title before him—at least for now—and so he would never think to question it? Could this be the reason Lord Valencourt was moving so quickly? Did he fear losing his inheritance, and so he sought to secure her dowry to save his own skin? Everything was such a muddled mess.

Taking in a shaky breath to calm her nerves, Olivia realized she wanted no part of any of this, for what would stop either her father or Lord Valencourt from taking advantage of her time and time again?

What she truly wanted was a life built on trust, honor, and . . . love.

She *wanted* love, and she feared the steady pounding in her heart sounded a lot like *Em-er-son.*

What was she to do? Could anything even be done? Had she complied with her father's demands for too long to even hope for escape?

"I see I have shocked you." Miss Yardley tittered, unabashedly intruding on Olivia's thoughts. Her smile was thin, as if she were enjoying catching Olivia off guard again.

"Not shocked." Olivia forced a smile, not wanting to give Miss Yardley the satisfaction. "Only enlightened."

Miss Yardley studied Olivia, her smile growing with every passing second. "Why, Miss Wilde, I believe your response has surprised even me."

Olivia highly doubted much of anything surprised Miss Yardley. She seemed to be a woman who thrived from knowing secrets and spreading the latest gossip. Olivia hoped her own name would be spared from the lady's tongue when next she decided to have any more of her so-called fun.

NINETEEN

Where is she? Emerson thought from his unobscured position near the entrance of the Cartwrights' ballroom. His eyes had been trained on the arched, double-doorway since his arrival, but Liv and her parents had yet to walk through them.

Inwardly, he felt like one of those caged, feral animals in Edward Cross's Menagerie, pacing the iron bars of its prison, while outwardly he attempted to maintain an indifferent, composed state. The constant flexing of his hand at his side was the only thing that betrayed his agitation. He needed to see her, needed to hear the spark of laughter from her lips to feel a semblance of ease.

"You cannot will her here," came Northcott's steady tone as he appeared alongside Emerson. "No matter how long or how hard you stare."

Emerson glared at his friend from the corner of his eye. "A fact I am well aware of."

Northcott nodded, seemingly undeterred by Emerson's dark mood. "You should come away." He paused as he glanced over his shoulder. "Others are beginning to notice."

Emerson followed his friend's gaze, catching a group of ladies studying him and talking behind the safety of their fans. "Let them talk," he said through gritted teeth, returning to his watch of the ballroom's entrance.

Nothing mattered but to see Liv walk through those doors. Gossip was as changeable as a pair of boots in this society. Once one subject was muddied, they would simply change to another.

"And Arabella?" Northcott asked.

Emerson nearly snapped his neck turning to look at his friend. "What *about* my sister?" he demanded. He noted his friend had called his sister by her Christian name, but he did not worry much over it. He trusted Northcott.

"Several times, she has made remarks about your behavior."

Emerson grumbled a curse under his breath. That would have been convenient to know before now. "And what have you said to her?"

He gave no answer.

Emerson cursed again. "You are supposed to be helping me."

Northcott maintained his indifference, though in coming to Emerson he showed that he cared. "She does not expect me to talk much."

"None of us do," Emerson muttered as he rubbed at the growing pain at the back of his neck.

"For me to do so now would only draw more suspicion."

"I believe she already suspects," Emerson replied. "Where is she now?" He turned to the side to get a better look at the ballroom, while also keeping an eye on the entrance.

"Dancing with the honorable Mr. Edward Trenor." Northcott nodded toward the dance floor. "You should discourage the match. It is said the Trenors are in need of serious financial gains."

Emerson nodded, the animal inside him rattling its cage as his memory went back to the ball where he had been forced to watch Liv dance with the gentleman. "Pull her away the moment the set ends."

"It would be best for you to do so."

Northcott was right, but Emerson could not abandon his post. "I cannot leave. If Liv should—"

"Valencourt isn't here," Northcott said bluntly. "She isn't coming."

And the animal he knew to be jealousy raged within its cage.

Whipping around, Emerson grabbed the lapels of Northcott's black evening jacket and shoved him a few steps back until he was stopped by the nearby pillar. A few feminine gasps rippled through the small crowd nearby.

Emerson knew he was overreacting; his anger was not for Northcott, he just happened to be the one in Emerson's reach when all he could see was red.

Northcott slowly lifted his hands and pressed lightly against Emerson's forearms to remove Emerson's grip. He showed not the slightest hint of fear or fight. His dark past had no doubt made him into such a man. "Your fight is not with me, Emerson."

There it was again. Lord Northcott's aggravating calm and collected indifference, while the animal inside Emerson wanted to unjustifiably rip him into shreds. He felt so out of control, and he did not know how to release his grip.

"Here we are," Bradbury said jovially, wedging himself between Emerson and Northcott. He wore a forced wide smile as he took Emerson by the shoulders and turned him. "Look who I found."

Emerson's mother stood before him, both concern and worry written across her face. But all the animal could see was pity.

Shoving out of Bradbury's hold, he growled, "You brought my mother?"

Bradbury shrugged, maintaining his forced, beaming smile. "Every man needs his mother." He turned to Northcott. "Do you not agree, Beasty?" he asked, no doubt trying to diffuse some of the tension.

Northcott raised a dark, skeptical brow, and then added to Bradbury's ridiculous conversation. "Have we ever met your mother?"

Bradbury scoffed. "Of course not. She does not like London." He held up a hand to shield his sly grin from Emerson's mother. "Which is why I prefer it."

And just like that, the role of ringmaster fell naturally to Bradbury, relieving a minuscule amount of tension in Emerson's shoulders.

"Then how can you say 'Every man needs his mother'?" Northcott pressed.

"Because most mothers are nothing like my mother." He paused, as if he had just thought of something. "Actually, Beasty, you should be able to relate. You know, after your mother went after your father's brother and . . . " Bradbury made a single stabbing motion with his hand. "Well, you know . . ."

Emerson's breath was knocked from his lungs as his eyes fixed on Bradbury.

Blood drained from Bradbury's face, and instant regret flooded his features. Emerson was suddenly grateful he had shoved Northcott into a somewhat secluded corner, and he prayed that the pillar had hidden them from the others in the ballroom.

"That is to say . . . I mean . . ." Bradbury stumbled over his words. "What I meant to say was, I am sure she was a good mother before she—" He clamped his hand over his mouth and looked to Emerson's mother with pleading eyes.

She cleared her throat, and with a calming smile, looked to Bradbury and Northcott. "What I am sure Mr. Bradbury wished to say—before his mouth ran away with itself—was that perhaps a mother can get through to her son when no one else can. Thus, 'Every man needs his mother.'"

"Yes, that," Bradbury said, pointing toward Emerson's mother.

She gave a sympathetic smile to Bradbury, and then turned expectant eyes on Emerson.

"There is nothing to discuss," Emerson said.

"Must I assume that Lord Northcott stumbled and that you merely helped him by stopping his fall with a pillar?" She narrowed her eyes at him.

His pride bristled. He was no longer a boy to be scolded by his mother, but a man. A man with responsibilities and expectations. A man, who without a doubt respected and loved his mother, which was why he held his tongue.

She seemed to understand his struggle, and she held out her hand to him. "I would like to dance."

Emerson felt a swift blow to his chest. His mother and father had ignored convention in their marriage, always choosing to save a dance for one another. For his mother to ask him now—for him to step even further into his father's place—was a bittersweet bite to take.

"I would be honored," he managed to get out through a tight throat.

She softly smiled in return, a sheen of tears building at the corners of her eyes. He was a selfish excuse for a son to forget that his widowed mother was fighting her own internal battles.

Taking her hand, Emerson tucked her fingers into the crook of his arm and led the way to the dance floor. With each step, the number of whispers behind fans diminished, but that did nothing to calm the raging war inside his head.

He found them a spot in the line forming for the dance, the tension in his shoulders easing when he witnessed his mother receive a kind smile from a friend.

"I should have asked you to dance the first ball after our return," he told his mother the moment their paths crossed in the dance.

"We were both finding our place," his mother said with an understanding tone, though there was sorrow in her eyes.

The dance required them to step apart and pair with another partner, which gave Emerson time to reflect on the past few months. His return to London had been veiled in the shadow of his father's death, only to be shown a glimpse of light with his every encounter with Liv. He did not want to lose that. He *could* not lose that.

"Arabella told me about the day you were introduced to Lord Valencourt," his mother said when they came back together. "I knew then that you ran the risk of finding yourself in the very situation you are in. What I did not anticipate was the severity of your reaction."

The dance required them to crisscross with another partner. While they were apart, his mother stared intently at him until they came back together.

"You must accept the fact that you will have to interact with the gentleman before this all plays out. I suggest you find a way to control your reactions to him before you risk damaging your own reputation. Or worse, damaging your sister's reputation as well as Olivia's."

Emerson nodded his acknowledgment, though the jealousy burning inside him wanted to argue against it.

"Remember what your father would say: 'A level head, a level course.'"

"A level head, a level course," Emerson repeated, the thought of his father extinguishing any fight he had left.

His mother was right. This was about more than just him. He would leave the matter be for now, but if Liv did not attend the Twickums' ball the next evening, he could make no promises as to his reaction.

TWENTY

The moment Olivia entered the Twickums' ballroom, her skin felt clammy, her head ached, and her stomach felt as if it might drop to the floor at any moment. Which meant either she was nervous about seeing Emerson or she had suddenly contracted yellow fever.

Both reasons were plausible, but neither of them preferable for the evening that lay ahead. She still did not know what to do about her feelings for Emerson. Even if she could somehow convince her father to look into what Miss Yardley had said about Lord Valencourt, it did not mean that her father—who was not in attendance tonight—would abandon his desire for her to marry a title. He would simply continue his hunt for another. And Emerson did not have a title.

She knew she should listen to her mother's advice and distance herself from Emerson for the rest of the Season. No good could come from encouraging an attachment. But the part of her that had come alive with her participation in the game wanted to do otherwise.

She could be sensible about it. All she needed to do was

remind herself that anything she or Emerson did or said was about the game—could *only* be about the game. If this was to be her last Season before she married, she wanted to make the most of it.

Looking over the ballroom, Olivia sought out Arabella before fear or doubt could change her mind. She had missed the previous ball, and her friend would be able to tell her where she stood in the game.

"Do you see the Lathams?" she asked her mother, rising up on her toes.

Her mother eyed her warily. "Is that wise?"

"I am looking for Arabella," Olivia said with forced calm, though she felt annoyed by her mother's subtle, though accurate, accusation. "I promised Arabella I would spend some time with her since we did not attend the Cartwrights' ball." It was not exactly a lie; she would have made such a promise had she seen Arabella between the Cartwrights' ball and now.

Her mother hesitated, causing Olivia to worry. She needed to play this game. "Very well, you may go. But I do not want you disappearing as you often do and risk your dances with Lord Valencourt."

She gave a sigh of relief and kissed her mother on the cheek. "Thank you, Mama. I will be back."

"See that you are . . . for both our sakes." Her look carried a warning—one that Olivia had every intention of following. She knew what she was doing was reckless, but so far she had been able to play the game safely.

Her mother pointed out where Arabella stood with her mother, and Olivia was off before her mother or her guilt could stop her.

Getting Arabella away from her mother proved to be a simpler task than her own escape. In fact, Arabella met her halfway, an excited smile upon her face.

"Am I glad to see you," she said, grabbing Olivia by the hand and pulling her quickly in another direction. "I was beginning to worry you were not coming—again." She did not stop until they were a good distance from both their mothers.

"What did I miss?" Olivia asked, a thrill running through her at the thought of the game. And at seeing Emerson, but she was not going to think about that.

"At the Cartwrights' ball? Regrettably nothing." Arabella let out a huff.

"What do you mean?" Olivia asked.

"Emerson was in a mood, and somehow—without even asking my opinion—we *all* decided not to play. But now that you are here, I can begin the game." She spoke with such excitement, Olivia nearly missed an important piece of information.

"Are you saying that you are *it*?"

"I am," Arabella said with a mischievous smile. "But do not worry. I have a bigger catch in mind. My brother has evaded me ever since the start of the game. I intend to catch him before the evening is through."

"May I help?" Olivia offered. She would have to return to her mother soon, but this would at least give her some excitement before her dance with Lord Valencourt.

Arabella's smile grew, and she looped her arm through Olivia's. "Shall we *give the devil his due*?"

Olivia could not help but laugh. "*Henry the Fourth*, and your brother is not the devil." He was quite the opposite, in fact, and for reasons she did not want to name, the thought of him sent a burst of heat unfurling through her chest.

"Are you sure about that?" Arabella raised a questioning brow. "He seems to be enjoying tormenting you as of late."

The heat climbed up her neck. She wanted to look away, but Arabella was watching her closely. As if she was, like Olivia's mother, suspicious.

Instead, she squeezed Arabella's arm in the crook of her own and said with an air of innocence, "To the devil then?" She winked and motioned for Arabella to lead the way.

Arabella was off like a horse bolting through the night. The crowd around them grew thicker with every hurried step. A few times, Olivia was forced to apologize to the people she had inadvertently knocked into whenever her foot caught in the flowing material of her gown. The last one in particular was an old matron with the most intimidating quizzing glass.

"*For goodness' sake,*" Arabella said to Olivia. "Are you even lifting your feet underneath all that gold and lace?"

"*Henry the Eighth,*" Olivia replied dryly, stubbornly slowing her pace for two—maybe five—steps. "Perhaps if you stopped jerking me about and actually allowed me time to help you look, I might not stumble so much on my gown."

Arabella slowed her step and arched a brow at Olivia. "Would you be sad if your gown was somehow damaged?"

Olivia's lips twitched. "Perhaps we should go faster."

They laughed together and resumed their search, though at a more manageable pace for both of them.

Olivia's gown was a soft cream, which would have been lovely had her father not insisted it be accentuated by a sheer gold overdress that hung just below the hem of her gown.

Dark gold lace rimmed the cuffs of her sleeves, and gold beadwork threaded around her neckline. The gown would make even a Greek goddess envious.

"Finally," Arabella hissed with excitement, picking up her pace.

"What?" Olivia asked, as she tried to keep up with her longer-limbed friend. "What is it? Did you see your brother?" Her foot caught again on her hem, but she was able to quickly recover. "Arabella, you must slow down."

"And risk missing this opportunity?" Arabella shot Olivia a quick, sly glance over her shoulder. "Not on your life." She wiggled her thin brows, her golden-brown eyes dancing.

"What opportunity?" Olivia asked, trying to see what her friend had found. Her heart picked up its pace until it matched the rhythm of her steps.

Arabella did not stop until they were hidden behind one of the white pillars framing a large painting. She pointed a finger into the ballroom so Olivia could follow its direction. "This chance."

Through a small break in the crowd, Olivia noticed a small circle of familiar gentlemen. It was the Brooks's Brotherhood—as Olivia had once overheard Mr. Bradbury call themselves. The Reckless Redhead, the Brooding Baron, and—she swallowed hard—Emerson. She would know that brown, tousled hair anywhere. She used to think it boyish, but now she saw it for what it was: untamed and handsome.

Handsome to the point where her heart no longer pounded but skipped several beats. Handsome in a way that left her lips and her mouth so parched she couldn't form words.

"—And it will be as easy as that," Arabella said with a smile, recapturing Olivia's wandering attention.

She had missed most of what her friend had been saying, though one word from the few she had heard stood out from the rest. "*Easy?*" Olivia repeated.

"Yes, *easy*. The opportunity is there for the taking." She pointed again to the unsuspecting gentlemen.

Why were they all together? It would take away from the chase of the game. So why had they chosen to do it now?

"It's *too* easy." The words slipped from Olivia's lips before she could even finish thinking them.

"What?" Arabella's eyes widened.

"Think about it." She stepped closer to the pillar to make a more thorough study of the gentlemen. "It makes no sense for the game for them to all be standing together. It has to be some sort of trap."

"They would not dare," Arabella said, her eyes boring into the gentlemen's backs. After a few moments, she gasped. "They did!"

"Where? What do you see?" Olivia stood on her toes, placing her hand on Arabella's shoulder to push herself even higher, but all she could see was the three friends standing in a half circle with their backs to them.

"Look about waist high," Arabella directed. "Between my brother and Lord Northcott."

Olivia focused her attention where Arabella had directed. That was when she saw it. The perfect trap. For there, perfectly tucked behind the three friends, stood Mr. Hampsheer.

The man stood slightly taller than the average person's waist, which was why she and Arabella had missed him at first glance. He was a difficult dance partner for many reasons. The extreme height difference, and his love for in-depth conversation, made any social interaction awkward. Dancing with the gentleman meant talking to the top of his balding head or risking permanent back damage from stooping to meet his eyes.

"Oh, they are clever." Arabella rolled her shoulders and tsked.

"You cannot possibly be thinking of going over there." Olivia's eyes bulged even as Arabella took a step toward the gentlemen.

"We cannot do nothing. They will think us cowards," Arabella said, glancing at Olivia over her shoulder, daring her not to follow.

Letting out a frustrated breath, Olivia followed. Her friend might be bullheaded, stubborn, quick to act, and reckless at times, but more than anything she was loyal. A quality Olivia strived to have herself.

Coming up to walk alongside Arabella, Olivia whispered to her, "If Mr. Hampsheer even looks as if he might ask one of us to dance, I will not hesitate to offer you up as a sacrifice."

Arabella grinned. *"All's well that ends well."*

Olivia stopped, perplexed. This was not the time for Arabella's Shakespearean riddles. "Wait. What does that even mean?"

Arabella did not stop to answer her question.

Letting out a frustrated breath, Olivia followed her madcap friend. She might not know Arabella's plan, but no doubt, it would be entertaining.

Lord Northcott was the first to look over his shoulder and spot their approach. He did nothing more to give them away, but the slight turn of his head still drew the others' attention.

Arabella stood at the edge of the group next to her brother, while Olivia took the open position between Lord Northcott and Mr. Bradbury. She hoped Lord Northcott would make the perfect shield between her and Emerson, but she swore she could feel Emerson's eyes upon her. Her skin shivered at the sensation.

"Good evening, brother," Arabella said, greeting the rest of the circle with a quick smile.

"Good evening to you, sister," he replied, his tone sounding overpleased, though Olivia did not have the courage to look directly at him. "You know Mr. Hamp—"

"Have you ever read Shakespeare, Mr. Hampsheer?" Arabella said, moving in faster than one could blink.

Mr. Hampsheer reeled back and stuttered, his eyes shooting back and forth between Emerson and Arabella. Mr. Hampsheer typically dominated every conversation; though he was short of stature, he was not short on intelligence.

Arabella's dominance of the conversation was graceful and swift, removing any opportunity for Mr. Hampsheer to ask either of them to dance. At one point, when she continued to speak about her favorite plays without stopping to take a breath, Mr. Bradbury went so far as to silently applaud her over Mr. Hampsheer's head.

"Some would argue it is cruel to do nothing when a person is being tortured," Emerson whispered into Olivia's ear. He had managed to change places with Lord Northcott without interrupting the group's conversation. His arm brushed against hers, and her shivers changed to heat. She prayed it would stay confined to her arm and not travel to her cheeks.

She met his gaze, forcing her lungs to take in a breath. He watched her with a warm, teasing grin, and the floor felt as if it had fallen from under her feet. A steadying pressure appeared at her lower back, the rescuing touch of his hand, and her heartbeat quickened.

"Are you not standing in the same circle?" Olivia challenged, trying to act as if his touch did not affect her.

This can only be a game.

Her reminder did nothing to ebb her awareness of him, forcing her to take a small, imperceptible step away from his touch.

The corners of his mouth turned slightly downward, and he returned his hand to his side. A tense awkwardness followed, and Olivia felt entirely at fault. Regardless of the unsettling emotions creating havoc inside her head, she did not want to ruin the game.

"How long do you think Arabella will continue?" she asked, offering him a shaky, but genuine smile.

"If the past is any indication," he said on a slow exhale, "I would say a lifetime."

They both looked to one another, and hesitantly laughed, the previous awkwardness abating.

"You should do something to save Mr. Hampsheer," she whispered to fill the silence. It was not because she missed his playfulness—or his attention. "His head looks as if it might burst."

"*I* should?" Emerson said, drawing back in a look of mock innocence.

Olivia could not help the smile that tugged at her lips at his ridiculous display. She suspected this trap had been orchestrated by him. Especially if Arabella had never tagged him before, the sibling rivalry would take precedence over the game.

"Yes, *you*. Or do you deny that you had a hand in this situation?" She placed her hands on her hips and tilted her head to emphasize her challenge.

He flexed his jaw, which did nothing to hide his amusement. Crossing his arms over his chest, he looked down at her with warm, daring eyes that had her heart soaring as well as twisting.

"I will have you know that *he* was the one who approached us. Besides, you should be grateful I do not intervene. Mr. Hampsheer will never ask my sister to dance now." He leaned close, his breath softly stirring the wisp of curls about her ear. "Which leaves only you."

With Emerson so close, Olivia had to lock her knees to hold herself in place. Her heart beat loudly in her ears, and it took her much longer than it should to collect herself.

This can only be a game.

Olivia let out a shaky breath, grateful when Emerson pulled back, though he watched her closely. She needed to say something that would remind them both of their circumstances.

"It is fortunate for me, then, that I may decline if Mr. Hampsheer should ask. I am promised to Lord Valencourt for two dances."

Emerson's smile faded. "He isn't right for you, you know."

"If only it were a choice of whether someone was right or whether they were wrong." She forced a smile, not wanting to completely put a damper on the moment.

Emerson opened his mouth as if to say something, but then must have thought better of it, and closed it.

TWENTY-ONE

Disappointment settled in Olivia's chest, which was ridiculous; it was not as if he would argue against her point. They both were choosing to be sensible about it.

"I had best return to my mother," she said, suddenly wanting a moment to herself. Arabella appeared to have the situation well in hand with three players in the circle to choose to tag, and perhaps after Olivia's own dances with Lord Valencourt, she could return to play the game.

She picked up her skirts and turned to leave, but Emerson's hand stopped her, his fingers firm around her elbow.

"What are you doing?" she asked, looking down at his hand and then up at him.

He stared at her with alarming intensity, doing nothing to adjust his hold. His grip wasn't painful, but it was strong enough to show he had no intention of letting her simply walk away.

"Mr. Hampsheer," Emerson called out, cutting off Arabella's ongoing rant. Pulling his eyes from Olivia's, he addressed the group. "If you will excuse my friends and me? We have a previous commitment to see to."

Mr. Hampsheer sputtered for a moment, his eyes still darting between Arabella and Emerson. "Of course. Of course," he managed to say, though he sounded as if he was not certain what he had agreed to. The poor man had been out of his depth the moment Arabella arrived.

Mr. Bradbury was kind enough to help the gentleman along with a small nudge on his shoulder, along with a recommendation of a lady Mr. Hampsheer should seek out.

Lord Northcott, as usual, said nothing.

"That took you long enough, Latham," Mr. Bradbury said while dusting off his hands. "I was beginning to fear the man would never recover his senses, after the way your sister prattled on. Luckily for me, I have been around her enough to be immune." He shot an unrepentant grin at a scowling Arabella.

Emerson appeared completely uninterested in Bradbury's banter, and instead looked at Lord Northcott. A silent exchange passed between them, Lord Northcott nodding before offering Arabella his arm. Arabella took it, but not before looking to Olivia for some sort of insight. Olivia shook her head and shrugged, feeling just as unaware of what was happening as Arabella.

Emerson slid his hold from Olivia's elbow down to her hand, which he placed into the crook of his arm. He took a path along the edge of the ballroom that led to a set of double doors that opened onto a terrace.

"My mother will be in the ballroom," Olivia cautioned.

"I am aware," Emerson replied, pulling one of the doors open.

Olivia braced herself for a burst of brisk night air. Instead, she was met with a wave of humidity along with the slightest taste of dirt in the air. Her senses on alert, she entered a brilliant room made entirely of glass walls. Tilting her head upward, a small gasp escaped her lips as she stared up into a starry night sky.

"What is this place?" she asked in a hushed tone.

Emerson led her out across a short, stone terrace to the top of a stone staircase. "Admiral Twickum prefers the sea, while Mrs. Twickum prefers her orangery," Emerson replied, as he guided Olivia down the steps.

Behind her, Olivia heard Arabella mention something to Lord Northcott about the room as if she had been there before. "How do you know of this place?" Olivia asked, her curiosity growing.

"My mother and Arabella are often invited here for tea," Emerson replied, as if it were nothing.

All Olivia could think was if her father ever saw or heard about such a room, he would have one built—and one even more grand than this.

When they reached the bottom of the steps, Emerson led them onto a sandstone walk that held a square-based fountain at its center. Plants with budding white and pink flowers cascaded down three of the four sections of the fountain, while a stone statue of Poseidon with his trident stood proudly atop it.

Potted orange trees, ferns, and palms were staggered about

on the far side of the fountain, filling the room with the most delicious scents.

"Why did you bring us here, Emerson?" Arabella asked as soon as the group gathered near the fountain. She released Lord Northcott's arm and moved to stand next to Olivia, whom Emerson had placed between himself and the fountain.

"I suspect a possible defector is in our midst," he stated, looking Olivia straight in the eye. He folded his arms across his chest, and Lord Northcott and Mr. Bradbury stepped up to stand on either side of him, as if they were judge, jury, and executioner. "Do you know what happens to a crew member who defects?" he asked Olivia, surprising her with a crack in his serious demeanor.

Mr. Bradbury looked ready to burst into laughter at the ridiculous shift in mood, while Lord Northcott looked as stoic as he always did.

"Are you talking about pirates?" Arabella asked, apparently in on a joke that Olivia could not understand. "Like from the stories Father used to tell us when we were children?"

"A childish punishment for the defection during a childhood game," Emerson justified, still holding Olivia's gaze.

"Well?" Mr. Bradbury broke in, an exaggerated scowl on his lips. "How do ye plead, Miss Wilde?" he asked in an absurd affectation of a pirate.

"How do I plead?" Olivia repeated, looking around the group. "This is madness."

"A madness you agreed to play, Liv," Emerson reminded her, stepping toward her.

Reflexively, Olivia took a step back, and the back of her legs connected with the cold stone of the fountain. "What are you doing?"

"I want you to find happiness." He stood directly before her, his gaze as intense as ever.

"And you believe I can find happiness in playing your silly game?" Her voice came out breathless, her heart pounding even harder, as if such a thing were possible.

He nodded slowly. "You could."

Olivia swallowed, her throat tightening. She wanted to believe him, but she did not know how it was even possible. All she had was that moment. Should she not make the most of it?

"Well then," she looked to Arabella, who she knew was still *it*. "May I?"

A sly grin grew along her friend's lips. "I do not see why not," she replied. They were about to bend the rules a bit, but in the end all would be fulfilled to complete a proper tag.

"What are you two going on about?" Bradbury asked in confusion.

"Only that . . ." Olivia paused, taking in a fortifying breath before nodding to signal Arabella.

Arabella nodded back before reaching out and tagging Lord Northcott who was closest to her.

"Lord Northcott is *it*!" Olivia squealed, picking up her skirts and bolting away from Emerson.

Grabbing Arabella by the arm, they ran for the safety of the other side of the fountain, laughing.

The gentlemen were slow to respond, though Lord

Northcott caught on first. He reached out to touch a still-stunned Mr. Bradbury. "You are *it*."

Mr. Bradbury laughed. He did not have to go far to find an easy tag in Emerson, who then looked to Olivia across the fountain with a roguish grin.

Within the blink of an eye, Emerson stepped onto the edge of the fountain and cut the corners by jumping across them, splitting the distance between them in a matter of seconds.

Arabella squealed in excitement and bolted, leaving Olivia to fend for herself.

Abandoned, Olivia panicked and foolishly ran in the opposite direction, thus singling herself out of the pack.

Emerson remained on the edge of the fountain, jumping the corners to keep up with Olivia's quick steps.

"Better run faster, Liv," he taunted her. "I'm contemplating throwing you into the fountain." He jumped down from the fountain's edge, now only a few steps behind her.

"Don't you dare, Emerson Latham," Olivia shrieked, her heart pounding with excitement. She had not felt this free since her childhood, and the thrill of evading capture kept her legs moving despite the restrictions of her skirts.

All too soon, Emerson's hand wrapped around her wrist, twirling her around until she found herself pinned between him and the fountain. The other players' laughter faded into the background as they scattered throughout the orangery.

Emerson took hold of Olivia's upper arms and tilted her backward so she hovered dangerously close to the fountain.

He leaned over her, his mouth close to her own, and

she could not look away. His smile grew, and his eyes briefly dipped to her lips.

"Are you going to let me go?" she asked, breathless. She could feel the water bubbling perilously beneath her.

"Not if I can help it." Slowly he pulled her upward, and her heart pounded in her ears.

He was going to kiss her.

She was going to let him.

"What on earth?" Olivia's mother gasped, breaking the spell between them.

Emerson's body stiffened, and his hold on her tightened as he lifted her the remainder of the way to her feet. They both faced the entrance of the orangery.

Olivia's mother stood near the bottom of the stairs, her shock and unease evident as she glanced behind her to where Lord Valencourt was silently watching and then back to Olivia.

"Olivia Mary Wilde, you will come with me at once," her mother snapped in a tone Olivia had never heard before.

Mortified and guilt-ridden, Olivia moved quickly to obey, only to find herself pulled back to Emerson. Her back knocked into his chest; he was breathing hard, as if he had just run a long distance. He kept a hand on her hip, the gentle pressure both steadying her and unnerving her. She prayed Lord Valencourt could somehow not see.

Emerson spoke to her mother. "Mrs. Wilde, if you will allow me a moment to explain. This was all my—"

"That is enough, Mr. Latham." Olivia's mother cut him off. Her tone brooked no further argument. "Olivia, come."

His fingers flexed at her waist, as if hesitant to let her go.

"Please," she whispered, begging for him to understand. This was all her fault. She should have pulled from the game when she first suspected her attachment to Emerson.

Ever so slowly, Emerson's grip slipped away, though the memory of his touch remained.

Walking quickly to her mother's side, she avoided the gazes of her other friends, not wishing to see what they thought of the situation. "Mother, I—"

"Not another word," her mother whispered with a clenched jaw. Clearing her throat, she turned toward Olivia's friends. "Mr. Latham, your kindness toward my daughter has been appreciated, but I believe it would be best if you showed your kindness elsewhere."

Olivia heard her mother's formal tone, and she might have believed her mother meant all that she had said, but she also saw her mother's shaking hands. No, the words sounded more like her father's, and it was obvious that her mother was doing what she thought would spare them all from his wrath.

Emerson remained silent.

Her mother pressed a hand to her back, leading her up the steps to where Lord Valencourt waited. He looked down at her with an unreadable expression, and she suppressed a shiver.

"My apologies, Lord Valencourt," she began, knowing her mother expected her to make things right. "I have no words for my thoughtlessness. All I can offer is my honest wish for your forgiveness." The words tasted like vinegar and salt on her tongue.

She felt depleted, utterly laid out before him as if she were some sort of bobble on a platter waiting to be chosen or rejected. She felt sick, realizing she was nothing more than something that could easily be tossed away.

"All is forgiven, Miss Wilde," Lord Valencourt said loudly enough for everyone to hear. He gestured for her to continue up the steps. The moment she passed by him, she felt his hand at her back. Unlike Emerson's gentle, reassuring touch, the baron's fingers dug through the boning of her corset to her skin, proving his strength and displeasure.

He was putting on an act for her mother. His real feelings of unhappiness were evident in his touch, reaffirming everything Miss Yardley had told her about him. He needed her father's money, and he was willing to do anything to get it.

Glancing over her shoulder at the life she was not certain she would ever see again, Olivia immediately sought out Emerson. She found him staring with hatred at Lord Valencourt's hand at her back, and for a moment, before Lord Northcott put a hand on Emerson's shoulder, she feared he would come after her.

TWENTY-TWO

A fire burned inside Emerson. It coiled around his muscles and fueled his pace as he took the steps into Brooks's gentlemen's club two at a time. The report he had been waiting for from his solicitor had arrived early that morning, and after reading its contents, he had sent word to Northcott and Bradbury, asking to meet.

According to the report's contents, Lord Valencourt had not been in possession of his title for very long, having only inherited his advancement into the aristocracy after the sudden deaths of his father's uncle and his father's cousin. The two previous barons were rumored to have drunk and gambled away everything that was not part of the title's entail, leaving Valencourt, the current baron, with nothing but the real threat of financial ruin. Liv and her title-hungry father were the perfect targets, and the so-called honorable baron had been quick to take full advantage.

Emerson had also discovered the Wildes were not the only family to be taken in by Lord Valencourt. A chilling rumor had been uncovered by Emerson's solicitor, accusing the baron of having had a previous engagement with an unnamed lady, who, as it so happened, also came from a family with a large fortune. The rumor claimed it was the lady's family who had cried off the engagement, following a violent altercation between the baron and a member of the lady's family.

Stepping into the club's cardroom, Emerson made straight for the private tables, where he saw a concerned-looking Bradbury and a solemn Northcott already waiting for him.

"I thought your note sounded angry," Bradbury said as Emerson took his seat. "But looking at you now, I would say you look ready to take on a colony of badgers."

Emerson clenched his jaw, in no mood to deal with Bradbury's jokes.

"Valencourt?" Northcott asked.

Emerson nodded, his hands clenched on his thighs underneath the table. He hated feeling so out of control.

"As you feared?" Northcott continued.

He gritted his teeth. "Worse."

Bradbury cursed underneath his breath, while Northcott's shoulders tensed. The trio fell into a dark silence. Several ideas of what Emerson should do filled his head, many criminal acts, and all reckless enough they would cost him what mattered most. His gut clenched at the very possibility.

"Should I be concerned that you have spoken fewer words than old Beasty over here?" Bradbury said, still trying to lighten the mood.

"I am not old. We are all of a similar age," Northcott flatly corrected him.

"Now that's a laugh," Bradbury scoffed. "With how you

spend most of your days, anyone might mistake you for their decrepit grandfather."

Indignation flickered in Northcott's eyes, vanishing before he turned his attention to Emerson. "Do you have a plan?"

Bradbury scoffed. "And, apparently, he has the memory of a grandfather. He cannot even remember that we were having a conversation."

Raising an annoyed brow to Bradbury, Emerson addressed Northcott. "None yet, but I need to find a way to talk with Liv." An act made nearly impossible now that her mother had forbidden him to see Olivia.

"Has your sister been able to see her?" Northcott asked.

"Not that I am aware of."

"Do Arabella and your mother have any social engagements this evening? Perhaps Miss Wilde and her mother will have the same."

Leave it to Northcott to come up with a sensible plan.

Emerson dragged his fingers through his hair, trying to remember what exactly had been discussed while breaking their fast that morning. "It was something to do with a private musicale or soirée—something of that nature."

"So let us go to this musicale-soirée thing," Bradbury said.

"We are about to have company," Northcott warned, watching something over Emerson's shoulder.

Bradbury turned his head and swiftly muttered a curse.

Knowing who it was without looking, Emerson stood and turned, his body ready for a fight.

Lord Valencourt was walking straight for them, his expression hard and his steps determined.

Behind him, Emerson heard the distinct sound of two chairs being pushed back across the wood floor, and he knew his friends stood with him.

"I cannot believe *I* am the one about to say this," Bradbury spoke, stepping up behind Emerson's shoulder, "but I would advise *not* striking the conceited prig. An all-out brawl will do nothing to help your situation with Miss Wilde."

A level head, a level course. His mother's voice echoed his father's words inside his head.

Bradbury was right—on both accounts—which was alarming, considering the source.

Clenching his fists at his sides, Emerson took a steadying breath and waited for Lord Valencourt to approach.

"Mr. Latham," the baron spoke as if he were addressing a servant.

"Lord Valencourt," Emerson returned, not bothering to hide his displeasure.

"A word?"

"By all means." Emerson offered the baron the open chair opposite him, though he would have preferred to hit him over the head with it.

The baron gave no thanks, nor did he acknowledge Northcott or Bradbury, as he walked around the table to take his seat. "I felt we should discuss the other evening."

"I am afraid you will have to refresh my memory," Emerson replied, taking his own seat. His friends sat in the chairs on either side of him. He knew exactly what the baron referred to, and he too had some things to discuss, but that did not mean he was going to take it easy on him.

Lord Valencourt pressed his mouth into a thin line, and he stretched his neck from side to side. "I can be a reasonable man, Mr. Latham. I accept that you and Miss Wilde have known one another for some time. And I accept that time has clouded both of your judgments as to what is deemed appropriate behavior between an unmarried man and an unmarried woman."

He leveled Emerson with a dark stare, though, if anything Emerson only became more annoyed.

"But what I will not accept is such displays of familiarity between the two of you from this moment on."

The instinct to lunge across the table and show the baron what he thought of his warning surged through Emerson.

Bradbury cleared his throat loudly, and Emerson felt the heel of his friend's boot press down on top of his own.

Emerson exhaled. "You speak for Miss Wilde as if you have the right to do so. Has the marriage contract been signed already?"

"It is as good as done."

The heat coursing through Emerson turned to ice. A fiery ice. He no longer wanted to simply fight the man, but to obliterate him. To ruin him in mind, body, and reputation as retribution for making such an egregious statement.

"'As good as done'?" Emerson repeated, tilting his head to mock Valencourt. "It sounds to me as if you have the cart before the horse. Especially when all it would take is for something from your past to get back to the lady's family and make them want to cry off."

He knew his threat was more bluff than truth, but Lord Valencourt need not know that. Emerson had known Joshua

Wilde long enough to have witnessed him use his large stature to intimidate in order to get what he wanted. Why would he care if another man did the same? Even if it was his own daughter, his only care was the title.

Watching Lord Valencourt, Emerson expected to see a flash of panic, anger, or malice. But what he saw instead cracked the ice that had already frozen his spine.

The baron's eyes darkened. The man was keeping a darker secret than Emerson knew, one that made Valencourt take on the look of the devil himself in order to keep it hidden.

And then, with the blink of an eye, the devil was cast out.

A stony expression settled over Lord Valencourt's face and with a calculated slowness, he leaned forward and collected the untouched deck of cards from the center of the table. "What is it they say about showing one's hand too early?" He split the deck in half and shuffled them together. "Care to make a wager?"

"That would depend upon the game and the stakes," Emerson said, leaning back in his seat and crossing his arms over his chest.

"The game would be écarté." He paused to shuffle the deck of cards in his hands. "And there would be no . . . tangible stakes."

Emerson scoffed. Of course—the man was near bankrupt.

Lord Valencourt continued, unfazed. "Think of the game as more of a prediction as to who shall win Miss Wilde in the end."

Emerson narrowed his eyes on the baron, who casually continued to shuffle the deck of cards. He doubted the game had anything to do with winning Liv, but everything to do with Valencourt's pride. Emerson had obviously wounded the baron's pride the night of Twickums' ball, and he would be more than happy to chip away at it again.

"Very well. I accept." It would feel good to knock the titled fop off his pedestal.

A wolfish grin crossed Lord Valencourt's face as he removed any card lower than a seven from the deck. When the baron finished, he set the deck in front of Emerson. "Your deal."

Ignoring Lord Valencourt's dismissive tone, Emerson picked up the deck and shuffled through it a few more times simply to annoy the baron. Écarté was a trick-taking game where the highest suit or trump card won the trick, and five winning tricks won the game.

He dealt five cards to both of them, then turned the eleventh card over to stand as the trump. The queen of hearts—how fitting.

Lord Valencourt picked up his hand and took a moment to rearrange them. "I propose three."

"Accept," Emerson replied, watching as the baron discarded three cards from his hand and replaced them with three new cards from the deck.

Looking over his own cards, Emerson proposed two. The baron accepted, and Emerson made the exchange. Despite the fact that this card game held no tangible stakes, the air around them felt heavy and thick. Emerson *wanted* to win. Not just to poke at the baron, but to prove that justice could prevail in a world that favored rank and that a man without merit could get what he deserved.

Lord Valencourt started the first trick, laying down the ten of spades, to which Emerson followed with the ace of the same suit. The baron scowled, then discarded an ace of clubs, playing neither the suit nor trump, thus giving Emerson the first trick.

Emerson took his time collecting the cards and placing them to the side, enjoying the baron's irritation. The game was far from over, but it felt good to be the first to win.

Deciding on the knave of spades, Emerson started the second trick.

Lord Valencourt tossed down the knave of diamonds with the flick of his meaty fingers, proving to Emerson he had neither the suit nor a trump to win the trick.

Making a poor effort to suppress another satisfying grin, Emerson played the ace of diamonds to start the next trick.

The baron remained expressionless as he placed the king of diamonds on top. "You know, Mr. Latham, you and I are not that different."

"How so?" Emerson replied, throwing away a card and awarding the baron the third trick.

"We are both gentlemen thrown into our current positions by the sudden deaths of our predecessors." The baron held his final two cards close to his chest.

Emerson bit the side of his cheek to quell his anger toward the baron's assumption. "I think losing my father is very different than you losing a distant cousin who had the propensity to drink and gamble his life away."

Lord Valencourt shook his head and tsked, starting the next trick. "My, my—you are thorough. I shall give you that."

Emerson laid down his own card, and Bradbury groaned as Valencourt collected another win.

The baron grinned and slid the cards to the side. Grabbing the remaining deck, Lord Valencourt tapped the cards on the green baize tabletop and passed out five new cards to each of them. He turned over the eleventh card, revealing the next trump.

Looking at his new hand, Emerson's gut clenched. Almost all were low. If both their previous hands had not consisted of so many higher cards he would have good reason to feel nervous, but he knew Valencourt was likely facing the same problem.

To discard all his cards for higher ones was a slim chance, which was why he only proposed to switch out two. Lord Valencourt accepted his proposal, and then proposed to switch out three of his own. The deck was now entirely used, meaning whoever won the most tricks this hand would be the victor.

Since Valencourt had started the previous hand, it was Emerson's turn. He played his lowest card and waited for the baron's move.

"You may think that because you know a few details about my family, that you know me." Lord Valencourt laid down a card that would continue the trick. "But allow me to inform you that while I might not have been bred to inherit my title, I learned enough to know that no son of a second son of an earl is any threat to me. With a title comes privilege, and that privilege will get me the financial backing of the Wilde family coffers."

Emerson clenched his jaw, and they played in silence

until the final trick. They were tied; the next winner would take it all.

Having learned cards from Bradbury, Emerson suspected the baron's final card should be lower than the one in his hand. There was a small chance he could have counted wrong or forgotten a card, but the pleased look on Bradbury's face had him feeling confident enough to turn some of Lord Valencourt's words back on him.

"If I may tell *you* something, Lord Valencourt," Emerson said, "you may think yourself my better because of your title, but if there is anything that life has taught us both, it's how quickly circumstances can change."

The baron's glare deepened, and his biceps flexed beneath his fitted jacket.

Emerson stared back, unflinching, as he waited for Lord Valencourt to play his final card.

The baron moved slowly, extending his arm over the table in order to lay down his card. The white face of the card flashed before Emerson's eyes as Lord Valencourt turned it over and laid it down for all to see.

Emerson's heart stopped.

The card before him was not lower than his, but the trump king.

Valencourt had won, and the injustice of it all crashed down upon him.

"What poor luck," the baron mocked as he collected the winning cards and reassembled the deck. "But we both know that luck has nothing to do with it. The better man always wins."

Lord Valencourt rose from his chair, and all Emerson could do was watch as he strutted out of the room.

"Bradbury, how . . ." Emerson's words faltered. He stared blankly at the abandoned cards, his mind replaying the game, trying to make sense of it.

"I do not know," Bradbury said. He grabbed the deck of cards from the table and divided the stack as if he knew exactly where to look. Within seconds, he pulled out a king of spades, not from the top of the deck where it should have been from their previous play, but from the middle.

"The dirty, cheating wretch," Bradbury hissed.

The paralysis over Emerson broke, and he lunged for the deck of cards in Bradbury's hands. He needed to see it for himself. Turning over the last four cards, he saw a second king of spades among them.

The baron was a cheat, and everything inside Emerson screamed to destroy him.

"I'm going after him," Bradbury growled, sliding his chair back.

Emerson grabbed his friend's arm to stop him. A plan was forming in his mind. One that would see justice done that would last past a single altercation.

"No, do not. Let him think he has won," Emerson said.

"What? You cannot be serious." Bradbury scowled, pushing Emerson's hand from his arm.

"It's not worth it."

"Not worth it?" Bradbury threw his arms up. "The man—"

Emerson held up his hand to silence his friend before he could draw the attention of everyone in the room.

"Emerson is right," Northcott said, eliciting an even deeper scowl from Bradbury.

"It is as you said," Emerson began. "Fighting will solve nothing. Valencourt has shown us his hand—more than his hand. He is hiding something darker than we know. I saw it in his eyes after I baited him about the rumor. He is desperate enough to disregard all honor in order to protect it. And now I know what I must do."

"What?" Bradbury asked, begrudgingly leaning back in his seat.

"I am going after Liv. Tonight. The game is over."

TWENTY-THREE

She was trapped inside a prison of her own making. Quite literally. Lord Valencourt sat far too close on her right side, while her mother sat sentinel on her left.

After learning of her behavior at the Twickums' ball, Olivia's father had broken everything in arm's reach and then issued her an ultimatum. Either perform the role of dutiful daughter and marry Lord Valencourt or be completely cut off, left with nothing but her own ruin on the cold streets of London. In his words: "What other use is there for a daughter?"

Luckily—if one in such an impossible situation could truly call it that—Olivia knew the baron had to propose, which meant that every note struck at the musicale that evening was like a steady cadence to her true self's demise.

"Are you enjoying the performance?" Lord Valencourt leaned down to whisper, his hot breath fanning across her ear.

Olivia cringed, and the baron appeared to notice. The corners of his mouth turned down, and his eyes narrowed.

"Forgive me," she whispered, trying to think of what her

mother would say. "I am afraid I was so taken by the music that your voice startled me." It was a bald-faced lie, but she found she no longer cared. What was one lie in what was sure to be a lifetime of many?

"One could say the same about your beauty," the baron replied with a smile that grew into a chilling, predatory grin.

Olivia resisted the urge to shudder, firmly believing everything about the baron was cold and calculated. Pasting on a smile of her own, she demurely offered it to Lord Valencourt before returning her attention to the performance.

The Addington sisters played another piece of music before Mrs. Addington announced it was time to retire to another room for intermission and refreshments.

Lord Valencourt rose from his seat. "Shall we?"

Her mother promptly stood, but Olivia found she could not. "You go, and I shall join you in a moment."

Lord Valencourt regarded her with a dark, questioning brow, informing her she would not get away from him so easily.

"I must make for the retiring room." It was an age-old trick every woman had employed at least once in her life to have a few moments to herself.

Valencourt dismissed her, his attention instantly focused on escorting Olivia's mother to the refreshment room before Olivia could say more.

She remained in her seat, waiting for the room to clear. At the first sound of silence, Olivia tugged off her white satin gloves and tossed them onto the chair next to her. The small, orange, crystal-like beads dangling along their hems had pressed red, painful marks into her skin. She marveled that money could buy so many things—except for comfort. Quite honestly her father's wealth had done nothing for her aside from burdening her with clothes she did not like and a future husband she did not want.

Leaning forward, Olivia pressed the palms of her hands into her eyes, knowing it was only a matter of time before her mother came looking for her.

"Liv?" A familiar, deep voice called from somewhere behind her.

Jerking her head up, Olivia saw Emerson approaching. His mouth was set in a slight frown, while his rich brown gaze searched her face, carefully, closely.

"What are you doing here?" she asked, shocked.

"We need to talk," he said, stepping around the row of chairs and taking one of her hands in his. He wore no gloves, the heat from his skin as it pressed to hers overwhelming her thoughts.

Pulling Olivia to her feet, he laced their fingers together before he began to lead her out of the room.

Her heart quickened with every step, her breath arresting in her chest for one wild moment, and then reality crashed back in.

"I cannot go with you." She forced the words out through trembling lips, pulling her hand away until she broke free.

Emerson stopped, his mouth pressing into a firm line. "You cannot or you will not?"

"You know it is because I cannot." Her eyes pleaded with him to understand, to have mercy on her heart already broken for a love that would never be. "Please, you must leave."

"Not until you hear what I have to say." A flash of determination lit his dark eyes, and he reached for her again.

She pulled out of his reach, and his nostrils flared.

"Speak if you must," she said, her chest feeling tight. "But know I cannot stay for long." Tears of anger threatened to break free, but she stubbornly willed them not to fall. Why was he not understanding? It was too late. Whatever it was or might have been between them, it never stood a chance.

In one swift movement, Emerson reached out and took her hand back in his. "It cannot be here." Not even waiting for a response, he pulled her toward the doorway, where Olivia was stunned to see Lord Northcott waiting. He stuck his head out into the corridor, then turned back to nod at Emerson.

Emerson pulled her into the corridor, where she was now unsurprised to see Mr. Bradbury keeping watch outside the door to the refreshment room.

"I cannot leave the musicale," Olivia protested, attempting to pull against Emerson's iron grip as another round of panic began to set in. Where did he intend to take her?

"Trust me," Emerson said, his pace never slowing as he pulled her away from the refreshment room. "We are only going somewhere we will be left alone to talk."

Opening the second to the last door in the corridor, Emerson led Olivia into a small, private sitting room and promptly shut the door. A fire blazed in the hearth, a chaise longue framing one side and a sideboard holding several different colored bottles lining the other.

The flickering firelight danced across the bottles, reflecting an array of greens, browns, and blues onto Emerson and her. If she was not feeling so high-strung at the moment, Olivia might have enjoyed such a mesmerizing sight.

"What is it you fought so hard to say, Emerson?" she asked, pulling hard enough to finally break free. She took a few steps away, wanting the distance between them.

Emerson glared at the space she had created between them, and then met her gaze. "Valencourt is not who you think him to be." His words echoed in the silent room.

That was it? That was what was so important for her to hear? So important to have her risk her father's wrath and sheer ruin if they were found alone together?

Shaking her head, Olivia let out a short, humorless laugh. The corners of her eyes stung, while a pain stabbed in her chest. "Do you think so little of me to assume that I am not capable of discerning this for myself?"

Emerson blinked, his frown turning into a scowl.

"Well, then, allow me to appease your conscience, and tell you that I am well aware of Lord Valencourt's history."

"You cannot marry him," he demanded.

Olivia's full anger ignited. "Go home, Emerson. You overstep yourself."

In three strides, Emerson crossed directly in front of her, his nostrils flaring and chest heaving with every breath. "Oh, I have not even begun to do so."

Not intimidated by his high-handedness Olivia took a step toward him, their bodies a mere breath away from touching. Her neck was tilted upward, the muscles along her spine and shoulders tightening. "Save your breath. I no longer wish to be moved about like a pawn in everyone else's game."

"This is no game," he ground out the words in a harsh rumble that she could feel emanating from his chest.

"Of course it is. It is *all* some sort of game. Everyone wants something. My father wants a title. Lord Valencourt wants my father's money. You want to be free of your conscience toward me."

"That is not what this is about." He stared at her with alarming intensity.

"Do you really expect me to believe that after what you came here to say? I see that I was mistaken and that your conscience is all that has mattered to you." Olivia snapped, her anger surging through her until she saw nothing but red.

The air in the room grew heavy with tension, the only sound the heavy breaths coming from both of them.

And then, in one flicker of the dancing flame, the frustration melted from Emerson's face. "You," he said, his voice hoarse and tight.

"What?" she asked, her own anger melting into uncertainty.

"You," he repeated. "That is what has always been important to me." His voice was unsteady, but soothing.

He raised his hand and pulled one of her curls from its confines. It was the barest of touches, but she felt it everywhere.

Olivia's heart pounded a frantic rhythm, and the heat she felt centered on her hand as Emerson's fingers gently intertwined with hers at her side.

"I had planned a much better way to tell you this." He looked at her with serious, earnest eyes. "I have wanted to tell you this for some time, but it never felt right. I wanted it to be right. You deserve more than rushed words in a room of someone else's home. But I am afraid if I do not say this now, I will be too late."

"Wh-What are you saying?" Every part of her body felt unsteady, including her voice. Could this really be happening? She knew she should stop him, but she knew she wouldn't.

"Liv." Emerson's hand slipped from her fingers. He set his palms at her waist, gliding them across the fabric of her dress until they locked together at the small of her back. His dark, penetrating eyes looked down into hers. "You are *it* for me." He bowed his head and claimed her mouth with a searing kiss, momentarily robbing her of breath.

The kiss was everything she had ever dreamed of and more. She was mesmerized by the touch of his hands—both soft and strong—as they slid up her back. He remained patient with her, almost teasing her until she pushed him to give her more. Standing on her toes, Olivia deepened their kiss. He pulled her hard against him, crushing her into his chest.

She pressed her palms to his chest and felt his heart pounding as hard and as fast as her own. It was a blissful and emboldening feeling to know she caused such a reaction in him.

His hands glided up to her shoulders until his fingertips gently caressed the column of her neck. Her body shivered in anticipation as his hand cradled her face. He tilted her head to the side, surprising her with how such a gentle touch could deepen their kiss.

And then, just as quickly as they had come together, she was harshly pulled away. She stumbled backward, her hips colliding hard with the sideboard. She scrambled to steady herself along the wooden edge as several glass bottles toppled over and fell to the floor.

Disoriented, Olivia heard the sickening sounds of flesh hitting flesh. Someone was fighting Emerson, and her stomach dropped.

Forcing her eyes to focus, she looked up in time to see Emerson land a blow over Lord Valencourt's head as the growling baron charged into him. His shoulders collided with Emerson's chest, the momentum knocking Emerson off his feet and into the chaise longue. Emerson was pinned on his back, his head and legs hanging over both sides as he fought to hold the baron's fists at bay.

Mr. Bradbury charged into the room, helping to throw a feral-looking Lord Valencourt off of Emerson. The baron stumbled backward, colliding into the wall that was Lord Northcott's tall frame. Northcott held back Lord Valencourt, while Mr. Bradbury did the same for Emerson, who was now on his feet and ready to resume the fight.

"Is this the kind of company your family keeps, Mr. Wilde?" Lord Valencourt spat over his shoulder in the direction of the door, blood dripping from the corner of his mouth. "Guttersnipes who work together to take advantage of your daughter?"

Horrified, Olivia turned toward the doorway and saw her father, his large arms crossed over his broad chest. His expression was dark and ominous, sending a foreboding chill down her spine.

Lord Northcott shoved Lord Valencourt forward, only to snap him back by his jacket collar. The barons stared one another down, though in that moment, Olivia found Lord Northcott the more intimidating of the two.

"I thought my wife had made it clear to you in regards to being around my daughter, Mr. Latham," Olivia's father said.

"As clear as the Thames," was Emerson's mocking reply. The skin around one of his eyes had already begun to sport a puffy, black-and-blue circle.

"I once considered you a man of intelligence," her father said, stepping fully into the room. "But I now see you are a fool. You have nothing to offer me which I cannot already possess ten times over. You will not win here."

"I am offering nothing to you," Emerson replied, squaring his shoulders and straightening his disheveled jacket. "Rather, I am offering everything I have to *her*." He turned to Olivia, the truth of his statement burning in the light of his eyes. "She deserves the right to choose for herself."

Olivia bit her bottom lip to keep the tears building behind her eyes from falling.

Her father's mirthless laugh sounded as cold as the devil's conscience. "Olivia will never have the right to choose." His dark eyes flashed to her with an even darker promise. "She knows what will happen to her—and to her relationship with her mother—if she walks away from me."

The floorboards beneath Olivia swayed and dipped, the truth behind her father's words twisting a sickening knot in her stomach. He would keep her from her mother, she knew he would. What she did not know was what else his volatile temper might do to exact his revenge.

Knowing she could make no other choice, Olivia turned to Emerson, her tears finally falling free.

A vein bulged at Emerson's temple as he stared down her father. He held his fists clenched tightly by his sides, and Olivia's heart suddenly sped in fear that the men might still come to blows.

Emerson's jaw flexed as if he intended to speak, but Mr. Bradbury quickly stepped up beside him and placed his hand on his shoulder.

Emerson jerked his head toward his friend, and Mr. Bradbury subtly shook his head. Emerson's posture did not change.

The tension in the room rose.

Then he took in a deep breath.

When he turned his attention to Olivia, she could see the struggle in his eyes. He wanted to fight this, he wanted to fight for her, but he held himself back. She wished she had the power to change the game her father was playing. She hated the unfairness of it all, and she hoped Emerson could see that in her eyes.

But this was no longer about her. This was about saving her mother. This was her choice.

"Olivia. Come," her father demanded, breaking the connection between her and Emerson.

Raising her chin, Olivia turned to walk in her father's direction, when her slipper connected with something hard and round. It was one of the fallen glass bottles, its smooth surface spinning across the carpet toward Emerson and Lord Valencourt. The bottle slowed, then stopped.

Olivia's breath stopped as well. The bottle's neck, like the needle of a compass, pointed her toward Emerson. She wanted to laugh, and then cry. Fate, it would seem, was directing her toward Emerson. And she would never have him.

Stepping over the bottle, Olivia crossed the room to stand next to her father.

He ignored her, as if she did not even exist, and addressed Emerson. "You should be grateful your father is no longer here to witness this, Mr. Latham. I, for one, would be ashamed to call you *son*."

Emerson's mouth pressed into a firm line, and he squared his shoulders. "If you truly knew my father, Mr. Wilde, you would know he would never be ashamed of me. In truth, he often wished for me to *live* and to be as *wild* as my heart wanted me to be."

Olivia pressed her eyes shut, Emerson's hidden meaning causing her heart and throat to ache as more of her tears streamed down her cheeks.

The sound of Lord Valencourt's steps filled her ears. She felt the crushing grip of his hand around her arm, but she refused to look at him.

"Go with Lord Valencourt, Olivia." Her father ordered, and she obeyed.

TWENTY-FOUR

Emerson waited for Mr. Wilde to step out of the room before lowering himself onto the chaise longue, the simple movement robbing him of breath. His left side had taken the brunt of the baron's initial ham-fisted attack, and the pain radiating there had become more than he could take.

"What happened?" he asked Bradbury the moment he could take in half a breath.

"Mr. Wilde showed up out of nowhere a moment before Lord Valencourt came out of the refreshment room looking for Miss Wilde," Bradbury said, sitting next to Emerson. "They both noticed Northcott and me standing in the corridor, and there was not much else we could do without causing a scene. The moment Lord Valencourt saw you with Miss Wilde . . . He moved quicker than I could react."

Emerson tried to raise a questioning brow, but the motion proved difficult with the swelling around his eye.

"In my defense," Bradbury continued, "even I was not anticipating such an ardent scene, and I knew what you were trying to accomplish in here." He looked Emerson over, and grimaced. "I hope those few moments with Miss Wilde in your arms were worth it."

Emerson grinned despite the pain. "Every one."

Bradbury chuckled and shook his head. "I assume you have a plan to get Miss Wilde and her mother out of this predicament or else you would have ignored me and not let her go."

"I have the beginnings of a plan," Emerson said, wrapping his arm around the ache in his left side. "I'm going after her. Tonight."

Bradbury's eyes widened. "Tonight? Valencourt must have hit you in the head harder than I thought. You are in no condition for avenging."

"I have no other choice. She means *everything* to me."

Bradbury shook his head and gave a low whistle. "Lud, if I was Lord Valencourt, I would be heading straight for Gretna Green after seeing you with Miss Wilde."

At that thought, Emerson let out a string of curses, shooting out of his seat. The sheer pain of the motion doubled him over, and Bradbury helped to ease him back into his seat.

"No need to injure yourself further, you besotted imbecile. Northcott called for his carriage the moment Mr. Wilde walked down the corridor. He will follow them, and then send for us."

Emerson sent up a grateful prayer for having such loyal and quick-thinking friends.

"Miss Wilde must have your cats all tied up in a cradle." Bradbury laughed. "You did not even notice the big hulk of a baron was missing."

"My apologies," Emerson drawled. "As you have been so

kind to point out, I am currently sporting a pathetic one-eyed version of blind man's bluff, thus some things have escaped my notice."

"No need to fear, good sir. Thou shalt still have a chance to win *fair maiden's* heart." Bradbury winked.

"Arabella would be proud," Emerson replied. He dared not laugh for the sake of his ribs. He slid forward in his seat and grunted. "Now, I need to get myself up off this chaise."

Most of his body ached, and he groaned as he regained his feet.

"Again, sorry about that." Bradbury grimaced, rising up to offer Emerson a hand.

Emerson waved him off. "I did it to myself." He stepped over a few of the fallen glass bottles. The way their reflected colors had danced across Liv's creamy skin and pale hair just before they kissed was forever fixed in his memory. "I had not intended to kiss her until after I had the chance to tell her everything."

"You did not tell her everything?" Bradbury asked in disbelief.

"Not even the half of it," he said, breathing through the stabbing pain in his side.

"She has to know you will come for her," Bradbury said, heading for the door. He promptly stuck his head out, holding his hand up to stay Emerson's progress while he checked to make sure the corridor was empty.

Bradbury had put words to Emerson's greatest fear. He was not certain if Liv knew he would come for her, especially after what her father had threatened.

British law protecting the rights of a husband were nearly

ironclad, making it almost impossible to do anything for a woman in Mrs. Wilde's circumstances. But what Joshua Wilde did not know was that Emerson had an extensive family of "Old Maids," as they called themselves. It seemed the Latham females were destined to outlive every one of their husbands. With such a vast selection to pick from, Emerson would be able to place Liv's mother in any one of their homes for a time, changing up her location enough to keep Joshua Wilde a few paces behind, even with the man's resources.

Now all he had to do was get them out.

"Time to go," Bradbury said, intruding on Emerson's thoughts. He regarded Emerson carefully. "Will you be fine on your own?"

Emerson appreciated his friend's concern. He knew how bad certain parts of his body ached, and he could only imagine how bad he must look to someone on the outside. He let out a deep sigh, instantly regretting it. Sparks of fire ran up his side, forcing him to take smaller breaths to help alleviate the pain. "I can manage." His pride answered for him.

Bradbury grimaced in sympathy.

"Go," Emerson said, waving him off. They had already taken up more time than they should. He hoped Northcott or one of his groomsmen were waiting outside with information.

They encountered no one from the musicale except a footman, who looked at Emerson's condition with a questioning glance as he returned their hats and coats. Bradbury slipped him a coin or two—probably more "investments" from Emerson—for his silence, and they were soon out into the chilled night air.

Emerson had to focus on descending the few steps. Even

that simple movement caused him pain, not as much as he felt when Valencourt punched him, but it was still hard to ignore.

There was no sign of Northcott or his carriage, leaving them no choice but to proceed on foot in the hopes that Joshua Wilde had taken his family home.

"So, have you come up with any more of a plan?" Bradbury asked, no doubt to fill the silence between them. There were still carriages traveling the roads and a few people walking along the pavement, but London at night was nothing compared to the noise London could stir up during the day.

"I know the ending," Emerson replied. He was trying to keep the conversation light, though he felt anything but light on the inside.

Bradbury lifted his gaze to the night sky. "And you call me shameless when talking in jest."

"I believe I have called you many things, Bradbury, but never that."

Bradbury opened his mouth to, no doubt, give his rebuttal, when a carriage pulled up alongside them. The silver crest of the Northcott house flickered as it passed beneath a streetlamp, and Emerson immediately picked up his pace, clutching his side in pain. Bradbury matched his stride and only moved ahead to open the door the moment the carriage stopped.

Stepping inside the dark space, Emerson sat opposite Northcott, while Bradbury took the seat next to him.

"Where is she?" he asked. He hissed in pain as the carriage jerked into motion.

"Wilde's Mayfair residence. I left a groomsman behind to

watch the house." Northcott paused, and somehow Emerson knew his friend was not done yet. "Valencourt remains with them."

Emerson clenched his jaw, determined to fight through the pain that momentarily numbed him to anything else but the passing of time, which felt as if it would go on for an eternity.

"Do you have a plan?" Northcott asked, his face mostly covered by shadow.

"He knows how it ends," Bradbury jumped in, his smile showing as the carriage passed beneath a streetlamp.

Northcott ordered his driver to stop a few houses before their destination. They got out and joined the groomsman-turned-spy huddled behind the trees directly opposite the Wildes' home.

"Anything?" Northcott asked his groomsman.

"Not much of anything, my lord. No one else has come nor gone. Been movement in some of the windows, but I could make nothing out."

Northcott nodded and sent his man back to the waiting carriage.

They all stared at the large house with its many windows filled with light.

"I could walk up to the house and have a look around," Bradbury offered.

"I would not risk it," Northcott advised. They were risking their position now; three fully grown men standing behind a winter-ravished tree were hard to miss.

"Well, we cannot just stand here all night," Bradbury pointed out as he began to fidget against the cold. "You might not have much to live for, Northcott, but some of us actually enjoy life."

Northcott, as usual, made no reply.

"I will check at the servants' door," Emerson said, the makings of a provisional plan forming inside his head. "Most of them know who I am. Maybe I can get some answers."

Emerson had suspected some of Joshua Wilde's uncommon group of servants might have more allegiance to Liv and her mother than to their master. It seemed he would have to test that belief.

"Wait. Look there," Northcott said.

He pointed in the dim darkness to a figure walking down the front steps of the home. The man wore the livery of a servant, though he walked with the confidence of a lord.

"Mr. Latham?" the man called out. The figure then headed across the empty street toward them.

Recognizing the voice, Emerson stepped out from behind the cover of the tree. "Mr. Jenson, is it not?" he asked, recognizing the unconventional butler. His heart hoped, while his senses remained on guard.

"Aye." The butler crossed his arms over his chest. "Come ta rescue our Miss Wilde?" He spoke in a neutral tone—not threatening, but not warm or welcoming either.

"And her mother too, if I can convince her," Emerson replied. He took a chance and held out his hand.

The butler raised a brow, staring at the offering before reaching out to take Emerson's hand. "Sounds ta be a good plan ta me. What canna butler and a few loyal servants do ta help?"

"Is Miss Wilde all right?" Emerson asked immediately.

"Shook up a bit. But she be with her mother in the parlor next ta the master's study. The baron be with the master, plottin' and plannin'."

"Any chance you could get me to her?"

"Happy ta get you inside the door, and a few other things if we can. Just can't get caught helpin'. Jobs like these be hard ta come by for the likes of us."

"I understand," Emerson replied, grateful to be given that much support. He was already off to a better start than he thought he would be, though there was still much to figure out.

His biggest challenge would be getting the ladies out without causing an all-out brawl. He was in no condition for another fight, and while he wanted to execute an invasion worthy of the Danes, he would have to settle for something similar to the Trojans, but without the benefit of a large, wooden horse to hide—

Emerson's thoughts ceased. The last word echoed inside his head.

Hide.

Could the answer be so simple? It was a long shot with all the unpredictable variables they would encounter. But with Jenson's knowledge and control of the household, they could take steps to prevent most of them. It was risky, but he could think of nothing else.

Turning back to his friends, he asked, "Anyone up for a little hide-and-seek?"

TWENTY-FIVE

Olivia stared at her ghostly reflection in the glass of the parlor room window. Everything around her was swallowed inside a deep, cold, blackness. Her face was overcast with shadow, while the flickering flames from the hearth behind her outlined her taut frame.

How fitting that reflection felt—to be swallowed by a darkness while a sliver of hope still burned to be free.

She stood firm in her decision to leave with her father to save her mother, but that did not mean she could not still hope to find a way to save herself and her mother from their fate.

They were being held captive inside their own home while her father and Lord Valencourt discussed Olivia's future in the very next room. Jenson had been in once to see after them, but her father had immediately ordered him and every other servant out of the room.

"Olivia," her mother said, her visage slowly forming over Olivia's shoulder in the window's reflection. "Come away from the window, sweetheart."

"I will," Olivia replied, emotionless. She was not quite ready to resign herself to the sofa and nervously await her father's decision. The act of standing was her little rebellion.

Her mother seemed to study her for a moment, worry creasing her brow in her reflection. "Will you not tell me what happened?"

When Olivia had left the Addington musicale with her father, she had been unsurprised to find her mother already sequestered in her father's carriage. She had been concerned then, as she was now, but at least here they could speak freely. The carriage ride home had been painfully silent.

"I do not know where to even start," she replied, a flood of emotions washing over her. How could she tell the story to her mother when Olivia herself was not sure where it had even begun?

"You were found once again with Mr. Latham?" her mother softly prodded.

Olivia nodded, the darkness in the window growing into light as her mind replaced its bleakness with the memory of their kiss. A pressure built in her chest, and she pressed her hand to the spot, as if she could simply push it away. Now was not the time for despair. She was not married to Lord Valencourt yet. Until the moment she was, she would believe she still had time.

"I had hoped to spare you from this," her mother said, her hand coming to rest on Olivia's shoulder. "What you think you feel for Mr. Latham will fade with time . . . and distance."

She turned to face her mother. "I do not think this feeling will ever fade," Olivia said. Tears she thought she had all cried out once again fought for release, and her voice quivered with emotion. "Nor do I want it to."

Her mother's eyes widened, shock flowing over her features. "You love him," she said on a whispered breath.

"I love him," Olivia said, saying the words out loud for the first time, relishing the taste of truth on her tongue—like sugar and lavender.

Her mother went still, her silence filling the room, her face draining of color.

"Mama?" Olivia's heartbeat quickened in her chest.

In the blink of an eye, her mother was moving. She picked up a large portion of her skirts and rushed toward the window. Her hands grasped for the bottom pull, though Olivia knew it would be useless. The windows were always locked. Joshua Wilde would never allow anything of his to be stolen.

"We have to get you out of here," her mother said, still struggling with the window, her breaths coming out in short, panicked bursts.

Olivia went to her mother and tried to pull her away. "Mama, stop. Stop this."

She stopped her struggle, but only to grab Olivia by the shoulders. "You will climb out this window, and you will run. Do not stop until you reach the Lathams. That man loves you, and he will take care of you. I know it."

Abruptly, she released Olivia's shoulders, momentarily knocking her off balance, and reached again for the locks on the window.

"No. Wait. Stop." Olivia grabbed for her mother, this

time with enough force to pull her back. "Mama, there is something you must know."

"Whatever it is, you may write to tell me later." She pushed against Olivia's hold. "Address it to Jenson; he will see that it gets to me."

Olivia realized the only way to get through to her mother would be to come right out and speak the horrible truth, and she hated her father even more for it.

"Father threatened me with you." The words burned her throat as she spoke them, their meaning rendering her mother as still as a statue.

A lifetime of fear flashed in her mother's eyes, and she wrapped her arms around her middle where Olivia's father's hands so often left their marks.

Nausea roiled in Olivia's stomach for what she must tell her mother next. "If I leave, I fear he will punish you in order to get back at me."

Her mother pressed her eyes shut, her lips quivering.

A chill crawled up Olivia's spine, and she reached for her mother to comfort them both.

But her mother pushed Olivia away. "It does not matter." Her tone was lifeless, but resolute. "You will go. I will—"

"I will not leave you," Olivia said, stopping her before the room could grow any colder.

Her mother held out her hand, stopping Olivia's approach. "Yes, you will." She took a step back, putting more distance between them.

"I will *not*," she insisted, a lump forming in her throat. "Because you are my mother, and I love you too."

Two tears fell down her mother's cheeks, quickly followed

by a third. "I wish I could have done more for you." She swallowed hard. "I failed you as a mother, I see that now. I should have fought for you to have a better life, rather than accepting what was once my own fate."

"You did all you could," Olivia said. "I could not have asked for a better mother."

Charlotte Wilde had beaten more odds than any woman of her upbringing. Born a tradesman's daughter, forced to marry the crass son of a ship's chief mate, and she still held herself with enough class and grace to equal the gentry and the aristocracy alike. It was a gentleman's world, and a lady could only try to find her place in it and hope to thrive.

"I did not do enough." Her mother's voice was a thin, dull thread, ready to break at the slightest pressure.

Taking her mother by the elbow, Olivia led her to the fire, unable to stand the cold dread that had settled over the room. She did not know what they would do. But she did know that she would not give up hope. For her sake as well as her mother's.

She had to believe love could conquer all. She had no other choice.

TWENTY-SIX

The plan was set. Jenson had been true to his word in getting them inside the house unnoticed. Most of the household staff were already abed, while those remaining could use the excuse they were simply following Mr. Wilde's orders to avoid the parlor.

The candles in the entrance hall and other rooms of the house were either extinguished or removed completely, leaving Emerson and his friends with the darkness needed to pull off their ruse.

"Are we even certain this is going to work?" Bradbury whispered into the shadows.

They were encamped in the parlor next to Mr. Wilde's study. There was just enough light from the moon to distinguish the outline of one another's faces.

"You are voicing this concern *now*?" Emerson asked with blistering sarcasm. The bandage Jenson had insisted on wrapping around his injured ribs drew tight as he turned to look at Bradbury who stood closest to the window.

Bradbury's smile flashed in the moonlight. "Just thought

it should be mentioned. It would make for a terrible ending if the knight-errant went after the lady and came back burnt to a crisp because of poor planning."

Northcott scoffed. "You are an idiot."

Bradbury scoffed in return. "And you are just jealous that I was the one to think ahead for a change. Watch out, Beasty, I am learning your ways."

"Could you two ladies have this out over tea another time?" Emerson cut in, knowing how long Bradbury could stretch one of his arguments out. "We still have a game to play."

"Oh, good," Bradbury said brightly. "So you do believe there will be a later."

Emerson looked to the heavens for patience.

No one said anything further—which was surprising for Bradbury—and Emerson took the silence as his opportunity to move forward with his plan.

Stepping up to the door, Emerson opened it enough to confirm the corridor was clear. There was no sound, nor any shadows moving along the darkened walls.

"Now, remember," Emerson said to his friends, "Northcott will draw attention to the third door on the right."

"And I will do the same, but at the second door on the left," Bradbury interjected. "That is, after I have accomplished the most daring part of this plan—drawing the wild boars out of the shadows."

"I will then go out the servants' door next to the sideboard," Northcott said, repeating his portion of the plan with calm confidence. "Then return back up through the servants' stairs to meet you and the ladies at the front door."

"Meanwhile, I shall be creating a ruckus in the music room, before taking the connecting door into the ballroom," Bradbury said with far too much excitement. "Where, after giving them a Herculean chase about the room, I shall escape out the terrace doors and meet all four of you at the carriage for our escape."

Emerson took a small, steadying breath. "And with any luck, Mr. Wilde and Lord Valencourt will only have one or two candles between them to try to find you and not enough brains between them to catch you."

"The brains part was never in question," Bradbury said. "But if we are captured. Northcott is deaf, and I only speak Greek."

"Greek?" Emerson asked. "Why Greek?"

"Because the few Greek words I remembered from Eton are utterly useless, so I figured it would be the same for them. That way the conversation would go nowhere."

"Idiot," Northcott grumbled again.

"You know, Beasty, you should look into some English courses yourself. You seem to know—and use—only a few words."

"We will only use that plan as a last resort," Emerson said, cutting Bradbury off before he could torment Northcott further. "Now, let's get going."

Northcott left without a word. Bradbury, on the other hand, paused in the doorway.

"If, for some reason, I do not make it out of this, I demand you name your first son after me." He stepped halfway out, then turned back to Emerson with a wink. "Northcott can have the second son."

Then he was gone, stolen into the corridor's darkness.

Emerson stayed back, shaking his head and silently chuckling to himself. Little did his friend know that if he was lucky enough to have two sons, that request would be happily granted.

"Well, good evening to you gentlemen," Bradbury's boisterous tone echoed throughout the corridor. He appeared to have made it into Mr. Wilde's study. "Nice evening for a game, do you not agree?"

Loud, angry shouting quickly followed, and—if Emerson was not mistaken—a piece of wooden furniture had been thrown. He hoped Bradbury had made it out of range in time.

"Well, that was not very nice," Bradbury called, followed by hurried steps that faded down the corridor.

The sound of two heavier sets of boots quickly followed, and then stopped in front of the door Emerson still hid behind. He held his breath, and listened.

"Why is it so blasted dark in this house?" Mr. Wilde's voice thundered. "Jenson? Devil take it, Jenson, show yourself."

"You are wasting time. We can go after him ourselves," Lord Valencourt growled, and their footfalls moved on down the corridor.

The plan sounded like it was working.

Waiting another few seconds, Emerson stepped out of his hiding place. He entered Mr. Wilde's study, hoping neither gentleman had chosen to circle back to check on the ladies.

If so, coming in through the connecting door would at least give him the element of surprise. He figured he could land one good swing before the pain from his injury would drop him to his knees.

Emerson approached the connecting door that led to the parlor and placed his ear to the wooden panel, trying to make out any male voices.

Hearing nothing, he reached for the handle and pulled the door open. At first the room appeared to be empty, but then his eyes reached the other doorway and he saw Liv and her mother staring at him with wide, blinking eyes.

"Emerson?" Liv said on a heavy, exhaled breath.

"Yes?" He crossed his arms over his chest and leaned with one shoulder against the doorframe, as if he had dropped by for an everyday visit and not for a daring rescue. On the inside, though, his hands itched to take her in his arms, and his lips burned at the thought of another kiss—one that would certainly require him to beg for her mother's forgiveness at a later time.

"What—how—? What is happening?" Liv finally managed. Locks of her beautiful spun-gold hair had fallen from their pins, making her look the perfect picture for adventure. He could not wait to untuck a few more.

"Did you truly believe I would not come for you?" he asked, easing himself from the doorway.

"I—I did not know," she said, her voice quiet and trembling.

He gave in to temptation and came to stand before her. Cupping her face in his hands, he leaned in until his lips were a breath away. He stared straight into the beautiful blue depths of her eyes.

"I will always come for you," he whispered, and, so she would never doubt it again, he sealed that promise with a gentle kiss.

Pulling back, Emerson stopped short as he saw tears rolling down Olivia's cheeks, her eyes fighting not to meet his. Something was wrong, and he needed to know what. "Liv?"

With a shuddering breath, she stepped away from him. "I cannot go with you."

"Why not?" Emerson asked, taking a step toward her, refusing to be parted from her.

She took another step. "I will not leave my mother." She turned her head and looked at Mrs. Wilde, whom Emerson had selfishly forgotten was in the room.

He felt like the biggest reprobate in the world. Here he was, holding Olivia in his arms and stealing a kiss, while she still carried the burden he was here to remedy.

"I am here for the *both* of you," he said, looking to Liv and then her mother.

"How?" Liv asked, taking another step back and reaching for her mother's hand.

Mrs. Wilde watched him carefully, though Emerson noticed how she did nothing to pull Liv closer to her.

"I wish I had time to explain."

Liv continued to hold fast to her mother, her hesitancy reflected in her silence.

"I need you to trust me when I say I have aunts who will take her in and care for her until your father can either be reasoned with or gives up the search." They both looked at him as if he had sprouted a second head. "I promise, I will explain it more at another time, but we only have until—"

The sound of discordant piano music filtered through the open doorway. The game had entered the music room, which left only the ballroom. Time was running out.

"What was that?" Mrs. Wilde asked, her eyes widening in alarm as her gaze shot toward the door.

"With any luck, *that* is Mr. Bradbury leading your husband and Lord Valencourt in a game of hide-and-seek."

"Is everything a game to you?" Olivia asked, a faint smile playing at the corner of her lips.

He closed the space between them, relishing the heat he felt from her body. "I will play any game as long as it gets me to you." He brushed his knuckles back and forth over her cheek in a tender caress, and he felt her lean into his touch.

Her mother cleared her throat, a soft, chiding smile upon her lips, making Emerson feel like a child caught stealing pastries from the kitchen.

"Right." Emerson awkwardly cleared his throat, the action straining at his tender ribs. He winced, his left arm touching his side.

"Are you badly hurt?" Liv asked, worry written all over her face as she placed a comforting hand on his arm and then moved it up to gently touch the swollen flesh under his eye.

"Just a minor injury." He placed his hand over her hand on his cheek, and momentarily leaned into her soothing touch before removing it. "Nothing to worry about," he said with a forced smile before moving for the door.

Looking out into the darkened corridor, Emerson was relieved to see the unmistakable form of Northcott waiting near the front door, while muffled, angry voices could be heard at the opposite end. There was no way of knowing how much time they truly had, and unwilling to risk losing any more of it, Emerson motioned for Liv and her mother to join him at the door.

Liv linked her arm with her mother's, which was likely for the best. If he touched Olivia, he would not be able to stay focused, and they were not out of danger yet. Choosing to take up the rear, he bid the ladies to make their way toward Lord Northcott, while he watched and listened for any sign of threat.

The ladies had barely reached Northcott when Emerson heard the deep, guttural growl of a man on the prowl. Heavy steps picked up their pace, the sound echoing in the marble corridor, their owner undeniable.

"Latham!" Mr. Wilde bellowed, his rage shaking the walls. "Do you really think you can come into my home and take what belongs to me?"

"Get them out," Emerson yelled to Northcott, before quickly placing himself between the dark shape of a stampeding bull and the ladies.

"No!" He heard Liv yell, and his gut clenched as he listened to her struggle. "Let me go. I am not leaving."

"Get her out, Northcott. Now," Emerson ordered, keeping his eyes trained on the dark form drawing ever closer.

Liv continued to argue, despite her mother's pleas for her to leave. In the end, her stubborn arguments were silenced by the sound of the door closing.

With Liv safely out of the house, Emerson focused on the now-visible, rampaging Joshua Wilde. Emerson's eyes darted around his surroundings, looking for anything to use against him. He spotted a nearby table, small and spindly and barely wide enough to hold a single vase of white roses.

Emerson doubted it could bring down a man with such violence in his eyes as Mr. Wilde, but he had no other options. He would have to time his attack perfectly, and he prayed his ribs could withstand such an action.

At the last possible moment, Emerson reached for the table, clenching his teeth against the searing pain, and brought it down over Mr. Wilde's head.

The man's body hit the floor with a heavy thump, the wooden table splintering into pieces. Emerson would have feared him dead, except that, after a moment, Mr. Wilde tried to push himself up. But then a deep groan came from his mouth, and he went limp.

Emerson approached Joshua Wilde's unconscious form. Broken glass, bent and broken rose stems, and a puddle filled with white pedals were scattered around him on the floor.

He clutched his throbbing side before bending down and examining Mr. Wilde's head. A large bump rose on the top of the man's forehead, and blood trickled down from a long gash. With any luck, it would be hours before Mr. Wilde would wake to a splitting headache and enough memory loss to keep him puzzling as to where his wife and daughter had gone.

Straightening, Emerson spoke to the pathetic form at his feet. "They never *belonged* to you." He paused, taking a small, calming breath. "They were gifts you should have lived your life for, not them for you."

"How touching." Lord Valencourt's derisive laugh cut into the room.

Emerson's head jerked up, hissing out a pain-filled breath as he saw Lord Valencourt leaning against the balustrade, his arms crossed in front of him.

He pushed off the balustrade and slowly began to remove his evening jacket and roll up his sleeves. "You never know when to give up, do you, Latham?" There was bloodlust in his eyes.

Emerson adopted an expression of cool indifference, not wanting the baron to know how much pain he was truly in. He doubted he had enough strength to take the brute down, but for Liv he would fight until his last breath.

Lord Valencourt took the time to pop the knuckles on each hand. "I am going to enjoy telling everyone at the club how the better gentleman won."

"No one could mistake you for a gentleman," Emerson replied. He kept his jacket on in order to conceal his injury, though he knew the fabric would restrict some of his movements.

"I am going to make you eat those words," Lord Valencourt snarled, coming straight for him.

Emerson had enough time to raise his fists before the words "Eat Shakespeare!" echoed inside the entryway.

The baron's large mass crumbled to the floor in a heap, revealing Liv, standing behind him, a large and ornate book in her hands. Her shoulders rose and fell with every breath, an entire side of her golden hair had broken free from its pins, and her cheeks were flushed from exertion.

"Arabella was right." She paused to take in a deep breath.

"Shakespeare *is* always the answer." Liv offered him a half smile, her expression bordering on playful.

Emerson could not return the feeling. He knew he should be grateful for her rescue, but all he could think about was how she could have been hurt. "You should be at the carriage with Northcott and Bradbury."

Olivia looked over her shoulder as Bradbury raced the last few paces behind her.

"Deuced hard to reason with that one," Bradbury said, his hands on his knees as he struggled to catch his breath. "And even harder to keep up with her after I have run the length of this home several times over."

Emerson's frustration only grew. There was no knowing when Mr. Wilde or Lord Valencourt would come to, and he wanted to be gone before they did.

Pressing his mouth into a flat line, Emerson went to Liv and held out his hand for the book. "We *will* be discussing this at another time. We need to leave."

Liv squared her shoulders and met his angry stare before handing him the book, the strain from the sudden weight paining his ribs.

She would never apologize for her decision to come back for him, he could see that in the intensity of her eyes, and he did not know whether to be secretly proud or infuriated.

He made it as far as the pavement and past a few neighboring houses before his anger won out.

Emerson pulled Liv to the side, and with his free arm, he turned her to face him. "You should—"

"Oh, good," Bradbury interrupted, coming up to stand next to Emerson. "Have it out with her now, before she gets it into that fanciful head of hers that she can crash our plans whenever she pleases."

Emerson shot a dark glare at his friend.

Bradbury's smile faded. "Oh, uh—right. I will just go—" He awkwardly cleared his throat as he looked around, his eyes stopping on Northcott and Olivia's mother, who were waiting at the carriage farther up the street. "I will just go over there."

Emerson waited for Bradbury to leave before turning his attention back to Liv. "You—"

Liv cut him off with a defiant glare. "Do not tell me I cannot do something when you are unwilling to do the same."

"What?" he said, both confused by her words and outraged by her stubbornness. She could have been badly hurt.

She took a step toward him and poked a finger into his chest. "You came for me. Do not tell me I cannot come back for you."

Emerson stared down at the fiery, beautiful creature before him, and his anger melted away. A traitorous smile crossed his lips. "Heaven help me."

He had said from the start he wanted someone who would challenge him, and here she was.

Her hand slowly flattened against his chest, and she stepped closer to him, causing his heart to beat faster for a reason other than anger.

"I could not leave you," she said, a beautiful smile blooming upon her lips.

Her words did him in, dissipating the last of his anger. Without a second thought for the pain of his ribs, Emerson reached for her, pulling her into his arms and resting his chin on top of her head. Her hair held the hint of the scent of rose water, and somehow that intimate knowledge seemed to soothe his pain.

He allowed himself a moment to selfishly soak in the feel of her against him. Pulling slightly back, he placed a finger under her chin and tilted her head toward his. Their eyes locked.

Bending down, his mouth hovered over her lips, their breath mingling. "I love you, Liv," he whispered, before sealing his words with a kiss.

Her lips were warm and soft as they moved against his. It was nothing like their rushed first kiss. He took his time, becoming lost in the feel of her against him.

Slipping his hands to the back of her head, he did what he had wanted to do earlier in the parlor—removing all of her hair from their pins. Her curls cascaded over her shoulders, wild and free in the night breeze. He tasted her soft gasp as he threaded his fingers through her silken locks.

She leaned into his touch, and he felt her hands gliding up over his shoulders to rest at the nape of his neck. Her fingers traced mesmerizing circles on his skin, and he let out a deep sigh of his own.

She giggled against his lips, and, as a man who knew his limits, he slowly stepped back from her.

Self-consciously she smiled up at him, as if suddenly shy about her reaction to his kiss.

Dropping one hand from the side of her face, he gently lowered the other until he could stroke her lower lip with the pad of his thumb. His gaze never left hers.

"Emerson?" Her voice was little more than a whisper, but it drove his heart into a galloping pace.

"Yes, Liv?" he asked in a low voice, holding his breath in anticipation for her next words.

"I love you too."

A smile pulled hard at the corner of his lips, and he saw its reflection in her beautiful, bright blue eyes smiling up at him. He took hold of one of her hands, pulling it up to his lips to place upon her palm a chaste but ardent kiss. He would remember this moment until the end of his life, because this moment was no game—it was real.

TWENTY-SEVEN

Olivia paced inside the Latham's private family parlor, the too-long, white nightgown Arabella had given her threatening to tangle around her feet. She had not seen Emerson since late last evening, when his mother had taken one look at her son and immediately sent for a doctor. Emerson had been rushed one way—though not without protest—while Olivia and her mother had been helped into other rooms.

Now, hours later, having found little sleep, she paced a line in the carpet, anxious and guilt-ridden. Emerson had been hurt because of her, and while it had been everything heroic and reckless, she feared what Emerson's mother would think once she learned Olivia was the reason. She could not imagine what a mother—who had also recently lost her husband—would think of her son putting himself in such danger. Olivia prayed his injuries were nothing too serious.

Arabella had been stunned into complete silence after Olivia told her what had happened, which was something she would have never thought possible.

The door to the parlor opened, followed by the graceful

entrance of Mrs. Latham herself. She held a silver tray in her hands upon which rested a tall, silver pot and two white cups.

"I was surprised to hear you were already up," she began, walking straight for the sofa and setting down the tray on the short table in front of it. "My mother would recommend adding milk and sugar to a cup of boiling water to help with sleep." She motioned for Olivia to sit next to her. "But I thought this might do better instead."

Mrs. Latham picked up the pot to pour, a rich stream of drinking chocolate spilling from its short spout and filling each white cup. She smiled, offering Olivia a cup.

"Thank you," Olivia said, softly clearing her throat to get the words out. She took the cup, hating the way her shaking hands betrayed her anxiousness. "How is Emerson?"

Mrs. Latham paused, her cup stopping partway to her lips. Was there a slight tremble to her hold? Bringing her cup the rest of the way to her lips, Mrs. Latham took a sip and returned her cup to its saucer. "The doctor believes Emerson will make a full recovery in time, though the color of the bruising on his left side leaves room for concern." Worry and fear for her son were unmistakable in Mrs. Latham's eyes.

Olivia nodded, consumed by guilt. "I see."

She seemed to study Olivia for a moment before speaking. "Do you know what he told me the moment I saw the bruising?" Her voice sounded distant, as if she were back inside that moment, though her eyes watched Olivia carefully.

Olivia shook her head, her hands clutching the cup.

"He told me that if he had to, he would do it all again, because it got him you." She paused, tears shining in her eyes. "And I could not fault either of you for a love like that."

The tears threatening at the corners of Olivia's eyes broke free, and she found herself enveloped in a hug that took away so much of her guilt.

"Should I have cause to worry?" Emerson's deep, relaxed tone came from the parlor's doorway.

Olivia pulled from Mrs. Latham's embrace, turning to find Emerson's handsome form leaning one shoulder against the doorframe, one arm wrapped around his injury. "Tears and . . . chocolate?" he asked with a high-arching brow.

"Perhaps," his mother replied, collecting her cup of chocolate and casting him a goading look before taking a small sip. "It is much more fun to keep you gentlemen guessing."

Emerson's lips twitched, and his gaze slipped to Olivia.

Her heart fluttered as she fully took him all in. He stood in only his white shirtsleeves, dark-green breeches, and boots. The sight of him in such casual dress along with his freshly washed, tousled hair made her cheeks flush despite the glaring bruise around his eye.

He straightened from the doorframe, his smile receding into a tight line at the movement and his eyes briefly narrowing in pain.

His mother quickly rose, going to his side. Olivia made to follow, but only got as far as standing before she paused. It was a moment for a mother and her son, and it warmed Olivia's heart to watch Emerson wrap his free arm around his mother, reassuring her that he was healing and would be all right.

Mrs. Latham studied him for a moment and then rose up to kiss Emerson on the cheek. She excused herself from the room, leaving the door fully open.

Emerson looked to Olivia with another one of those half grins that tripped up her heart. "Are you always going to keep me guessing?"

Olivia's mind went instantly blank, his words making no sense as he crossed the room to her in four long strides, his eyes briefly dipping to her lips.

"I beg your pardon?" she asked, her hand unconsciously playing with the nightgown's ties below her throat.

"From before. My mother said ladies like to keep men guessing."

"Oh." Olivia softly smiled, shaking her head. "I actually do not know anything about that."

Emerson chuckled, his arm tightening around his side. "Well, for someone who does not know, you are doing a good job of it right now."

Olivia tilted her head, unsure what he meant.

"I am trying to know what you are thinking, Liv," he whispered before leaning down to press a kiss on her cheek.

Heat rose into the spot where his lips had touched her, and she feared her entire face had turned bright red. She wanted to get him back for teasing her. Luckily, an idea quickly came to mind. Clearing her throat, she met his gaze.

"Your mother had thought to celebrate our engagement, but I had to inform her that we were not truthfully engaged."

Emerson's grin immediately faded, and he took her by the arm as if he feared she would leave. "Yes, we are."

"Did you ask me?" she said, doing her best to hold back a triumphant grin. Getting at him had been all too easy. "I fear I do not remember the moment."

"My apologies," he said in a wry tone. "After all my

Herculean efforts to save you, and both our confessions of love, that small detail must have slipped my mind."

"I can assure you that none of your efforts went unnoticed. But a lady does like to be asked."

"Then by all means, I shall rectify that." With a wide sweep of his arm on his good side, and an overexaggerated groan, Emerson painstakingly lowered himself to one knee. He took one of her hands in his and cleared his throat. "Olivia Mary Wilde. Will you be my wife? To laugh with me. To play ridiculous games with me."

A giggle burst from her lips, and she covered her mouth with her free hand. He caught on rather quickly, but instead of turning teasing eyes to her, he looked at her with a heat that warmed her from the inside out.

"To raise a family with me. To grow old with me. And to love me, as I swear to always love you."

Happy tears filled her eyes, and she took in a deep breath. He had laid out the perfect future for her, no lies, no sacrifices—well, maybe a few since she would need to let him win occasionally for the sake of his pride. But it was perfect for her, and most important of all, he was giving her the choice.

She didn't respond. She couldn't seem to find the single word she wanted to say among all the emotions she was feeling. A tear slipped down her cheek.

Emerson was instantly on his feet, wiping her tear away with a gentle hand.

"Is that a yes?" he asked softly.

He was such a good and honest man, and she would thank the heavens for him for the rest of her life.

"Yes." She had barely exhaled the word before her lips were completely consumed by his kiss.

He claimed her mouth, and she returned the kiss, pouring all the love she carried for him into that embrace.

Eventually, he pulled away and leaned his forehead against hers. "Now that we have that settled, we should discuss our immediate departure for Gretna Green."

"Are you well enough to travel?" she asked, reaching for his injury.

"I am well enough." He smiled, as if that would reassure her. "Until we are married, your father legally has control over your life—an issue I want to see rectified as soon as possible. Besides, I thought we could return home by way of Bath. We could enjoy the healing waters, while also seeing your mother settled with one of my aunts."

"Bath?" Olivia asked, stunned. "But that is hundreds of miles out of the way."

Emerson shrugged one shoulder. "I see it as a few extra days for your bridal tour."

"And what of your family? We will be gone for several weeks."

"My mother has agreed that it is best to stay behind so Arabella does not miss out on the remainder of her first Season. She also insists upon a party when we return to celebrate with our family and friends."

"Is it wise while my father is still in Town?" A shiver of unease went through her, and she reflexively wrapped her arms around her middle.

Emerson reached out and ran a comforting hand up and

down one of her arms. "Northcott has promised to keep an eye on my family—and yours."

Olivia eyed him skeptically, not daring to believe Joshua Wilde could be managed so easily. She half-expected him to burst through the Lathams' front door at any moment, demanding his property be returned.

"And I may have received word from Jenson, explaining your father's bedridden condition. Trust me, now is the time. And once we are married, we shall face whatever is to come—together."

Hope filled her chest, the threat of her father becoming a distant memory,

"To Gretna Green, then?" She smiled, a thrill shooting right through her.

Emerson leaned his head down, a heart-quickening smile upon his face as he gently brushed their noses together. "To Gretna Green, my dear future Mrs. Latham."

ACKNOWLEDGMENTS

Thank you to my little family. Especially to my husband, who is my greatest fan and strictest critic—I love that you quote my characters with me. And to my dad, who has always stood beside me and cheered me on. To my mother-in-law and father-in-law: thank you for your patience, your support, and the endless hours of babysitting you endured while I tried doing something just for me.

Thank you to Shallee McArthur, who came into my life when I wasn't even certain a girl like me should be on this journey. Without you, I never would have found a writing community, enjoyed so many writing retreats, or had the courage to write something as crazy as this.

Thank you to Camille Smithson and Kiri Patterson for being the best critique partners a girl who struggles with feelings could ask for.

And last but not least, thank you to Shadow Mountain for taking a chance on little old me.

DISCUSSION QUESTIONS

1. In the beginning, Emerson assumes Olivia is aware of his attempt at a secret courtship, but he soon learns he is mistaken. He comes up with a different plan to court her by using the game of tag. Why do you think the game worked when the traditional method did not? Which method of courtship—traditional or unconventional—would you prefer?

2. Emerson nicknames Olivia "Liv," or "Liv Wilde"; however, at the beginning of the book, due to her family circumstances and society's expectations, she's unable to do anything like *live wild*. How does her character change and grow throughout the story? Do you feel she lives up to her nickname?

3. Bradbury makes a wager in the betting book that involves Emerson, a pig, and a stolen waistcoat. Right before they are ready to make good on the bet, a frustrated Bradbury tells Emerson that he made the bet to help his friend find his way again. In what way did going through with the wager help Emerson work through his grief over the loss

of his father? Do you think the experience helped in his ultimate goal of winning Olivia?

4. The *ton* refers to Northcott as the Brooding Baron, and throughout the story he is depicted as quiet and observant. Yet his friends do not appear to be wary of him. Why do you think that is? Do you think there is more to his character than meets the eye?

5. When Olivia doesn't show up to the Cartwrights' ball, Emerson becomes extremely agitated. Bradbury brings Mrs. Latham to him, saying that every man needs his mother. It is clear that Bradbury doesn't feel the same way about his own mother but knows it will help Emerson. What does that say about Bradbury's character? How is the relationship between Emerson and his mother unique?

6. When Mrs. Wilde realizes that Olivia is in love with Emerson, she admits that "she should have done more" to spare her daughter from a similar fate she endured. Olivia argues differently and refuses to leave her mother behind and run to Emerson. In what ways did Olivia's mother help protect her daughter from the actions of her husband and Lord Valencourt?

7. The theme of the story shows that love conquers all, though not without sacrifice and pain. Do you agree that love is worth the trials to get to happily ever after?

8. There are several children's games played or named throughout the story. How many did you remember?

ABOUT THE AUTHOR

JENTRY FLINT is a bookworm-turned-writer with the propensity to try just about anything. She has a true love of history and believes a good quote can fix most things. She lives in southern Utah with her husband and two daughters—who, naturally, are named after characters from books.

Her favorite things in life are flavored popcorn, her grandmother's purple blanket, and curling up on the couch to watch a movie with her husband. *Games in a Ballroom* is her debut novel.

GAMES

in a

BALLROOM

OTHER PROPER ROMANCE REGENCY TITLES

NANCY CAMPBELL ALLEN
My Fair Gentleman
The Secret of the India Orchid

JULIANNE DONALDSON
Edenbrooke
Blackmoore

LEAH GARRIOTT
Promised

ARLEM HAWKS
Georgana's Secret

JOSI S. KILPACK
A Heart Revealed
Lord Fenton's Folly
The Vicar's Daughter
Miss Wilton's Waltz
Promises and Primroses
Daisies and Devotion
Rakes and Roses
Love and Lavender
The Valet's Secret

MEGAN WALKER
Lakeshire Park

JULIE WRIGHT
A Captain for Caroline Gray